Take Out the Jocks
a feminist revenge comedy

Finalist, Satire/Humor Category: "Your book was chosen by our judges for demonstrating exceptional literary craft, excellence, and innovation."

— STORYTRADE BOOK AWARDS, 2025

Runner-up, Wild Card Category

— LOS ANGELES BOOK FESTIVAL, 2024

Take Out the Jocks

a feminist revenge comedy

MICHAEL NEST

Take Out the Jocks: a feminist revenge comedy

Copyright © 2023 Michael Nest

Although some characters in this book say words that are quotes from real persons and some events are inspired by real incidents, the characters and events themselves are entirely fictitious.

Library and Archives Canada Cataloguing in Publication
Nest, Michael, 1966–, author
Take Out the Jocks: a feminist revenge comedy
Issued in print and electronic formats
ISBN 978-1-7381840-1-9(paperback); ISBN 978-1-7381840-0-2(pdf)

Cover by Michael Nest, with assistance from Merrily Weisbord.
Image of 'Diana the Hunter' courtesy of ArtDecoCollection.com.
Photo of clouds courtesy of Kathy Main.

Media and other inquiries: info@michaelnest.com

CONTENT WARNING

In this work of crime fiction, female characters have a narrative purpose that does not include being murdered.

No jocks were harmed in the writing of this story.

SPRING 2018

1

IT WAS MID-AFTERNOON when the reporter pulled into the trailhead parking lot at Coates Ravine. His editor had hastily assigned him after receiving a police tip that a young man's body had been found by a kayaker. A story was needed for the six p.m. online edition update and for hardcopy the next day. He checked he had his notebook, pen, and phone, and made a mental note of possible photos to take at the scene and questions to ask any police officers guarding it.

Thirty minutes along a wooded trail, yellow and black tape blocked the path. A state trooper stood beyond it. This was the point where the man had gone over the edge.

The reporter waved. "Hi there. I'm Wyatt Bell from the *Mossberg Gazette*."

"Henry's new guy?" asked the trooper. "I liked that piece you did on the police charity helping out the church on Fifth after the fire. We've got a great community here."

Ingratiating himself with police officers was usually good for information down the track, Wyatt had found. "Thanks. You guys do great work. What's your name?"

"Trooper Chase."

"What happened here? Who's the guy?"

"We can't announce it yet. The medics are down there at the river right now. They're bringing a chopper to winch him out, then we'll notify family."

Wyatt took in the broken wooden rail and noticed Chase was standing in the middle of a bunch of footprints. He knew there were three options for how the man had gotten to the bottom of the ravine: fell, jumped, or … "Was he pushed?"

"Not this guy. He was a football player. You're going to have yourself a story when you find out who it is."

The radio on Trooper Chase's chest crackled to life: *Chase? We've secured the body. Radio the chopper. It's Branson Vanburg. His driver license was in his pocket.*

Chase grabbed at his handset. "Ok. Will do."

Wyatt recognized the name immediately: Branson Vanburg, who had been cleared of rape charges four days earlier. Vanburg's acquittal was the lead story that day. The *Gazette's* chief editor, Henry Konig, insisted on writing it himself, extolling the integrity of the American justice system and enthusing that a brilliant football career had been safeguarded.

But Vanburg was now dead at the bottom of Coates Ravine.

FOUR DAYS EARLIER

KATE RAN THE light as it turned red, flooring the accelerator as she absorbed the news on the radio: *Local football star, Branson Vanburg, was this afternoon acquitted of all rape charges in Mossberg Criminal Court. In his ruling, Judge Nossel said there was insufficient evidence to prove lack of consent and he found the witness for the prosecution to be unreliable. Judge Nossel's statement included regret that the Vanburg family had experienced the inconvenience of a trial. It'll be fine spring weather for the open day at Fort Byrd this weekend …*

The rest of the news went unheard as Kate contemplated what this case—yet another acquittal—meant for Mossberg. She pulled into Seyram's driveway and walked around to the back, the smell of cooking wafting through the kitchen window. Looking through the French panes, she could see Seyram busy over the stove, singing.

"It's me," Kate called as she took her boots off and walked into the kitchen.

The rhythmic funk of Asa's "Dreamer Girl" filled the kitchen as Seyram bopped toward Kate and they embraced.

Seyram, Kate, and their friend Carly had been having dinner at each other's place every few months since they moved back to Mossberg at around the same time twenty years earlier. Kate and Carly were very capable cooks when it was their turn to host dinner, but didn't try to compete with Seyram, who could never resist putting on an elaborate spread. There were three dinner rules: other household members had to be out (this meant husband and children in Seyram's case and, in Carly's, her daughter Summer); the host cooked whatever she liked, no complaints allowed; and they brought their own drinks. Kate was a dedicated drinker of Corona beer with lime, Carly loved her sauvignon blanc, and Seyram was the mistress of mocktails—although once a year she let herself sip a beer or champagne. They ate around seven, then spent the evening eating, drinking, laughing, and catching up on each other's news and on the latest happenings in the world: politics, books, entertainment, arts, far-off disasters, and events closer to home.

"What are you cooking?" asked Kate. "It smells spicy but I can tell it's not a curry."

Seyram laughed. "My days of competing with your mom are *over*, so it's definitely not a curry. I've made a pear, gorgonzola, walnut, and spinach salad, then I'm going to grill tilapia—you're getting a whole fish each and you better eat it all—and that comes with jollof rice, grilled vegetables, and shito sauce. The jollof is Nigerian-style, but the sauce is pure

Ghanaian—that spicy, dark paste. That's probably what you can smell. I'll put the fish on when Carly gets here. Cheers."

Seyram tapped her glass against Kate's opened beer bottle.

"What's for dessert?" asked Kate.

"English trifle. I know that sounds weird, but the sugar and cream go really well after the chili. It's in the fridge."

Kate opened the fridge and saw a magnificent English trifle, with blueberries and strawberries layered in a glass pedestal bowl. "You know, don't you, that Carly and I never eat lunch when we have dinner at your place?"

Kate felt the warmth of Seyram's company and kitchen, and she was beginning to calm down after the news on the car radio, but Seyram could tell something was wrong.

"You look distracted. What's up?"

"Did you hear the news this afternoon?" asked Kate. "About that kid Branson Vanburg?"

"That's the rape case, right?"

"Yeah. Sometimes I want to burn this town to the ground, even though I know I've got a comfortable niche here."

"Carly sent me five texts asking if I'd seen the news, but I deliberately avoided it by cooking and listening to music. Did they announce the verdict?"

Just then a blond, bobbed head went past the kitchen window and seconds later they heard the back door open. "Hellooo!" Carly exclaimed. "I'm not late! Summer has a new boyfriend who actually picked her up *on time*, which meant I could get away as well."

Carly fumbled to get her boots off amid her oversized scarf and loose coat, and Kate came to her assistance, taking each item as it was passed to her. Carly gave Kate a squeeze and walked over to Seyram. "Great music. This is Asa, right?"

"Dreamer Girl," replied Seyram. "I float right out of Mossberg when I hear this song."

They hugged and Carly stood back and looked at Seyram. "You're going all out West African this evening: the music, and I'm sure I can smell …" Carly sniffed the air. "…is that jollof? And I *love* that dress—pink and red—gorgeous! And those gold earrings."

Seyram laughed and touched her earlobes. "My Ghana gold! I spend my days dressed in a white lab coat in a bland, sterile place. Home's where I let loose." Seyram owned and managed Mossberg's clinical hematology laboratory.

"You still have your nerdy glasses," piped up Kate. "And your hair is so sensible that it's just begging for extensions or braids. Or a wig."

"Oh, no, that'd never do. That's not me," said Seyram, patting her short natural Afro. "Now, Carly, you've been texting me all afternoon. Kate told me there was an announcement about the rape case."

"Yes, it depresses me so much. Vanburg raped Wendy Fieldhouse's daughter Colette, and the judge acquitted the asshole. There goes justice in Mossberg again."

"That's why I ignored your messages. Sometimes I feel so mad, I want to run out of the house shouting 'These girls are our daughters! I'm going to *destroy* you!'" Seyram checked herself; Kate and Carly exchanged glances.

Seyram took a breath. "Instead, I listen to music and cook. So, let me serve up dinner, and let's talk after."

Returning to Mossberg, Pennsylvania, after years away at graduate school and then establishing her career, Seyram and her husband, Felix, an accountant, had bought a 150-year-old farmhouse. Once on the outskirts of town, the property was now surrounded by small acreage developments. They had renovated, repolished, and repainted the all-wood house, but never changed the original floor plan. This meant the kitchen remained a large separate room at the back of the house, in the middle of which was the long wooden table where Seyram prepared and served food, and welcomed family and guests.

Carly and Kate sat while Seyram put the tilapia on to grill. They started with the salad, and slowly but surely the food disappeared as they talked.

Kate put her feet up onto a neighboring chair—the only person Seyram ever allowed to do this—and took a swig of beer. "Imagine if the people murdering, harassing, and assaulting women across the country said they were part of an organized network that wanted to destroy Americans' freedom—to terrorize them. We'd be outraged. Congress would pass special spending bills and the Army Reserve would be mobilized to patrol the streets and ensure peace and safety. Instead, it just keeps happening over and over again. I feel like the MeToo movement is passing us by before anyone in

Mossberg has even heard of it, let alone cares what it is. I'm so fed up with this town."

"Well," said Carly, "we had that march against sexual assault that I helped organize last September. A hundred people turned up. That was pretty good for Mossberg."

"Yes," said Seyram, "but do you also remember how it got politicized? The mayor said, and I quote, 'In some countries these ladies would have been greeted with bullets. It is a triumph of democracy they were allowed to march.' That was the headline in the paper: *Triumph of Democracy: Feminists Not Shot*."

"I'm trying to focus on the *effort* we made," Carly protested. "At least we got some coverage. Next time hopefully even more people will come, and the *Gazette* will run a story on *why* we're marching."

"Sorry," said Seyram. "I feel like Kate at the moment. I was so happy when Felix agreed we should move back to Mossberg to start a family and be close to Mom and Dad. Now I wonder what kind of influences they're getting from this town."

"Are we *un*happy?" asked Carly.

"I'm unhappy with the way women are treated," said Seyram. "In our private lives we're happy—I've got Felix, and Nana and Kofi; you have Summer. We all have jobs—and Kate's the mistress of everything she does."

"I run a hardware store," said Kate. "I wouldn't romanticize it."

"But you love your job and you're good at it, and the store is a destination for every do-it-yourselfer within a radius of fifty miles. What I'm wondering about," Seyram continued, "is what kind of values my children—or any children in Mossberg—are absorbing from a community whose ideas about women and men are stuck in the fifties. I encourage them to aim high at school and be ambitious, but Nana's friends tell her she shouldn't try to be smart because boys only like pretty girls. And Kofi sees that the way to be popular at school is to play sports or goof around in class."

Carly gave a wry smile. "Terrible for the mom who never once in her life got anything less than an A."

"But that's part of the problem!" exclaimed Seyram. "I'm not just fed up for my kids, I'm fed up for myself. I've spent my life trying to be an achiever, but nothing I do changes anything."

"Seyram, you *are* an achiever," said Carly. "You run a successful business, your kids are polite and smart, despite what you say about them not trying hard enough, and you're the most together person I know."

"But I'm sick of it!" Seyram clunked her juice down on the table. "I'm sick of smiling at clients who are unreasonable; sick of trying to be the perfect mom when Mossberg's standard for perfection is a Stepford Wife; sick of being a volunteer at a church where men make the decisions and women are just the 'volunteers.' I'm even sick of being nice to Felix—and he's the best husband ever. I'm tired of being ... *contained.*"

"If you're saying you want to have an affair," said Kate, "then you really are having a crisis. You've been good all your life because you were taught that's how to get on. Now you've realized you could've been a total bitch and ended up in exactly the same place. In fact, you might have ended up being Anna Wintour in New York if you'd been *more* of a bitch."

"For goodness' sake, I don't want to have an affair ..." Seyram shook her head, her voice trailing off.

"Since we're confessing," said Carly, "I'm tired of being meek. I thought I'd grow out of it, but bullies still frighten me, and the worst thing is they know it. I see them looking at me and thinking *She's a pushover*, and they're right. I read in the news about young women who freeze with fear and agree to get into strange men's cars and then get assaulted. Everyone says, 'Oh, she must have wanted it, why else would she get into the car?' But that could be me."

"You left David," said Seyram. "That took courage."

"No. He left me. I never had the courage to go, even though we both knew the marriage was over. We just didn't love each other anymore. He did me a favor by leaving first—and I'm glad he did." Carly clutched her head. "God, I'm even grateful I got dumped! How pathetic." She had tears in her eyes. "You know the harshest insult Summer uses when she's mad at me? It's not 'I hate you.' It's 'You. Are. *Weak!*' She's had me figured out since she was five. How can I encourage Summer to be courageous when I can't stand up for myself? I already warn her to be careful at night and she's only fifteen."

"You're being too hard on yourself," said Kate. "What about your pottery? It's sold all over the country for thousands of dollars. You make these big, bold, amazing objects. I don't have anywhere near your creativity. Or Seyram's smarts."

"But that's the problem. Yes, I make these ceramics that turn people's heads, but I wish I had that courage in dealing with people."

Despite Kate's valiant attempts at encouragement, they sat there in a funk, exasperated with themselves and their town.

"Sometimes I'd like to turn the tables and make men scared," said Carly, "just for a week, so they know how it feels to go out at night, or to come home late, or to walk alone in the woods, worrying about being assaulted or murdered."

Kate sat up. "Let's do it. Let's make *them* scared. Send a warning about what will happen if they keep treating women the same way."

"Strike terror into them!" Carly exclaimed. "What do you think, Seyram? I know you're Miss Goody Two-Shoes, but we've been waiting years and no one else in Mossberg is ever going to take action. All we ever do is support the victims after the fact."

Seyram hesitated. "I'm just thinking about Kofi. He's not far off being a young man."

"Kofi is ten!" said Kate. "He's the sweetest boy I know."

"But that's only because you know him. Our neighbor, Mrs. Jeffers—you know the one across the road with the oak tree in the front—had her cousin visiting from Indianapolis.

Mrs. Jeffers went shopping, leaving her cousin alone, when Kofi and his friends started fooling around in the street. Her cousin called the cops on them."

"*What?*" Kate and Carly exclaimed in unison.

"I'm not kidding. A police car arrived, siren wailing."

"What happened?"

"Luckily it was Trooper Chase. He high-fived the kids then knocked on her door and asked where the troublemakers were—in that order. Nothing too urgent in Mossberg. The cousin, looking terrified, said 'They're standing behind you.' I could see it all from my doorstep. Trooper Chase looked at the kids, then the cousin, then back at the kids, then back to the cousin, totally confused. He then realized what was going on and, to his credit, introduced each boy to her by name. He knows them from baseball. Apparently, she'd reported a group of Black men trying to break in. Total nonsense, of course—Kofi said they were chasing each other and ran onto Mrs. Jeffers' lawn—but I knew what she was doing. There's Kofi, a ten-year-old kid, with a couple of his friends who are pretty dark, but what she saw was a group of thugs breaking into her house."

"But that's terrible!" said Carly. "Did you raise it with Mrs. Jeffers?"

"I didn't need to. She called me personally, very apologetic. She knew it was prejudice about Blacks—and young men as far as I'm concerned. Look, Kofi and the other boys on this street are a bunch of goofballs, and the entire street knows it, but the idea they are all culpable for Mossberg's sexual violence problem is ludicrous. We can't just randomly target young men."

Kate and Carly looked at each other, chastised.

"But," Seyram continued, "I think we're getting closer to who should be our target. Who are the heroes—the role models—in this community? It's all the sports stars. Mossberg must have more jocks per capita than anywhere else in America, and they behave appallingly. Send them a warning and everyone gets the message."

Now it was Kate's turn to protest. "We can't just attack people because they play sports."

"No," said Carly slowly, nodding her head in agreement. "But we also know that individual sports stars like Branson Vanburg are predators—I don't care what Judge Nossel says. So you're both right: we can't just target all young men, and we can't just target men who play sports. But we can target jocks, the sexual harassing kind."

"Let's do it!" said Kate. "Let's take out the team captains."

Seyram was confused. "You mean *date* them? I could be Branson Vanburg's mother!"

"Jesus, Seyram, I mean take him out of action. Hurt him!"

"Who?"

"Vanburg and those other those jocks who swagger around Mossberg and think they can treat women however they want."

"Whoa, whoa, whoa! What are we trying to accomplish here? The courts, the college, the police—that's the system that barely lifts a finger in response to complaints. Isn't targeting *them* a better idea?"

Carly interrupted. "What about the men who run Mossberg, like Roger Konig, the mayor, and his brother at the *Gazette*, Henry Konig—and that asshole Councilor Jeffers? Why target jocks when it's the old men who block change?"

"We can't fix the old men," said Kate. "And, right now, *today*, it's the young men who are assaulting women, not the old guys," said Kate. "Yes, the system is upheld by Mayor Konig, Councilor Jeffers, Judge Nossel, and the institutions they run, but they'd just be replaced by clones. We have to turn things on their head. The only way to provoke Mossberg into action against sexual assault is to make men scared—*personally* afraid."

"Why us?" asked Seyram. "None of us has ever been sexually assaulted, nor our children. We're not like those moms who are driven to kill a man because their kids were abused."

Kate was exasperated. "I don't need to be raped to take action against sexual assault."

"Wouldn't it just make us vigilantes?" replied Seyram.

"You want us to wait another century until there are enough women in the legal system to improve justice? Or go on marches for a few more decades?" asked Kate.

Everyone fell silent.

"We've got to have limits," said Seyram finally. "Make them scared first and see if that works. And we can't just go for all jocks, just like we can't just go for all young men. The soccer captain, Angel Hernandez, goes to my church and is kind to everyone. He tutored Nana and Kofi in Spanish. He's nothing like Branson Vanburg. We need a priority list and I'd make Vanburg target number one."

Kate laughed. "If Angel Hernandez is respectful to you and other women, and patiently tutors your kids, then by definition he isn't a jock. Knowing the Hernandez family, he's probably taken some pre-marriage vow of chastity and isn't allowed within two feet of a girl outside a church hall. We can cross him off the list. So, let's have some limits. Agreed." She rubbed her hands together. "But Seyram, you need to move on from being good. And Carly, you need to move on from being meek. Putting the fear of God into Mossberg's jocks is the perfect project."

"What about you, Kate? What do you need to move on from?" said Carly gently.

"What about me? And this isn't about me anyway."

"You need to fall in love again," said Seyram.

"Not even," said Carly. "Have crazy sex if you like, but you need to let someone else in."

Kate harrumphed. "Hmmm, we could learn about that from you."

Seyram burst out laughing. "Kate and I still have PTSD from that camping trip to the Poconos. You and David were at it like rabbits all night, keeping everyone awake."

"We were twenty, stuck in a tent in a forest," protested Carly. "What were we supposed to do?" A dreamy look came over her. "Wow, that brings back good memories. And what about you, Seyram, insisting on sleeping apart from that boyfriend of yours so he couldn't get his hands on you. I still remember how despondent he looked when you announced it was bedtime and dove into Kate's tent."

The three of them were laughing now.

"Seriously, Kate," said Carly, reverting to her gentle tone. "You need to move on from Tracy and what happened on prom night."

3

GRACE SCHMIDT COLLECTED her thoughts and arranged her notes on the table. She was next in line to speak at the Mossberg Town Council meeting—to argue for an increase in the budget of Sisterhood House, the women's resource center she ran. Grace made a similar pitch every few years, usually without success. This year she had decided to be more dramatic in laying out what was at stake in terms of basic safety, and had enlisted some younger people to help, hoping their earnestness and energy would persuade the councilors. Sitting in the audience was Carly, who was on the management committee for Sisterhood House and had come along to support its budget pitch. As Grace rose to speak, Carly caught her eye and gave her the thumbs-up.

"Thank you, Mayor Konig, and thank you Councilors," said Grace. "Since 2013, nine women have been murdered in our town. We don't feel safe walking around, particularly at night, and this includes your mothers, sisters, and daughters. Sisterhood House receives an average of five referrals a week— women and children experiencing some kind of harassment or violence. That's 250 referrals a year, which is a huge number for a single organization in a town our size. We support complainants to make reports to the police, but the police rarely make it a priority to investigate such cases. Occasionally we have the resources to provide legal assistance when a matter goes to court. But this support costs money.

"I am here today to ask you for more funding. A budget increase of ten percent—that's only $7,000 per year—that would allow us to extend our pro bono legal clinic from two nights a week to three. The extra money would go to heating and electricity, as well as allowing us to provide an additional thirty nights of emergency shelter annually. That's equivalent to ten additional weekends of food and accommodation for a mother and two children.

"I've invited three students from Mossberg College's Safe Space Alliance to tell you about their experiences and their perspective on the importance of Sisterhood House: Tanisha Carter, Bao Zhang, and Beth Katz."

Councilor Jeffers, known for quizzing anybody who appeared before the council, interrupted. "Excuse me, miss, just before the girls speak, could you remind me what your organization actually does? You know, we go through this grant process every three years, and I'm so old I always forget the details of each request."

"Of course," said Grace with a tight expression. She sparred with Councilor Jeffers at every council meeting and knew, despite Jeffers' claim to have a poor memory, that he remembered everything.

"Thank you," continued Jeffers. "Now, the ... *Sisterhood House*, I think you call it. It encourages women to leave their husbands, is that correct?"

"No, Councilor Jeffers. If a woman finds herself in an abusive relationship and chooses to leave for her safety and the safety of her children, our organization will help her find emergency accommodation, and give her food and very small amounts of money for things like cabs, phone calls, and personal items. If she chooses to take legal action because of the abuse she suffered, our free legal clinic will give advice about her options for reporting a crime and pursuing it in court. We also provide a space for people to hold meetings and other get-togethers."

"If a woman *chooses* to leave? So, you'd describe your organization as supporting women's right to choose, is that correct? You are pro-choice."

The chamber was dead silent.

"Well, the term *pro-choice* is commonly used in a completely different context that I think has nothing to do with what we're discussing here."

Jeffers changed tack. "You're aligned with the Hashme Organization, aren't you?"

"Excuse me?" Grace was confused. "We're independent, and I don't know the Hashme Organization.

"Come, come, miss. It's all over the internet. Trying to get a foothold in Mossberg and turn the tables on men. Encouraging girls who get themselves into bad situations to complain instead of taking responsibility. The Democrats fund it. Hashme."

The penny dropped. "Councilor Jeffers, do you mean the 'hash' MeToo movement—which encourages women to talk about harassment and abuse?" Grace turned to Mayor Konig. "It encourages women to use social media and the courts, to denounce abusers and advocate for change."

"Well, that doesn't seem fair," said the mayor. "Where do the men get to complain about women?"

Grace was speechless.

Jeffers continued. "How would you describe the values of your organization?"

Grace replied carefully. "We believe that everyone has rights under the law and that these include the right to not suffer any sort of violence. I describe Sisterhood House as embodying the best of American values, not least of which is letting individuals live peacefully and freely in society, with access to equal justice and a right to happiness just like in the Constitution."

"Miss Schmidt, the mothers you assist, they're not all married, are they?" said Jeffers.

"We don't ask if they are married, and it makes no difference to the help we provide. In short, we have no idea."

"Why don't you ask if they are married? Surely a pact signed under God is worth something?"

"It has no bearing on our decision to assist them."

"And do you help many—what's the fashionable term?— women of *color*?"

"We don't collect statistics on race or ethnicity. As I said, we help anybody who needs it, assuming we have the budget."

"Well, you must be able to make an observation." Jeffers gave a chuckle. "After all, colored folks stand out in Mossberg!"

Grace bit her lip. "I would guess about one-third of the women and children we help have African American, Latin American, or Asian heritage."

"One-third? Well, that's astounding!" Jeffers took his glasses off and looked around the chamber. "Clearly something is going on that such an overrepresentation of coloreds comes to you, because at the last census Mossberg was *eighty-seven percent* white."

"Interesting you are so aware of that statistic, Councilor Jeffers. What I will say is that people of color in Mossberg are poorer on average, and women in poorer households are more likely to need help when leaving violent relationships. So, we see more poor women, proportionally, than middle-class women. In Mossberg that means more women of color."

"What I'm putting to you," said Councilor Jeffers, "is that Sisterhood House dedicates itself to helping single mothers who, in light of Mossberg's demographic makeup, are disproportionately non-white. And you enable *married* women to exit from their union to the men of Mossberg. You do this because of a set of values that could only be described as anti-family." Jeffers turned again to the chamber. "We've heard these arguments before. You all know that I believe this organization should be defunded. I want to emphasize to the council, yet again, that we are harboring a huddle of *pro-choice feminists* in our midst. Our values—and Mossberg's community—are under threat. At a tipping point!" He got louder. "Hashmes are building networks under our nose! Young people no longer go to church! Immigrants are taking over downtown! And women walk around in yoga pants! My cousin from Indianapolis visited recently to stay with my sister, and in broad daylight a gang of thugs tried to break into my sister's house—while my cousin was there sitting alone! *What is happening to America?* Thank God we have Fort Byrd Army Base to protect us!" Out of wind, Councilor Jeffers collapsed into his chair.

Taking advantage of the pause in proceedings, Grace turned to Mayor Konig. "Perhaps, Mayor, our three students from Mossberg College could now say their piece?"

"Yes, let's keep moving. Bring on the girls."

The students were even more nervous in the wake of Grace's exchange with Jeffers. They'd never addressed an audience outside of college before and this issue was personal. Tanisha had wanted to be an engineer until George Floyd's death. She loved the idea of designing and building things, but Floyd's killing had electrified her. Tanisha wondered if the methodological approaches used in engineering could be used to reform institutions like the police, and had started the local Black Lives Matter chapter. Bao had begun their transition after high school, but leaving those years behind hadn't made it much easier at college. Mossberg College had kind, supportive professors, and the Safe Space Alliance was a godsend and a great place to make friends, but they were conscious of people throwing them looks and insisting on calling them "Miss." Beth was the current energy behind the Safe Space Alliance. She had pioneered its relationships with off-campus organizations like Sisterhood House, as well as the college BLM chapter. She was a fourth-generation New York City feminist, but even she had to take a deep breath as she looked out at this cynical audience.

Carly, sitting alongside the students, sensed they were nervous. "You can do this," she soothed as they rose. "Just pretend it's a class presentation." But Carly herself never could have done it. *Where do young people get such confidence?* She admired them and wished that, just once, she could publicly take a stand on a matter of principle.

Tanisha stood first. "Sexual assault, verbal assault, stalking, and indecent exposure are common in this community. Last week there was an attempted rape on Main Street after the bars closed. The week before that a woman jogging out near Coates Ravine was groped. And the week before that a young mother pushing a stroller in the early afternoon had obscenities shouted at her by a carload of guys coming into town from Fort Byrd. We know women, gay, and transpeople on campus who report things to the police or to campus security, and nothing ever seems to happen. Black women in particular have a really hard time getting the police to take their complaints seriously. We're always told there's not enough proof that the guy intended harm, but we also know men from the frat houses and the army base joke about how easy it is to get away with harassment. We want this to stop."

Bao got up next. People in the gallery shifted in their seats and glanced sideways at each other. "Harassment is not a 'women's problem.'" Bao made quote marks in the air. "Everyone deserves to be treated respectfully, and the problem lies at the feet of perpetrators of disrespect. I'm an ally of Sisterhood House, and it needs more allies. People like you: citizens and businesspeople in the local community who care about Mossberg's reputation, who want to transform it into a town safe for everyone. We're asking you to be allies by supporting Sisterhood House and increasing its budget."

Then it was Beth's turn. "Hello, everyone. I'm Beth, the president of the Safe Space Alliance. I could be your daughter in college, going out with friends on a Friday or Saturday night. But you need to know that Main Street is not always a nice place." She gestured to Tanisha and Bao. "Last Friday we three were outside Starbucks and were harassed by a bunch of drunk guys. Improving safety on campus and in town means working together—with the town council and with the police—and we want to do that. And we want *you* to make that possible. Sisterhood House has a vital role in Mossberg, even though you may not always see it for yourselves. It identifies town locations that need better security, it supports women who need help making reports to Mossberg Police, it provides emergency shelter … and it desperately needs money to continue operating. Please support Sisterhood House, approve this budget increase, and make our community safe."

There was muttering in the public gallery.

"Our community is already safe for *families*," someone called out.

"If Main Street is not a nice place, what's a nice girl doing there?"

And from the back of the room: "If you want to be safe, maybe you should spend less time having coffee with transsexuals on a Friday night and more time in the college library!"

Beth jumped to her feet. "Last week in that library a man pulled out his penis and urinated on one of the couches! Campus security called the police, who let him go because he said he was on medication that made him think he was at a urinal. He wasn't even charged with a basic misdemeanor! Sex-related complaints are not treated seriously in this town."

The meeting dissolved into shouting.

"Why are we hearing about men's toilet habits?"

"Give us a real issue to discuss!"

"Mayor, why are you taking up people's time with this nonsense?"

Tanisha, Bao and Beth made a hurried exit, followed by Grace and Carly. The five of them regrouped in the parking lot.

"I'm so sorry, Grace," said Beth. "I lost my temper. I totally messed up."

"No, no, *no*. You were *great*," said Carly. "I wish I had the guts to stand up like that."

"Carly's right. You all did great," echoed Grace. "Councilor Jeffers is an old adversary, and he knows how to get an audience riled up against anything that smacks of progressive reform." She gave a bitter smile. "Like helping poor women leave violent marriages."

"But what about the House? Does this mean it's going to close?" asked Tanisha.

"Not at all. I've run Sisterhood House for twelve years and been through these threats to withdraw funding multiple times," said Grace, reassuring and sanguine. "Despite what Jeffers says, most councilors support what we do. Our regular grant money is secure, and about thirty percent of our budget comes from donations and bequests anyway, so Sisterhood House isn't going to close. It just means we can't extend our services."

"They made me realize one thing," said Beth. "We need to make connections between the college and the army base."

Grace let out a laugh. "Don't tell me you also think—what did Jeffers say?—we should *thank God Fort Byrd Army Base protects us and upholds our values!*"

They all burst out laughing.

"Who realized we feminists were so dangerous?" Beth had her humor back. "I guess the point is that the base commander is influential in Mossberg. And there are quite a few women there. Forming a relationship can't hurt. I tried to reach out a couple of times last fall, but the only organized women's groups they have are sports teams, and they never got back to me."

Several months earlier, in a bar on Main Street, Beth had approached a group of five women who all looked to be in their twenties. It was easy to spot military personnel because of their neat hair and clothes, and the way they carried themselves: contained and fit. Beth figured it was a good opportunity to try to connect with them. She introduced herself, explained she was at Mossberg College, and wondered about life at Fort Byrd. They asked politely what she was studying.

"How the women's movement has changed American institutions," she told them.

They looked blank.

"Look," said Beth, fishing in her backpack, "this is what I'm reading." She held up the book and read aloud the title: "*Faithful and Fearless: Moving Feminist Protest Inside the Church and Military*. It's amazing!"

Awkward silence.

Beth asked what they did. Three were training to be explosives detonation experts and had served previously in Afghanistan. The other two were Stryker combat vehicle drivers retraining to become M1 Abrams tank systems engineers.

The five army women returned to their beers and resumed their conversation. Beth was dismissed.

4

IT WAS SEVEN forty-five a.m. when Branson Vanburg pulled into Coates Ravine, "Blurred Lines" by Robin Thicke and Pharrell Williams playing on the car sound system. It was a beautiful spring day and Vanburg was on cloud nine. He leaped out of his truck—a brand new Chevrolet Silverado his father had bought him to celebrate. Four days earlier he'd been cleared of all sexual assault charges. *That bitch!* In his closing statement, the judge had apologized for taking up "this decent family's time."

The case for the defense focused on Colette Fieldhouse's behavior at the party. Vanburg's lawyer grilled her about her short skirt and low-cut top, and why she'd worn such clothes. He asked if she regularly drank alcohol with men she didn't know. She explained that she'd been invited to the party by a friend, another young woman, and thought it was just a gathering to meet people. Vanburg's lawyer then quizzed her about her arrival at the party, because witnesses had said that on entering the house she kissed her friend on the lips. The defense argued all this behavior suggested she went to the party for sex and wanted to have sex with Vanburg ... or any other man willing to fall into her trap. Vanburg's lawyer argued that the kiss on arrival was provocation designed for male arousal. Furthermore, even if Colette was silent during the sex with Vanburg, this was neither his fault nor his responsibility. Rather, it was a sign of her lack of responsibility for their encounter. The judge asked Colette, "Why couldn't you just keep your knees together?" As for Vanburg pulling her out of his car and leaving her in a bus shelter in the middle of the night, well, Vanburg's lawyers argued that he wanted her to be in a place where she could get home safely, and he had to go to football training early the next morning. In sum, the defense argued Vanburg had shown responsibility (to himself), and had broken no laws.

The all-male jury agreed.

Pushed for comment by the media pack outside the court, Vanburg's father, Tilman Vanburg, shouted "I thank the jury for this verdict. My son should never have faced jail for twenty minutes of action with some girl. Because of all this stress, he will never again be his easygoing self."

Mossberg had its jock back, even more heroic to many because of the persecution he had endured—a hero and a survivor.

Throughout the whole saga, Vanburg remained captain of Mossberg River's football team. "Innocent until proven guilty," coach Sterling insisted. During the court case, and especially in the hours after his acquittal, Vanburg received hundreds of messages of support, including one from coach Sterling saying he was a sure thing for a four-year football scholarship at Mossberg College. Freshman year. It was going to be big. Bring on the game; bring on the parties; bring on the girls.

Vanburg regularly came to Coates Ravine for an early morning cardio workout. A six-mile loop trail wound through forest, crossing back and forth across the ravine on footbridges. He trained there during football season with his buddies. They joked they were a wolf pack: howling in unison when they spotted a woman up ahead, slapping at her ass as they ran past and yelling, "Nice tits!" She was always terrified—"Stop it! What are you doing?!" she'd whimper—and they'd run off laughing. The older ladies were the most fun: always so shocked.

He squatted to tighten his laces, arranged his shorts to make his packet comfortable, and took a swig of water. He turned right to run the path counterclockwise. This way he could do the hilly section first, then do sprints on the long, flat, final stretch on the opposite side of the ravine, before crossing back to the parking lot.

There was only one other car parked there, a blue Mazda2. Vanburg sneered—a chick's car—and bounded off, singing the lyrics to "Blurred Lines".

5

CARLY'S BLUE MAZDA2 had turned into the Coates Ravine parking lot at seven thirty a.m. She, Kate, and Seyram got out and stretched in the fresh air, a woodpecker tapping in the distance. When the weather was good, they came here early on the weekends, typically continuing whatever conversation they'd left off when they last met, interspersed with periods of silence while they walked fast for several hundred yards.

They always did the circuit clockwise, turning left at the trailhead and crossing to the opposite side of the ravine to get into a rhythm on the flat, before working up a sweat on the hilly section, on the way back to the parking lot.

"You know what we decided at my place—about targeting the jocks in this town? I'm having a real crisis about this," said Seyram. "It was easy for you to suggest it, Kate, but you've always been the bad girl. I was Daddy's girl who never did anything wrong, and Mom tells me I'm the best mother ever. I love *following* rules, not breaking them."

"You still are good," replied Kate. "You're saving your daughter, and Summer, from sexual predators by getting them before they fully hatch."

"The problem is," said Carly, "this entire town is in its comfort zone. Women have low standards for men, and the men are happy with the status quo. That's what makes the three of us so pissed. After school we got out of our comfort zones: we left, went to graduate school, or got jobs elsewhere, and eventually decided to come back on our terms. But our past is all around us and Mossberg hasn't changed—the social rules haven't changed, and they're never going to unless someone shakes things up."

Two miles into their walk they rounded a corner onto a long straight stretch of path that ran right beside the ravine's edge. Several hundred yards ahead, a young man was running fast toward them.

Carly noticed him first. "That's Branson Vanburg up ahead. Look at him running free!"

"I'm not going to change course for him," said Seyram. "Keep walking straight."

Vanburg reached them at a clearing where there was a bit more room for him to pass. Exuding confidence, he flashed them a smile. "Ladies."

Kate couldn't contain herself. "Lady, yourself, rapist."

The word dropped like a ten-ton weight into the clearing.

Vanburg pulled up sharp. "What did you call me?"

"I called you a rapist, asshole," said Kate. "You should thank your lucky stars you had those good ol' boys on the jury. You assaulted Colette Fieldhouse and now you're running around free as a bird."

"Who the fuck are you? They were a jury of my peers."

"That's the problem. It was a jury of *your* peers."

"Colette Fieldhouse went to that party to get laid. Chicks love football players." Vanburg smirked. "Want some like she did?" He hauled on his crotch. "Come get it."

Vanburg leaned back against the wooden rail separating the path from the ravine, spreading his arms along the top. It could have been a scene from a magazine shoot—handsome, muscled man, chiseled features, healthy glow—except for the leer.

Carly felt exactly the way Vanburg intended. Even in the company of two tall, grown, women, she quailed.

Seyram couldn't believe her ears. She'd been raised to be polite to elders—in church, in school, in the family. Always. Who was this young man who thought he could speak to them like that—so confident, so crude, so dismissive of what he'd done, in front of three adult women?

Kate took out a cigarette and struck a match, staring right back at Vanburg.

The staccato of a woodpecker sounded in the distance.

The smell of burning made Seyram's head clear. She assessed what was in front of her: a six-foot-four 250-pound jock. But Seyram herself was not petite ... and she had the element of surprise because Vanburg thought he was master of the situation. Immediately behind him the land fell sharply into the ravine. No one else was around.

Seyram pushed her glasses up her nose and made a tentative step forward.

"What are you doing?" Carly had a panicked voice.

"Seyram, are you mad?" Kate hissed.

A hard look came over Vanburg's face and his hands went to his waistband.

"Ladies, get in line."

Seyram stepped forward again, bent as though to kneel, then charged like a bull.

All Kate and Carly could remember was Vanburg doubled over Seyram's back, his eyes wide, and his mouth forming an 'O' in surprise as Seyram propelled him back, up, and *out*— into space. Arms and legs flailed in the air, followed by three seconds of silence before a loud *crack* came from below.

A single leaf drifted down to the burbling river. The woodpecker hammered away.

Seyram teetered on the edge, grabbed the post to steady herself, then stepped back and smoothed her blouse. Turning to Kate and Carly, she fixed them with a defiant look. "Like I said, I'm tired of being good. Let's take out the jocks." She turned and headed back to the car.

6

THE THREE OF them walked hastily, not saying a word. Seyram strode ahead; Carly and Kate struggled to keep up.

As they reached the parking lot, Carly couldn't contain herself. "Seyram, say something! What happened back there? I thought we were going to make men scared first."

"I don't know!" Seyram almost shouted, fierce and upset at the same time. "I saw the way he looked at us and I thought *Branson Vanburg is an unrepentant rapist.*"

"Was," Kate replied drily. "Start up the car, Carly, and let's talk on the way back to town. We need to get out of here. If anyone asks if we saw anything, the answer is no. We just did our normal walk, OK? No one else is here; no one else has seen us. Let's keep it that way."

They piled into the car, Carly reversing out, ready to turn into the road. Kate continued to take charge, leaning forward from the back seat to give instructions: "Carly, take the long way back into town. There's less chance of passing another car and it'll eat up a bit of time, so you won't get home too early and have to explain why."

As Carly put distance between them and Coates Ravine, they started to relax.

"How can you think so clearly?" asked Carly, looking in the rearview mirror at Kate. "I'm shaking so much. I would have just sat in the car and cried—or called the Automobile Association. I really thought he was going to attack us at one point. Seyram, are you OK?"

Seyram's hands were trembling in her lap, and she was still breathing fast. "I'm just processing what happened. When he spoke so crudely, it's like the rational part of my brain stopped. And I've got a sore skull from head-butting him."

The three of them broke into nervous laughter.

"If we ever go to court, that's our defense." Kate was matter of fact. "An accused rapist ran head-on toward us, and we were terrified he was going to attack. Sounds like a reasonable defense to me."

"Then we can't lie about not seeing anyone out here," said Carly. "We either saw him and thought he was going to attack us, or we have to say we didn't see a thing."

"You're right," agreed Kate. "Let's lie about it. Agreed? We didn't see a thing. We did our usual full loop and got back to the car at our usual time of nine thirty."

"But maybe someone else will arrive and start off on the trail the same direction as he did. They'll say they never crossed paths with anyone, which means we can't have done the full circuit."

"What have I done?" exclaimed Seyram. "We're already stumbling over lies!"

"Listen, we need to keep it together." Kate was thoughtful. "We don't know if someone came and went from the parking lot while we were walking. They may have seen Carly's car, so we can't lie about this when Vanburg is found. When the news breaks, let's call the police to say we were in the vicinity. This is the story: we did exactly the walk we did. Seyram, you got blisters, so we turned back, and you took off your shoes in the car. That's why—in case Felix or the kids see you—you're going to arrive home not wearing shoes. Carly, drop me off right outside my door, so no one sees me going inside."

"But I am wearing shoes," said Seyram in bewilderment.

"Yes, but we need to get rid of them. Yours too, Carly, and mine."

"These are my favorite sneakers!" said Carly. "It's totally legitimate that we were exercising there. And that's what we were doing."

"No, Kate's right," said Seyram. "It's one thing to say we were walking the trail, but quite another if the police get shoe prints from the exact place Vanburg went over the edge and those prints match our shoes. It's evidence all three of us were at the crime scene."

"I know a great place to get rid of them," said Carly. "I'm firing pottery in the kiln tomorrow. It'll be a few thousand degrees by noon. Leave your shoes in the car when I drop you off and they'll be ash by lunchtime tomorrow."

In the back, Kate broke into a sweat. "Thank Christ I care enough about the environment that I don't toss my cigarette butts away. You know how I lit that smoke? I was going to flick it at him, but then I stuck the butt in my fanny pack out of habit." Kate unzipped it, and sure enough, the butt was wrapped in foil that she kept for precisely that purpose. "It's got my DNA on it for sure." She rubbed her temples in relief.

KATE AND CARLY had been friends since the day Kate's family moved to Mossberg from New Jersey and her mother came to the local grade school to enroll Kate. As a child, Carly had been in love with textiles and fashion, so when Mrs. Bajwa turned up wearing a pink embroidered salwar kameez—traditional Punjabi women's wear of long, loose shirt and baggy pants—with a copper and turquoise floral design laid out in beads and sequins, Carly fell head over heels in love. Mrs. Bajwa had forced Kate to also wear a salwar kameez: "So you look nice for your new friends." Kate, born and bred in the suburbs of New Jersey, wanted to wear jeans and a sweater, and knew the salwar kameez was a mistake the second the other kids laid eyes on her.

"Are you from Africa?" "Are you starving?" "Do you ride camels?" "Does your dad have four wives?"

Kate had a standard response to these questions: "Get lost, putz!" None of the kids in Mossberg knew what a putz was, but they could tell it wasn't good to be one.

Carly had much less confidence. A quiet girl, she spent much of her time with her own thoughts or doing crafts. At seven, she was already bored by her classmates' utilitarian clothes and even more utilitarian imaginations. She leaped at the chance to make a friend from exotic *elsewhere*.

Kate, shunned by other students for being too Asian/African/New Jersey/non-Christian, was relieved to have any friend. Knowing Carly's family, the Schumers, also gave Kate entrée into a non-immigrant American family, even if they weren't exactly representative of Mossberg. When visiting Carly she loved the opportunity to explore their house unattended—Carly in the bathroom or lost in fashion magazines; Carly's mother grading papers in her book-lined private study and sipping a mug of steaming coffee; and Carly's father whistling in his pottery shed in the garden. Kate tiptoed around their house, agog at a framed newspaper cutting of Mr. and Mrs. Schumer dancing naked in front of the stage at Woodstock; at Mr. Schumer's plaster cast of Mrs. Schumer's belly and breasts when hugely pregnant with Carly, which hung proudly in the living room; and, in their library room, at records, books and objects—an eagle feather, a Mesoamerican clay figurine, a Finnish kantele stringed instrument, and Turkish wall tiles.

What Kate most liked at Carly's house was the atmosphere. Carly's dad was a potter who made barely a dime at weekend markets, but he kept their house and garden shipshape, loved cooking, and made a happy comfortable home for his wife and daughter. While making dinner he would say things like, "Think about being an astronaut or another Marie Curie." Carly's mom, an English professor at the local college, always asked Carly and her friends what they were reading and encouraged them to join the Peace Corps. Half of Mossberg,

Pennsylvania, had German names, but the Schumers were the only hippies.

In 2016, Carly's parents retired to New Mexico—"One of the few states out west where Hillary thumped Trump," said her dad. Tears still came to Carly's eyes when she remembered waving goodbye as their car rolled out of her driveway and turned west, but she knew it was for the best. Her parents had bought an adobe house in the high desert ten miles outside Santa Fe. "We can't take the cold anymore, Carl, and I'm tired of shoveling snow," her dad told her. "New Mexico has this amazing light and all these beautiful adobe buildings—and artists everywhere."

"And the plants and birds are just beautiful," said her mom. "We're going to sit on the back terrace, reading books and looking at the landscape. It'll be heaven! Remember, it's only a half-day plane ride away and we'll be back in the summer when the desert gets too hot."

The Schumers had been Kate's stalwart supporters during her youth when she rebelled against her parents. Her biggest argument with them began innocuously enough: it was about a haircut. Kate adopted her current look—the one she'd keep for over thirty years—the month she finished high school. k.d. lang's album *Ingénue* was all over the radio and, inspired, she transformed her long, glossy black hair into short back and sides, with an almost-quiff on top. Her parents were horrified. She started calling herself Kate instead of Katiya, her "real" name. And she vowed to never again, anywhere, wear a salwar kameez.

"You'll *never* find a husband!" wailed Juneeta, her mother. Her father jibed, "An American if you're *lucky*." Totally rational until then, her parents lost it when a chance for grandchildren appeared to be slipping away.

Kate's haircut and brown skin sometimes confused people. Up close, when people were paying attention, they nearly always thought she was gay. Kate wore jeans, stood tall, and walked with confidence. She wanted to signal what she was and was relieved when people "got it" without needing explanation. It saved time and occasional confusion— although she took cruel pleasure watching others stumble in embarrassment. But she'd also lost track of how many times when entering a restroom she'd been greeted with "This is the ladies' room!" or, alternatively, being taken for the janitor. At Mossberg River Golf Club, where she'd been a member for a decade, she still occasionally got a cheerful "Hiya, buddy" from male players, followed by a sheepish "Sorry, lady."

Kate's only visible concession to her heritage was a tiny gold nose stud completely disproportionate to her magnificent nose. The stud was a riposte to the white-girl, ski-jump noses that had stuck themselves in the air around her at school. Kate was out and, goddammit, so was her nose, unafraid to bring attention to itself.

Her aunts—Kate had four, who stuck their own noses into the entire family's business whenever visiting—thought this a terrible error of judgment.

"Why draw attention to your nose? It's one of your bottom three assets!"

"Take out the stud, grow your hair back, and use it to cover your face!"

"What husband wants a wife who jabs him with her nose every time she leans in close!"

"It's not a nose stud you need, but a nose *job*!"

Kate knew her family meant well; it was just the way they expressed themselves. They were from a long line of community leaders near Pathankot in Punjab, and when she finally came out to her parents—which was more of a muttering about how she was never going to marry a man— her mother told her it was the first breach of family honor in one thousand years.

Kate's two brothers, having thrown themselves into their studies and not shown the least interest in women until their early thirties, eventually married and delivered up five grandchildren. With the pressure off, Kate assumed the responsibilities of a dutiful daughter as her parents aged and was welcomed back at the family table as a beloved, if unfathomably odd, family member. Smoking and the L-word, however, stayed outside.

Kate and Carly met Seyram in ninth grade, on their first day of high school, although they would have met even if they weren't in school together because Seyram and Kate's dads turned out to be colleagues. Both were civil engineers for the Pennsylvania Department of Transportation and worked out of the Mossberg depot.

The reason Seyram moved to Mossberg wasn't her father's job, but her mother's. Ellen was a biotechnology expert and had pioneered biogas plants in Ghana. She was recruited into an academic job by the University of Pittsburgh. Ellen spent Tuesday to Thursday teaching and in the lab in the city, but on Mondays and Fridays and at weekends was at the family home in Mossberg doing administration, grading papers, writing scientific articles, and preparing for classes. It would have been more convenient for them to live in the city, but Seyram's dad, who had never previously been to the United States, was convinced Seyram would be recruited into a gang if they moved there. Ellen, who had traveled, knew this was silly. Nevertheless, once he got his job in Mossberg, ringed on three sides by forested hills and with its bucolic suburbs unwinding beside a river, the family decided it was the place to make their home.

Juneeta Bajwa thought Seyram, with her impeccable manners and studiousness, was the perfect role model for Kate, although she wondered how Seyram's family arrangements had produced such a child. "Such a pity you don't have brothers," she told Seyram, whose reply shocked her: "Ma says her PhD was her first child and I'm lucky to even be here."

"Don't you miss Mommy during the week? She must feel guilty going off to work at dawn every Tuesday. How do you eat when Daddy is in charge?"

"I went to boarding school in Ghana, so seeing Ma four days a week is wonderful. She does a heap of cooking after church on Sundays, and we heat that up during the week for dinner, but I prepare lunches for Dad and myself every morning. Thank you for the lovely dinner, Mrs. Bajwa."

Despite their different personalities, the three girls hit it off and spent hours in each other's homes. Just as Carly was enraptured by Mrs. Bajwa's clothes, Seyram was enraptured by her spicy cooking and she spent as many meals as she could in the Bajwa household. Similarly, Carly and Kate felt at home at Seyram's place, although for different reasons. Having an academic mother and a father who was around a lot felt normal to Carly, and she and Seyram were single children who had learnt to find their own fun. The laughter in the Boateng house was infectious, although it was even more enticing to Kate after the seriousness of her own home, where parental attention focused on her brothers.

The girls' parents came to know each other well from the dropping off and picking up of daughters from each other's homes and setting extra places at the dinner table. Seyram's and Kate's fathers were particularly friendly with each other, and all the parents were constantly bumping into each other at the supermarket or gas station, or at medical and dental appointments. They felt the loss when the Schumers moved to New Mexico, but the parents were thankful their daughters remained close friends.

WYATT BELL CALLED his editor in chief, Henry Konig, as soon as he had cell phone reception back at the Coates Ravine parking lot. "Mr. Konig, they've got the body. It's Branson Vanburg, the football player we did the story on four days ago. I overhead the police confirming his name."

Konig let out a low whistle. "Son, get back here on the double. We need this story written up ASAP."

Wyatt had graduated from the journalism program at Drake University a year earlier, working at the *Des Moines Register* over the summer on the agricultural beat—weather, commodity prices, farm corporation buyouts, machinery stories, and the Iowa State Fair. He came from a farm, so these stories were familiar to him. But his girlfriend, Emily, got into Mossberg College's renowned Public Health program, and he followed her east to Pennsylvania. His dad wasn't happy: "What type of girl expects her man to follow her?" His mom whispered in Wyatt's ear, "Don't listen to your father. I wish I'd had a career."

Within a few weeks of arriving, Wyatt got a job at the *Mossberg Gazette*. It was very different from the *Register*. On his first day, he expected an orientation and a stack of stories to read to give him a sense of the *Gazette*'s style and editorial expectations. Timidly, he knocked on Henry Konig's door.

The *Gazette* was a small local newspaper with an online edition and biweekly hard copy editions. Wyatt was the first reporter it had hired in almost twenty years, and he was the youngest on staff by about fifteen.

"Good morning. Mr. Konig? I'm Wyatt, your new reporter."

Henry Konig had his elbows on his desk, his head resting in his hands. He looked up at what appeared to be a twelve-year-old: fresh-faced and earnest, clutching a pen and notepad. A memory flashed of reading bedtime stories to his children. Straightening in his chair, he said, "Son, get me a Tylenol. They're in the cabinet behind reception."

This was such an unexpected response Wyatt wasn't sure the command was meant for him. He tried again, "Mr. Konig, I'm Wyatt Bell. Your new reporter."

"Goddammit, I heard you, son. I'm asking you to bring me a Tylenol!"

Wyatt scurried away and came back a minute later with a box of pills.

"Thank you." Konig took two with a gulp of water. "Now, sit down. I've got the FBI coming to see me this afternoon from Pittsburgh. Someone has reported some comments about females posted on our articles as a hate crime. What the hell happened to the First Amendment?"

Wyatt could tell the question was rhetorical.

"So now the FBI are involved. Apparently, they're going to track the servers and identify the fellas doing it. Meantime, the board tells me I have to spend money I don't have, hiring a girl to monitor the comments and delete the bad ones, otherwise we might be taken to court. Christ, I wish ladies would grow a pair!" Konig thumped the desk, making Wyatt jump in his seat. "That's your first assignment. There's a march happening this morning, from a place called Sisterhood House to City Hall. They're calling it the 'March for Change.' I want you to cover it and find out what they're complaining about; what they want changed. It's the MeToos, or some such thing."

At nine fifteen a.m., Wyatt walked out of the *Gazette* office to cover Mossberg's inaugural #MeToo March Against Assault. The organizer, Grace Schmidt, was happy to see a journalist and encouraged everyone to talk to him.

Wyatt got to work recording vox pop segments for the online edition. "Why are you marching today?"

"To bring attention to sexual assault in this town."

"The institutions that run this town—the council, the courts, the police, the churches—need to know that women and girls, and the gay and trans community, are tired of harassment and injustice. We need their help to do something about it."

"To support other women across America and around the world. Women who refuse to be silent about harassment they've experienced."

Wyatt returned to Grace and asked, "What do you hope the march will achieve?"

"We want people to realize that sexual harassment and assault is a local issue, not something that happens in far-off cities. Survivors can live with emotional and physical scars for years, but perpetrators are rarely convicted in Mossberg. When they are, their sentences are usually light. We want to tell survivors that they're not alone, that they have supporters in this community, and we want to send a message to the courts that sexual assault is a serious crime."

The marchers were impassioned and happy, notwithstanding the seriousness of their cause: smiling and laughing with each other, waving placards, and raising chants. Hope was in the air.

Wyatt was taken aback by the reaction to the march along the route. Iowans were conservative, but they were outwardly polite; they kept their contempt in reserve. In Mossberg, while a couple of cars honked in support, the marchers were also vociferously catcalled; a driver wound down his window and spat, a second yelled, "Suck my dick!", and a woman shouted, "I'll pray you all find husbands!"

Wyatt made notes of the finale, which took place on the steps of City Hall: of the placards and chanting, and of women speaking about the importance of local support to give hope that the future could be better for others. He went inside to get municipal data on assaults, noting how different this story was to pork futures on the Chicago Exchange.

He spent the afternoon back at the *Gazette* typing up the article on an old box computer for the next day's edition. It was the first journalistic social analysis piece he'd ever written for publication. One thousand words, packed with quotes from the marchers, a photo of a forest of signs on the City Hall steps, and loads of statistics. Rates of sexual assault in Pennsylvania were among the lowest in America, but Mossberg itself was up there with Arkansas, South Dakota, and Colorado, although nowhere near Alaska. Wyatt had a gut feeling he was onto a good story: how a movement was trying to change powerful institutions. His final year college project at Drake had been on the campaign to improve health and safety for immigrant farm workers, and he felt he'd landed on his feet in this new town doing a story like this. He titled it *Groundswell for Change* and envisaged it next to a thoughtful opinion piece or letters to the editor.

Henry Konig hated it. "What are you, son, a socialist? Mossbergers don't want to read this crap. We love our community. What this march shows is that we can tolerate citizens who aren't proud of America." He reduced the article to 200 words and retitled it *Triumph of Democracy: Feminists not Shot*, putting it on the front page as a complete story. All analysis was cut. It had the most hits of any story ever on the *Gazette*'s website. Fox News interviewed Henry Konig for a segment on how Trump's presidency was energizing small communities to resist the radical left.

As he drove back to the *Gazette's* offices from Coates Ravine, Wyatt mulled his dreams of a Pulitzer Prize for Investigative Reporting. His failed *Groundswell for Change* article had been a harsh lesson.

"Henry wants you in his office," said the receptionist as soon as Wyatt arrived.

Wyatt walked in to find Henry Konig on the phone to his brother, Roger Konig, trying to ascertain the status of the police investigation.

"Have the Vanburgs been told? This will be my front-page story."

The mayor was on speaker. "The police chief just sent an officer to their house."

"Tell me the minute the family knows. What happened?"

"The cops don't know. This kid had his whole life ahead of him. I can't believe he killed himself and there's no way you can just fall off the path at Coates Ravine. You know the trail, right? It's where we used to jog for football training."

"You think he was murdered?"

"Who would want him dead? That girl probably had supporters, but women don't murder men. Can't do that kind of planning. Besides, everyone thought he was a hero."

Konig told Wyatt the kind of article he wanted and sent him off to write. At four thirty p.m. the *Gazette* was informed the family knew, and they were free to publish the story.

Local Hero Dies in Coates Ravine Tragedy

Local football hero, Branson Vanburg, was found dead today at Coates Ravine. A gifted athlete and popular leader, Vanburg captained Mossberg River High School's football team to many victories. There is speculation he lost his footing in a freak accident. Police say there are no suspicious circumstances.

No mention was made of the recent court case. As far as the *Gazette* was concerned, the waters had closed over that unwanted chapter in the community's life. Vanburg would be buried a proud son of Mossberg.

Wyatt spent that evening scrolling through social media. It was clear Vanburg had loads of supporters—even more than during the trial, when hundreds went online to express their support for him. But was there a disgruntled former girlfriend? A boy whose girl he'd stolen? A rival on the football team? Another victim of his abuse?

The mayor was right: there was no way you could accidentally fall off that path, through the rail, at that point on the trail. Vanburg had also just been acquitted, so he would hardly be in the kind of depressive state that might lead to suicide ... or perhaps he felt guilty that he had *not* been convicted?

Given what Wyatt knew about Vanburg's personality, guilty or remorseful feelings didn't make sense either.

And then there were all those shoe prints. He couldn't identify anything useful from the photos he took, but thought he could make out perhaps three or four different shoe print patterns—including narrow prints more likely to be from women's shoes. That meant at least three people were at that spot, including Vanburg. Maybe he *had* been pushed? Could a woman do that …?

9

FOR SIX WEEKS after Branson Vanburg's death, Seyram, Kate, and Carly barely spoke to each other. This was a record gap in communication over decades of friendship. However, they thought constantly about each other—about Seyram's ability to act so decisively and her unexpectedly fierce lack of repentance; about Kate's ability to think so clearly under pressure; and about Carly's tremulous determination that what had happened was the right thing even though it scared her.

The three of them occupied themselves with work in the lab, the store, and the studio, but this was mostly to distract themselves from their thoughts. Like that single leaf floating down into the ravine after Vanburg, the mental dust that had been stirred up also needed to settle.

Seyram went particularly quiet. She worked longer hours at the business, and at home lay on the couch surfing channels or swiping through Facebook and Instagram. She would surreptitiously gaze at Nana and Kofi over her glasses, wondering what world they were going to enter as adults, and if her and Felix's parenting practices would be enough to protect them.

Kate and Carly talked together a few times, mostly to see what the other was thinking about Seyram.

"When Seyram said she was tired of being good, I thought she'd smoke a joint, not kill someone," said Carly.

"I was hoping she'd let the kids have a Big Mac," replied Kate.

"I bumped into Felix with the kids in the Daineton McDonalds once. He was stricken when he realized I'd caught him."

"Did you tell Seyram?"

"Are you mad? People talk about Asian tiger moms, but African lion moms are worse. Her standards are exhausting."

"One thing's for certain," said Kate. "She sure knows how to knock a guy off his feet."

Finally, Carly could bear the lack of a get-together no longer and sent a text: *Hi you two. Come to my place this Friday after work for dinner. That's an instruction.*

CARLY WENT TO answer the doorbell. Seyram had driven in behind Kate and they were standing together in the entrance, which opened directly onto a brightly lit combined living area and kitchen. Carly's pottery kiln and studio were in a converted garage in the backyard, but she also used an old architect's drafting table in a well-lit corner of the living area where she sketched new designs.

Carly put an arugula, cranberry, almond, and parmesan salad on her round table, gave Seyram a glass for the mocktail she had brought, and opened the sauvignon blanc. "I've still got one of your Coronas from last time," she told Kate. "Let me open that, it'll be colder than the ones you brought."

"Do you need a hand?" asked Seyram.

"Nope. The sauce is already done—it always tastes better if you make it the day before. I just need to boil water for the pasta when we're ready to eat."

"What's for dinner?"

"Mushroom, garlic, and parsley sauce with fettuccine. Pretty simple, but I've got herb bread too, and there are baked pears for dessert."

Despite the anticipation of the meal, their mood was reflective as they sat around the table.

"OK, I'm going to say this first," announced Carly, taking a sip of wine. "How are you all doing? After Vanburg I've been feeling kind of shocked. Not regretful, just shocked. I'm wondering where we're going with this."

"I prayed," said Seyram.

"And what did God say?" asked Kate.

Seyram shot Kate a look. They'd stopped arguing about religion a long time ago—neither had changed her position and there was nothing new to say—but they had a kind of ongoing, unspoken dialogue that welled up occasionally.

"As you know, that's not how it works. God doesn't just pipe up with advice; that's the whole point of prayer. But, since you asked, I personally concluded that we've stopped a predator in his tracks. And I don't feel bad about it. I'm fed up with women and girls in this town being held hostage by fear.

And I'm willing to do something—something proactive—about it."

"What about you, Kate?" asked Carly.

"I cracked a beer and drank a toast."

Carly was shocked.

"Carly, grow up," Kate continued. "What else has ever changed this town? What we should do now is to plan who's next. You said you're tired of being meek. Embrace that."

Carly spluttered on her wine. "I didn't say I disagreed. Just that I'm kind of shocked that we've actually done it. That we're on … this path."

"Sounds like second thoughts to me," said Kate.

"I'm with Kate on this," said Seyram. "Lots of different men rape women for lots of different reasons. We can't 'fix' them or change them, because how could we even figure out who they are? That's for the psychologists. What we *can* do is make men scared to go out—too scared to attack women. Put them in our shoes—in Nana's shoes, Summer's shoes, Colette Fieldhouse's shoes. That's what my prayer told me."

"Sounds more like Durga," said Kate. "The Hindu goddess who drives evil from the world."

"I like that," said Carly, perking up. "Driving evil from Mossberg."

"If it makes men afraid of doing evil, that's OK with me," said Seyram. "Speaking of which …"

Both Carly and Kate had noticed that Seyram had brought a recent copy of the *Gazette*. They all found the *Gazette* an invaluable source of local news, but Carly and Kate registered it as odd that Seyram had a copy with her. With a flourish, she now opened the paper to the second back page and put it on the table.

"Do you remember the sports pages from a few months ago?" Seyram turned the article around so they could see the article properly. "It's Henry Konig's annual feature on Mossberg's Athlete All-Stars with a whole commentary on who could get drafted for the NHL, NBL, NFL, or MLB." She smiled knowingly.

Kate and Carly scrutinized the article, looked at each other, then back at Seyram, perplexed. Was she losing it? The article seemed so disconnected from the conversation they had just been having.

"Oh, for goodness' sake," said Seyram. "They're the professional sports leagues—hockey, basketball, football, and baseball. It's our shopping list."

Kate and Carly remained uncomprehending.

"A hit list! There are nine jocks featured in the article, including Vanburg. We can cross him off." Seyram grabbed a marker from Carly's drafting table and put a thick red line through his profile.

"Gosh!" Carly blinked a few times. "You're a step ahead of me. I invited you here so we could reflect together on where we're at, and here you are already planning who's next."

Seyram ignored this and steamed right ahead. "And did you see the *Gazette* online today? Preston Brock has just been charged with indecent exposure."

"Preston Brock!" exclaimed Carly and Kate simultaneously.

"Yes, him. He's also here on this list." She tapped his cameo on the page. "For golf and football."

"He's working at the golf club over summer," said Kate. "I see him occasionally when he does an early morning practice round before me. He's good."

"He was a shit of a kid," said Carly. "Used to take the school bus with Summer and harassed her constantly."

"Well, apparently he's progressed to flashing," said Seyram.

"He flashed Summer once," continued Carly. "I complained to the school and *his* parents kicked up a stink. Said I was making him feel discomfort about his body. About being a boy. His dad threatened to sue the school. Preston Brock Senior—he's one of the partners in that law firm downtown, Greene, Taylor & Brock. Principal Kohler convinced me to withdraw my complaint and I regret it to this day. Summer told me she thought mothers were supposed to protect their children and didn't talk to me for a week."

"His dad probably paid Henry Konig to include Preston in their article," snorted Kate.

"What I don't understand is why the *Gazette* named him," said Seyram. "Isn't he a minor? He captained Mossberg Hills High School to the football playoffs last season."

Carly, who kept up with school gossip through Summer, laughed. "Preston Brock is eighteen and a dumbass. He was on track to flunk high school two years back, because he never did any work, and Brock Senior was threatening to sue the school again if they failed him. Preston's problem is he wants to join the army. The principal at Mossberg River said that if he wants to join up—especially if he wants promotion—his best chance is to graduate with a two point five GPA. The principal recommended he repeat senior year to improve his chances. So, although he'll never get into West Point—thank God—he might be able to join a military cadet corps."

"However," Carly continued, lowering her voice, "Ms. Schafer, the art teacher, told me the principal wanted to keep him as football team captain for this season just finished, so the football coach cooked up a plan with the principal to get Preston's dad off their back and keep up the school's football reputation. And that's what happened: he captained Mossberg River to the playoffs—sixth year in a row—and he's joining the army in the fall when the trial should be over."

"How did you know about the trial?" asked Seyram. "The *Gazette* says the charges have just been announced."

"Summer is friends with one of the victim's friends. Her parents insisted on pressing charges. I'll bet you a hundred bucks Preston Senior hires the best lawyer he can find and they'll go for a jury trial. The defense will pick men—alumni of Mossberg River. The football coach and a dozen businessmen will supply references about how Preston is an outstanding young man with a bright future, who wants to serve his country by joining the army. Then they'll argue it was all a *misunderstanding*: Preston is emotionally immature, and he thought flashing his dick would be a kind of juvenile sexy gesture to share with the girl he loved. And now he's really suffering because she reported him to the police. And he'll get off. It makes me sick!"

Carly flopped back in her chair thinking of Summer, only to spring back up. "Summer's friends from Mossberg River say that in his repeat year he was an asshole. Bullied everyone, disruptive, sexually harassed girls, still did hardly any schoolwork, so full of himself … but was great at football, so got away with it all."

"So, the flashing harasser is going to join the army and sit out at bases like Fort Byrd, come into town on the weekend and wave his genitalia around." Seyram was appalled.

"Except," said Kate, "that he's on our—what did you call it?—our *shopping list*. I vote this is who we target next." Kate was firm. "He's just done a school apprenticeship in sexual harassment. We should stop him from being unleashed onto the world."

"To be honest, Carly, I thought that's why you invited us tonight," said Seyram. "To plan who's next. I've made up my mind: we should continue."

"I'm with you," said Kate. "But how are we going to do this?" She gazed around in frustration. "Wait a minute. What did I just say? *Preston Brock plays a round of golf before me*. It's his freebie practice before he starts work. Golfers are supposed to keep their distance from each other but if we can speed up, we could get him alone and take him by surprise." Kate pictured the course in her head.

"Do we … do we *actually* want to hurt him?" asked Carly. "I mean, I can't bear the guy, but he's also a loser who may fail school again. I feel like Vanburg's death just happened out of nowhere, and we don't necessarily need the same …". Carly paused. "We don't need to do that again."

"What do you propose?" asked Kate.

"Let's … confront him on the golf course and play it by ear."

"You want us to give him a free pass because he's stupid?" Kate's raised eyebrow expressed all the contempt she could muster.

"Don't give me that look, Bajwa." Carly was hurt. "I'm just saying we need to think about how far to take this."

Seyram intervened. "We still need a plan, even if we play it by ear. I'm all for roughing him up as a warning, but we need to get close to him. Kate, you said he's good at golf, right?"

"Really good."

"How about this? We come up close to him—which I know you're not supposed to do on a golf course—and then flatter him. Tell him we want to watch him hit a few balls. Then Kate, you ask if he can show you how to swing. He'll stand behind you, right?"

"Right. The person showing you pretty much stands behind you and encloses you with their arms while they show you how to hold the club."

"And—Carly—Preston will say yes to instructing Kate, right? From what you say he's got a monumental ego, so he'll enjoy the flattery."

"For sure."

"Perfect. That means when he's demonstrating, you Kate, will be in front of him, and you and I, Carly, are behind him. We've got him encircled, and we can all be holding clubs. I say we warn him that if he flashes another girl before he goes off to the army, we're going to beat his testicles to a pulp."

"You don't think he'll report us to the police, or club management?" asked Carly.

"A guy like that is going to be so embarrassed he was accosted by middle-aged ladies. My guess is he won't say a word."

10

Saturday was a perfect day for golf: late spring, with squirrels leaping in the trees, birds on the green, nests full of chirping chicks, and a hint of humidity but no breeze in the air.

Kate, with Seyram and Carly in tow, had set off at her assigned tee time, playing the first half of the course at a normal pace, and maintaining the usual golfing distance from the player up ahead, Preston Brock.

Kate, who knew the course well, had identified the best place to confront him as right near the twelfth hole. There was a distance of about fifty yards from the eleventh hole to a thicket, which one had to walk around to get to the twelfth hole's tee box. The bushes would shield them from any players behind them. Timing was going to be crucial. They had to get close enough to Brock to be able to close the gap within perhaps thirty seconds, but far enough away from other players that no one surprised them during their planned confrontation.

As Kate hit off from the ninth hole, they saw Brock up ahead already moving on from tenth. A surge of adrenalin coursed through all of them; this was their agreed point of acceleration.

"Let's go," said Kate.

Kate raced through the tenth and eleventh holes, then they rounded the bushes to come upon him settling into his toes and twitching the club ready to swing on the twelfth.

Brock was distracted by movement to his right. Thinking it was a woodchuck hiding in the thicket—one of his jobs at the club was to destroy their burrows to prevent them digging up the green—he looked to take note of where it went. Three women, slightly out of breath, arrived as if out of nowhere. Brock was irritated. He liked to do his free round in peace and had little patience with females on a golf course, especially if they intruded on his game.

"You're not supposed to be here," he said, speaking slowly. "Girls should keep away from the men while we concentrate." Brock nodded his head at them, encouraging them to comprehend.

Kate curled her gloved hand into a fist.

Seyram poked Kate in the ribs from behind and whispered, "Ask him for help."

"Flatter him, you idiot," said Carly under her breath.

Kate just couldn't do it.

Carly, who knew nothing about golf, stepped forward and gushed. "Oh. My. *God!* You're *amazing!* We saw that shot you did back there on the tenth hole and just had to come and talk to you. You're *really* impressive."

Brock reminded himself to take better note of his talents. He was usually impatient with golf grannies, but he would let it slide this time. "Thanks, girls." He winked. "It comes naturally."

Carly took a deep breath. "But aren't you a really talented football player too? You're Preston Brock, am I right? I can't believe you're *so good* at *so many* sports!" She put her hand on her heart and continued in a hushed tone. "Is it true you're joining the army? Talented *and brave!*" Carly conjured up a tear and blinked it away.

Brock had anticipated adulation upon return from foreign countries, but not before he had even departed. This was confirmation he was on the right path in life.

Kate wanted to puke.

"My friend Kate here is too shy to ask, but could you show her how to improve her swing?" said Carly. "She's admired you for a really long time."

Brock looked at Kate, making a mental list: *No tits, no make-up, no smile, over twenty-five. Perhaps she needs Preston's touch to improve her day?*

"It won't take a minute," urged Carly.

Kate gathered her wits. "Please, Preston! It'd be an honor."

He had never been able to resist flattery.

Seyram and Carly took hold of Kate's arms and guided her over to Brock, parking her in front of him. Carly gave Brock a gentle push in the back. "There you go."

He snuggled in behind Kate, his pelvis brushing her bottom, arms reaching around to lay his hands upon hers as she held the club. He felt a wave of arousal. Bringing his lips close to Kate's ear, he whispered, "Want me to grab you by the pussy?"

Kate sprang out of his grasp and whirled around. "*What* did you say?"

"If the commander-in-chief can ask for it, so can I!"

"What are you talking about?" said Kate, confused and angry in equal measures. "Who's your commander-in-chief?"

"*Our* commander-in-chief," Brock sputtered. "President Trump! You should be grateful he wants you."

He was serious.

"Oh, fuck this." Kate swung her golf club against Brock's knee. *Thwack!* He buckled to the ground, falling on his back at Carly's feet.

Brock groaned and opened his eyes, then suddenly giggled. He was looking directly up Carly's skirt. "Mmmm! Mommy pussy." He giggled again.

Carly stumbled backward, pushing her skirt between her legs.

"Seyram, hand the me the driver," said Kate tersely. "Carly, get out of the way." She grabbed the driver from Seyram and took her stance: feet firmly on the ground, toes two feet back from Brock's head. After a glance at an imaginary hole 200 yards into the distance, Kate brought the club to the top of her backswing, then swung down and through to finish ... the club stopped at Brock's right temple.

He went limp.

Carly gave a small scream, then she and Seyram stared open-mouthed at Kate.

Kate glared. "Mmmm! Mommy golf club."

"I thought we were going to send a warning," said Seyram.

"Me too," said Kate.

11

The *Gazette* Blared the news:

Grisly End for Star Athlete in Golf Course Murder

The article did not connect the deaths of Branson Vanburg and Preston Brock, but Wyatt Bell did. He identified them very clearly as jocks, and remembered their type swaggering around locker rooms and corridors at school and in college. He also remembered a recent *Gazette* article about local athletes. Wyatt searched the digital archive until he found the sports story that profiled Mossberg's future sporting stars. There they were, side-by-side: Vanburg and Brock. Just a coincidence?

When he raised the possibility of their deaths *not* being a coincidence with his editor, Konig pooh-poohed the idea. "Don't be absurd, son. Mossberg loves its sporting heroes. And young men die all the time. Just because two athletes lose their lives months apart doesn't mean there's a connection."

Remembering the photos he had taken in Coates Ravine where Vanburg had gone over the edge, Wyatt proposed another angle. "Mr. Konig, what about my photos of shoe prints in Coates Ravine? I'm sure they show evidence that at least three people were at the scene. Couldn't we do a story on the *Gazette*'s exclusive evidence being a possible key to solving

Branson Vanburg's death? We could suggest there might be a link to Preston Brock's death. It could even be an exposé on the failings of Mossberg's police department."

"Exactly, son," Konig responded drily. "That's why we're never going to publish that story."

Wyatt remained convinced there could be a link between the two deaths. He also had little confidence in the police department's ability to investigate these cases. He went back to social media, looking for friends or girlfriends Vanburg and Brock had in common—individuals who may have played on both Mossberg River and Mossberg Hills football teams, and therefore may have known both men—and any negative comments toward them from the same individuals. He resolved to track down a few friends and ask more about Vanburg's and Brock's private lives. Then, on a hunch he couldn't explain, he decided the best place to start was back at Sisterhood House: asking Grace Schmidt how victims, survivors, and supporters felt about men like Vanburg and Brock.

Like Henry Konig, who dismissed Wyatt's suggestions of a link between the deaths of Branson Vanburg and Preston Brock, the Mossberg Police Department also did not see a connection between their deaths.

Seyram, Kate and Carly had remained on the golf course, first waiting for the clubhouse manager to arrive and then the police, having called them both. After a cursory exchange with

Kate and Carly, Mossberg Police Department's Detective Schultz asked Seyram to come to the station to be interviewed—much to the women's surprise.

"Sorry, Detective," interrupted Kate, "but I'm the golfer. Shouldn't you be interviewing me? Seyram and Carly were just supporting me while I played. I saw him first if that makes a difference."

Schultz took immediate offense. "The police know who needs to be interviewed. That'll be all ma'am." Turning to Seyram, he barked "Come with me, please."

Seyram had a sinking, knowing, feeling upon being singled out. She gave a quick wave to Kate and Carly before walking with Schultz towards his police cruiser, mentally rehearsing the story they had concocted before anyone else arrived at the scene, should they be interviewed: *We rounded the thicket and saw a man lying on the ground, then called the clubhouse manager and 911.* Simple.

At the police station, Seyram braced herself in anticipation of a hostile interview. Much to her surprise, it was a peremptory affair and after no more than ten minutes of questioning, mostly to get background details about work and family, Detective Schultz said she was free to go. Seyram left the station and caught a cab home.

"I'm on my way home," she texted Carly and Kate. Remembering their resolve on the golf course to say nothing potentially incriminating over the phone or to appear too keen to get together, Seyram then sent a follow-up: "I'm busy over the next few days but see you at Kate's place as planned."

12

Kate lived in a 1930s apartment above an old haberdashery just off Main Street. The store sold menswear—suits, jackets, waistcoats, shirts, hats, shoes, cufflinks, belts, braces, ties, and tiepins—and was run by the founder's great-grandson, Giovanni, who was now in his sixties. It was a Mossberg institution and had managed to stay afloat despite the advent of the mall outside town and then of Amazon. Giovanni measured his customers, tailored the clothes for an exact fit, and entertained them, including the many wives and girlfriends who came in, insisting they take a seat in one of his comfortable stuffed armchairs while he made them a coffee on his espresso machine and talked about the latest event requiring formal menswear: a wedding, an engagement party or an award night, a corporate event or a christening, a prom or a funeral.

Giovanni's great-grandfather had built the business and commissioned the building. The apartment had been a comfortable residence for two generations of the family before Giovanni's father bought a car and decamped to Mossberg's new suburbs. Giovanni leased the apartment to Kate for nominal rent. In return, she kept an eye on the haberdashery over the weekends, reported any leaks, and arranged any maintenance.

The building had a large basement area that included parking for several cars. The apartment took up the entire upper floor. It had three bedrooms, two bathrooms, two gas fireplaces, a huge living room with internal French doors so it could be divided in two, a separate kitchen, a dining room, and a winter sunroom where Kate stored her bike, golf clubs, and hiking gear. A balcony extended past the back of the store, creating a cool place to sit during Mossberg's humid summers. The only furniture Kate had bought was a new bed. Everything else was original. The same heavy wardrobes, armchairs, Formica kitchen table and chairs, dining room furniture, and reading and standing lamps. It was a cozy, vintage-cool oasis where Kate relaxed after long days running the hardware store and kicked back in her time off.

Seyram and Carly were due for dinner in thirty minutes. Kate always had the easiest time preparing dinner because whenever her mom, Juneeta, a superb cook, found out Seyram and Carly were coming around, she insisted on loading her up with food. Juneeta adored Seyram and Carly, and was relieved that Kate had loyal, responsible friends from educated families. Juneeta found it hard to imagine anything crazier than not marrying and having children, but she was sure that whatever crazier things existed, Seyram and Carly had prevented Kate from doing them.

Kate's only contributions to the meal had been to buy freshly baked naan from the local Indian restaurant and to turn on the rice cooker, because that afternoon Juneeta had loaded her up with samosas, vegetable pakoras, lentil soup, lamb curry, goat curry, mango chicken curry, paneer tikka masala, vegetable malai kofta, three types of dal, raita, a gallon of lassi, a thermos of chai, and three boxes of sweets—gulab jamun, coconut rasgulla, and jalebi.

"Mom, stop! There's only three of us. I told them it was going to be a light meal."

Juneeta looked hurt. "You girls disappoint me. Again. So *happy* to be thin. And you, refusing your mother's food! Just get a knife and stab me in the heart."

Kate let out a sigh. "Mom, we *love* your food. But it's enough. Really."

Juneeta pursed her lips. "Make sure you give leftovers to everyone, especially Seyram. She has a family to feed. I want nothing left uneaten."

"You just want them to call you and say, 'Thank you, Mrs. Bajwa, for the delicious food.' You know they always do and you know they always will."

"They are good friends, Katiya. You are lucky to have them. An inspiration for their careers and their family situation."

Kate didn't take the bait. She was well past pretending she was ever going to make her parents happy on the issue of either her job or her family situation. "Thanks Mom," she said as she loaded up the car. "You know, you really are the best cook in the world."

Inwardly, Juneeta gave a triumphant smile. There was still a place in the world for a mother who wanted to feed her family.

All Kate had to do was turn on the oven to warm up the food and set out plates and cutlery. She opened a Corona and sat back in one of the armchairs, thinking about Carly's comment from a few months back …

LIKE HIGH SCHOOLS everywhere, prom night was Mossberg River High's event of the year. Kate—then still Katiya—had wanted to make a splash. A point. High school was coming to an end, and she had survived it and its hallways of lockers and catcalls because she was smart and sharp-tongued. Students knew better than to take on Katiya Bajwa. She had never been strong enough to beat them up physically, but she could produce a cruel jibe that other students remembered. Like the girl who made fun of Kate's mom's cooking and got lanced with "At least I'm not a fatburg!" The girl got stuck with Fatburg as a nickname. Or the pasty boy who insisted on greeting her every morning with "Hey, colored girl!" until Katiya responded with "Hey, mole rat!" Thereafter he was Mole Rat, and no one called Katiya "colored girl" again.

The armor Katiya created for herself gave her a liberty most students didn't have. She was called a dyke every other day— usually shouted anonymously from the schoolyard crowd— but she had self-confidence and didn't care what others thought. She thought being largely left alone meant that she could be as free as she liked; that she wasn't part of that teenage world of insecurities and peer groups. That was her mistake.

Getting a prom date was the drama of the year for most high school seniors. For Seyram and Carly it had been straightforward. Mossberg River High School had a total of two senior students in the science club: Seyram and a Malaysian boy, Kha Sang. Kha Sang asked Seyram to be his date and was immensely relieved when she said yes. They smiled at each other through their glasses, happy that this had been resolved so painlessly and they could get back to chemistry.

Carly was asked by David, her boyfriend at the time. They went on to marry—in college, far too young—staying together until David walked out twenty-five years later.

Katiya had no interest in safe options. Throughout high school she had a crush on the soccer captain, Tracy Devereaux. Tracy was a born athlete, lithe and limber, could run like a gazelle, had amazing hand-eye coordination, and could leap into the air to connect with any ball. Katiya plucked up the courage and asked her to be her prom date. Faced with beautiful Katiya, Tracy could only respond with a yes. Emboldened, they were the first same-sex prom couple in Pennsylvanian history.

Prom night happened almost the very evening two waves of the 1980s crashed together. Powerful women of music like Tina Turner, Annie Lennox, Madonna, and Aretha Franklin were strutting their stuff, and sexual fluidity was in the air—

Boy George and Grace Jones, and Martina Navratilova had come out a few years earlier. Kate and Tracy tore up the dance floor as hit after hit played: Starship's "We Built This City," Kim Wilde's "Kids in America," Kenny Loggins' "Footloose," Madonna, Bowie, Thompson Twins, Whitney Houston, Wham, A-Ha, The Pointer Sisters, and Prince. Just before midnight, Cyndi Lauper's "Girls Just Wanna Have Fun" came on, and Katiya and Tracy leaped into the middle of the dance floor.

That's when the jocks pounced. The whole night Katiya and Tracy had been oblivious to other students: the girls sniggering, the boys watching from a distance through narrowed eyes. But by midnight the boys had had enough of girls who had no need for them; of girls who just wanted to have fun. They encircled Katiya and Tracy, blocking them from escape, jostling them back into the circle—"Dance, you dyke!" "Keep jigging, bitch!"—taking turns to jump into the ring to grab Katiya or Tracy and propel them around, shoving them to the other side only for them to be shoved back again as if they were in a pinball machine. The boys sang along at the top of their voices, "Don't you just wanna have fun?" *Whack* across to the other side of the circle. "I just wanna have fun!"

This went on through "Girls Just Wanna Have Fun" and into Michael Jackson's "Thriller." An eternity. Carly screamed and Seyram pounded on the boys' backs, yelling at them to let Katiya and Tracy out. During the moment of silence after the maniacal laugh that concludes "Thriller," Mr. Williams, the gym teacher, heard screaming and came over to break up the circle. "You silly girls!" he admonished. "For goodness' sake, choose a single boy and dance with him. And boys, stand down! Go back to your dates."

Bruised and shaken, Katiya and Tracy fled the school hall. A week later Tracy took a Greyhound bus to New York City and never returned. Kate toughed out the remaining days of senior year, but the bruises on her ribs took weeks to fade. The openness and chutzpah that had seen her through school were replaced by a deflective outer shell.

Kate's reverie was interrupted by doors opening and closing below, then footsteps on the stairs leading up to her apartment. Her friends had arrived.

SEYRAM AND CARLY stretched out on Kate's vintage armchairs.

"I cannot eat another spoonful," groaned Carly, holding her stomach.

"Your mom truly is the best cook ever," added Seyram. "You know when I was a kid I literally used to dream about her spicy food—never tell Ma that."

Kate stood in the doorway to her enclosed balcony, smoking a cigarette.

They rested in silence, digesting the meal, Kate blowing an occasional smoke ring.

"You've been keeping us in suspense, Seyram," said Kate. "Tell us what happened in your police interview."

"Sorry, I didn't feel like talking about it immediately. I was more focused on your mom's cooking," said Seyram. "As we left the golf course in the police car, I was feeling stressed. But it was very straightforward. The detective didn't ask me a thing about anything concrete, like where I was when I first saw Preston Brock or whether we approached him, and he called me 'girl' twice. At the end, when I asked if he was going to interview both of you, he said, 'Nah, we don't spend too much time on the ladies.'"

"I still don't understand why he interviewed you and not me," said Kate. "I'm the golfer."

"I can tell you exactly. After he said he wasn't going to bother with you two, I politely asked why he'd interviewed me. He told me it was for the optics! He shrugged and said 'Keeps the chief happy.'"

Carly was aghast. "He *admitted* to racial profiling?"

"'We always interview nearby Blacks when there's a crime.' Quote-unquote," said Seyram. "It gets better—or worse. Within two minutes of the start of the interview, I told him what church I went to, figuring this might help with something. He actually said out loud 'Hmm, one of those churchy Black ladies,' and mock-waved his fingers in the air. I said 'I'm Catholic. We don't do that.' So, yes, he racially profiled me, but he also *church* profiled me and *lady* profiled me. Sometimes this town exasperates me."

"I'm lucky I escaped: a brown lady golfer."

"Schultz thinks women who play sports are a joke. He can't imagine you—or me or Carly—are capable of anything. At the end of the interview, he said 'Ladies should be careful on the golf course,' as though lightning might seek us out or we might trip into a bunker and be smothered to death by the sand. This probably means the police won't come knocking on your door. However, I worry about whether we left any clues, or if the police will catch up with us. We need an emergency signal that we need to talk."

Seyram was matter-of-fact, and her words caught Carly and Kate off guard.

Seyram continued, "The coroner found Branson Vanburg's cause of death to be inconclusive, although we really don't know if we left any evidence in Coates Ravine. But we *do* know Detective Schultz is on Preston Brock's case because of my interview."

Carly was shocked. "You think the police might want to question me too?"

"It's their job, Carly. We need to be careful, and we should expect it," said Seyram.

"But we phone and text each other all the time. Do we really need something else?"

"Seyram's right," said Kate. "For all we know, the police might already be bugging our phones. They know we were in Coates Ravine the same morning as Branson Vanburg, and we were the first to report Preston Brock's body on the golf course."

"Could my house be bugged? I mean right now?" Carly was stricken.

"I doubt it," said Kate. "Brock's been dead a week. They'd need a warrant, and they'd need to be able to get into your house. Have you been out much?"

"No. I haven't been anywhere. I've been working in my studio every day."

"Seyram's right," said Kate. "We need an alert system to signal we want to talk, but something that won't be obvious if we're under surveillance."

"Let's talk as normal," said Carly, "but if we need to alert each other to something, use our WhatsApp to ask if one of us has something like … eggs. We can say we want to make a cake."

"We could go to the store for eggs," said Seyram. "It needs to be something we wouldn't normally buy."

"How about a roasting pan," said Carly. "Seyram, you've got that huge pan you use for Thanksgiving and Christmas turkey. If we call and ask to borrow it, it means we need to talk."

"What if I need to talk?" asked Seyram.

"Ask us if we still need to use your roasting pan. The police won't know what our previous conversation was, so it should still sound like we're talking about cooking—and Kate and I can think up any kind of reply. We'll know you want to talk and that's what is important."

"Glad you two have this sorted." Kate laughed. "Mom has a trove of pots and pans, so I could genuinely reply that I'll ask her if she has anything."

"That works as a reply. We then text about dropping it off at someone's house or meeting at the café—that'll be our rendezvous."

"The other thing we should do," said Seyram, surprising herself at her ability to strategize like a criminal, "is maintain our routines. We should act and go about our daily business as normal."

Kate and Carly, in full agreement, suggested they continue their walks in Coates Ravine, their sessions with Kate on the golf course, and occasional coffees and dinners at each other's houses in between.

Despite being the one to emphasize the importance of routine, Seyram struggled to continue one part of her own routine: confession. As a Catholic, she regularly went to confession on Saturday afternoon, chiding Felix when he did not, and ensuring Nana and Kofi followed her example. But confession presumes the penitent is truly sorry and has resolved not to sin again. Seyram, valuing the act of confession, couldn't do it—because she wasn't sorry.

At first she came up with excuses: "I've got to prepare dinner," "I have a headache," "I've got to finish some paperwork from the clinic." Then, realizing these excuses were feeble, and also realizing that the *failure* to confess actually suggests there is something that *needs* confessing, Seyram decided she had to return to the confessional. But, because she didn't regret either Branson Vanburg's or Preston Brock's death, she couldn't make an honest confession about those things. Instead, she confessed she'd snapped at the children, been impatient with Kofi, been unreasonable with a customer … then one day she confessed that during a visit to Pittsburg Zoo she'd hadn't let the children look at the elephant. This one was strange even for Father O'Connor, who had heard it all.

"What precisely was your sin, my dear?"

It had been Seyram's subconscious talking. Her confession had ignored the elephant in the room.

"Forgive me, Father. My sin was that I selfishly wanted to look at …" She struggled to think of another animal. "… the Komodo dragons! They are such magnificent animals. It was selfish of me to put my interests before those of the children. This is all I can remember. I am sorry for these and all my sins."

Father O'Connor, always partial to a mother confessing she had put her own needs before those of her family, let her off lightly. "You must serve your family and remember their needs. As penance read Philippians 2, and for a week say a daily prayer against selfishness. You may also wish to return to the zoo, this time putting your children's interests before your own. Remember, elephants featured prominently on Noah's Ark. Visiting them at the zoo is an opportunity for you to teach your children about the Bible."

Seyram rushed from the box knowing that in the future, whenever she saw an elephant, she'd hear a woodpecker's staccato.

13

BETH KATZ LIVED off campus with three roommates in a house toward Fort Byrd. Driving home late one Saturday evening from a Safe Space Alliance meeting on campus, she saw someone stumbling on the side of the road. A drunk walking home, she assumed, glancing as she drew level with the person. She would normally drive right by but this time she hesitated. *That's what I'm supposed to feel—fear. Maybe this person needs help?*

On impulse she pulled over and reversed. She opened the window a crack, then suddenly realized the person was a woman. Beth got out and rushed over. "Are you OK?"

It was one of the army Stryker combat vehicle drivers she had met at the bar the previous fall. "Three guys attacked me," she said, trembling.

Her name was Beatriz.

"I'll take you to my place," said Beth, inwardly feeling out of her depth. It was one thing to create relationships between organizations and lobby for support services, but quite another to counsel a traumatized woman. She draped a duvet around Beatriz's shoulders. "Should I take you back to Fort Byrd? They've got a doctor, right? Someone you can talk to?"

"I can't face going back now," said Beatriz. "I've got a leave pass until tomorrow evening. Can I stay here?"

Beth went into her bedroom and called Grace at Sisterhood House. "Grace, it's Beth, Beth Katz. I've just picked a woman up on the road to Fort Byrd. She's a soldier there. Something bad has happened to her. I'm pretty sure she's been assaulted," she said, lowering her voice. "Can I bring her to the House?"

Grace dealt with such situations several times a week. "We don't have any accommodation at the moment. We got three new domestic violence clients today, eight children between them, and we've used up our budget for motel accommodation. If she's willing, you should take her to Emergency. Ask her gently. But, if you do go, don't just drop her off. You need to stay with her."

"OK. And if she doesn't want to go? We're at my house right now, but it's not a great place for her to stay. I've got roommates who have boyfriends, and we only have the living room for other guests." Beth wondered how she could run something called the Safe Space Alliance but live somewhere that may well *not* feel safe for some women.

"Give me five minutes. I'll call around and see if I can get anyone to billet her. We do that occasionally. Don't pressure her to talk or to do anything. Make her cocoa, or coffee, or soup."

THIRTY MINUTES LATER Beth was back in the car with Beatriz, who had declined the offer to go to Emergency. "I found somewhere you can stay tonight. It's totally safe and you don't need to go back to Fort Byrd. Do you know Sisterhood House in town?"

Beatriz had never heard of it.

"It's a resource center for women. They found you accommodation for the night. It's a private home, not at Sisterhood House itself, but it'll be totally fine and better than my place."

"Are you sure?" Beatriz hung her head in her hands. "God, this attack just came out of nowhere."

"The woman is called Carly. She's on the board at Sisterhood House. She's really cool and she has a teenage daughter. No husband lives there. Honestly, she'll take care of you, and in the morning you can decide what you want to do." Beth felt guilty at her relief that she could deliver Beatriz into hands more capable than her own.

CARLY BROUGHT BEATRIZ a mug of cocoa and sat down opposite her in the living room. "Honey, you don't need to say a thing, but if you want to talk, I'm here to listen."

The truth about Carly was that while she was determined to overcome her own "weakness," as she saw it, this very vulnerability meant people opened up to her. Summer, sitting in the corner of the living room feeling petulant that she had to give up her bedroom to a stranger that night, but also intrigued by the drama, recalled how her mom could get anyone to talk. A plumber once came to repair their boiler, and she remembered her mom describing the plumbing problem as they descended to the basement. A mere five minutes later as they came back up, the conversation had switched to the plumber earnestly describing difficulties in his sexual relationship with his wife.

Beatriz exhaled deeply, then nodded as though encouraging herself to speak. "A guy I know asked me out on an evening date. Not someone from Fort Byrd, a college guy. He seemed like a nice change from army boys. We're pretty different—he's a senior hoping to get into law school, and I'm a Stryker driver in the military—but we hooked up a few times over summer when I was on leave and, funnily enough, we got on well.

"This time was different. He was with three other guys—I didn't like them—and he behaved weirdly. They were all in the same college fraternity, Chi Omicron Kappa. I thought it was going to be just me and him, but the three friends didn't go away. At about nine forty-five they suddenly decided to call it a night, even though it was still early, and as though their departure was all preplanned. They offered me a lift to the base and got me to sit in the back seat, between two of them. That made me feel uneasy, but my friend was in the front passenger seat so I thought I was OK.

"Instead of turning into Army Road, they said they had to make a detour and headed toward campus. Then, as we got closer, I saw the driver exchanging glances with the other guys and I totally panicked. I screamed for them to let me out, but the two guys on either side of me started grabbing at me. My friend told me that if I didn't struggle, I wouldn't get hurt, and that really freaked me out—about what was going to happen. I bashed my palm into the nose of the guy next to me and grabbed the driver by the hair and yanked his head back. He stopped and I literally clambered over the guy I'd punched, opened the door, and fell out into the middle of the road … then they just drove off." Beatriz was sobbing. She shook her head. "That guy was my friend! I thought I was going to be murdered."

"Is that how you got those scrapes on your hands and elbows—falling out of the car?" asked Carly.

"Yeah, it really hurt. After they drove off, I didn't know what to do, so I just started walking back to Fort Byrd, then Beth stopped."

Carly became aware of Summer sitting in the corner, listening, instead of doing homework in Carly's bedroom as instructed. *Too late now*. "Summer, be a love and bring the first aid kit." Turning to Beatriz, she said, "I'll clean these cuts and put on some dressings, and I can give you a change of clothes—your shirt is missing some buttons. Did that happen when you were struggling with the guys?"

"I don't know. I'm not even sure what happened, exactly. The army trained me to go to war, but this caught me completely off guard."

"I've got some buttons that will match. Let me sew them back on." Returning with her sewing basket, Carly asked in a soothing tone, "Beatriz, do you want to make a report to the police?"

"What do I tell them? They never said exactly what they were going to do, and I panicked and lashed out. It all happened in a blur." Beatriz shuddered.

"If you want to make a report, I can go with you." Grace had called Carly and given her the heads-up about being a support person if needed. "You tell it just the way you told me, and the police officer will ask follow-up questions. Why don't you go to bed, and we can talk about it in the morning? You're perfectly safe here. You can lock the bedroom if you want or leave it ajar if you want to call out in the night. My door will be open, and I'll hear you if you need me."

Carly gave Beatriz a hug, a spare toothbrush, and a change of clothes. "You've got your own bathroom. There's toothpaste there, and a towel and washcloth in the cabinet. Help yourself."

MOSSBERG POLICE DEPARTMENT didn't have an officer specifically assigned to sexual assault crimes, nor did it train its officers in interviewing techniques for such cases. It was an issue Grace had raised at council meetings and with Police Chief Delaney numerous times without success. This meant people like Carly and Beatriz, who had come in Sunday morning to make a report, had to speak to whomever was on duty.

Carly and Beatriz were already in the interview room when Detective Schultz walked in. He recognized Carly—the potter, as he called her—from the golf course incident, and briefly looked at the young lady beside her. He put down his notepad and stared at the desk as he spoke in a dispassionate, impersonal tone. "My name is Detective Schultz. I understand you want to report an alleged assault." He looked at Carly. "Ma'am, please remain silent during the interview. Let the alleged victim speak." Schultz fumbled with the voice recorder and turned it on. "This will be recorded. State your full name and address."

In the silence that followed, Schultz looked at the two women. In his experience, women—especially young women—were predisposed to lying, incapable of telling the truth. His own daughter never told him a thing about her personal life, and he wouldn't trust her account if she did.

Taking a deep breath, Beatriz told the story as she had originally told Carly. Schultz asked some questions of clarification, occasionally jotting down a word.

Beatriz soon felt foolish. When she said she couldn't remember the names of her friend's three friends, Schultz said, "So, you willingly got into the back seat of a car with a group of men you'd never met before." It was a statement, not a question.

When Beatriz reported they told her she wouldn't get hurt if she didn't struggle, Schultz said, "But they didn't actually hurt you at all?"

When Beatriz said she'd panicked, striking out at the men beside her, Schultz said, "So, you assaulted *them*?"

Schultz looked up at Beatriz. "What were you wearing when all this allegedly happened?"

Carly opened her mouth to object, but before she could utter a word Schultz snarled, "Stay out of it, ma'am." He turned back to Beatriz. "Well?"

"I was dressed for a night out on a date!"

"I thought as much."

In frustration, Beatriz said, "You're twisting this! I *know* their intentions were not good. They were planning to do something."

Carly reached for Beatriz's hand and gave it a squeeze.

Schultz saw the gesture and sneered. "Thank you, miss. I'll write this up. We'll call you."

Beatriz and Carly left the interview room and Carly drove Beatriz back to Fort Byrd. Beatriz never mentioned to anyone ever again what happened. Schultz returned to his office, opened the bottom drawer of his filing cabinet, and flung his notes onto a pile.

14

Carly smelled the coffee as her percolator sputtered. She had invited Seyram and Kate around for a Saturday afternoon visit—unusually, because typically they got together over dinner, but her experience with Detective Schultz had rattled her.

In the days since the interview, she had alternated between rage and hopelessness. She had planned to use her time to make pieces for a forthcoming exhibition she was having at Mossberg College. Instead, she neglected her work and got lost in her thoughts about the way they had been treated. *Yes*, Carly thought as she stared at the spinning pottery wheel, *we fled that police station. Beatriz, a soldier, reduced to a version of me in the face of cynical, judging male authority*. One day, after hours of this kind of stasis, she pulled up her clay-spattered apron, pressed it against her face and screamed, smothering the sound so that Summer and the neighbors wouldn't hear. She had come to a resolution.

The three of them drank their coffee and helped themselves to Danish pastries, as Carly told Seyram and Kate about the interview.

She took a final sip and put down her mug. "We've got work to do. I've been wrestling with this, I know—and you know it too—but my mind is made up. I know we talked about targeting Branson Vanburg but then it just kind of happened. And then we talked about shaking up Preston Brock, but it got out of hand and he ended up … dead. We need to stop the hesitation. If the police are investigating—as you said, Seyram, that's their job—let's take the leap and do this while we can, no playing around, before they close in."

Seyram and Kate were attentive. This was a Carly they'd never heard before.

"I know who we should target, and I also know you're the only two people in the world I trust enough to do this," said Carly. "We've been together through thick and thin."

"You mean because of the accident when we were in college," said Kate ruefully.

"Kate, we didn't die," said Carly impatiently. "Any one of us could have been driving. It just happened to be you."

"Me who was dumb enough to drive into a snowbank and strand us in a blizzard for two days."

"You were the least drunk," said Carly. "I was drunk *and* stoned."

"I still say it should have been me," said Seyram. "It was my car and I'd had the least alcohol."

"You were also most drunk. The point is we survived," said Carly. "Seyram, you reminded us of all that survival stuff about running the car for ten minutes every hour to keep warm, huddling together, and keeping blankets over us. And Kate, you told us to pee in the lowest point of the car so it wouldn't go everywhere—only you could have thought of that. We wouldn't have got through it alone."

"That's what the snowplow guy said when he found us," said Seyram.

"He was right," said Kate. "I still remember being in the car with blood running from my nose and, Carly, you soothing me, saying 'Don't worry! We'll survive—and your mom will still love you.'"

"That was the marijuana talking," replied Carly. "Your mom would have strangled you."

"I was secretly thankful we weren't found for two days," said Seyram. "It meant the alcohol was out of our system when we got tested, and we could blame the icy roads and not have to fess up to a boozy weekend. My dad would have killed me for *that*."

"So, give it to us, Carly," said Kate. "We're in this together. What's this 'work' we've got to do and who do you think we should target?"

"Do you remember that awful assault case from two years ago? What was her name?"

"You mean Sydney Brown," said Seyram.

"Yes, Sydney Brown. She worked in a bar on Main Street. The Mossberg College football team captain, Cooper Hanson, raped her when she was walking home after her shift. She was a tiny thing but managed to get away from him by climbing over the fence that divides the parking lot off Virginia Lane from Ohio Lane. She fell down the other side and broke her leg. Then Sheldon Nossel came along, wanting to pee, saw her there, and then *he* sexually assaulted her. As she lay there with a broken leg. She remembered their faces and went to the police. After the emergency room."

"Did Hanson and Nossel plan it like that?" asked Kate.

"No," Seyram took up the story. "They didn't know each other. They met at the courthouse during the trial. Now they're teammates and best buddies."

"Summer says they call themselves the Captain and the Outlaw," said Carly. "Want to know something else? They're profiled in that *Gazette* article about Mossberg all-stars. Cooper Hanson's in that horrible fraternity on campus: Chi Omicron Kappa. The *Gazette* even mentions it in the article, about how it's the home of sports stars. Tell that to girls who escaped its claws. I'm telling you, doing something about those two is in the stars."

Kate couldn't believe she hadn't followed this in the news. "What happened at the trial? Why aren't they in jail?"

Carly took a deep breath. "Hanson's lawyers argued it was consensual and that Sydney Brown had asked him to rough it up a bit. You know, the 'rough sex' defense. They argued she panicked—with all the roughness—and ran away, climbing the fence and breaking her leg."

"Did the judge ask why Cooper didn't run after her to reassure her or check on her?"

"Oh, yes. Hanson said he tried but he was too drunk to climb over the fence. Said he called out, 'Are you OK?' and didn't get an answer so went home thinking it was just a bad date. The jury acquitted him of all charges. Insufficient evidence of nonconsensual sex and his word against Sydney's on the 'roughing it up' bit."

"What about Sheldon Nossel?"

"This is where it gets really bad. He said he thought her moans were just because she was drunk; that it was a lane where people actually went for sex—you know, from the bars. Which is true, they do. And he figured she just wanted it. He said he was sorry that he'd made a mistake, but he'd simply misread the signals. He pled guilty, obviously hoping for a light sentence."

"The signals of a broken leg? The jury accepted *that* defense?"

"Nossel's lawyers were smart. They skipped the jury and asked for trial by judge only. The judge agreed it was nonconsensual, but said that the assault was minor in nature, that Nossel couldn't have known her leg was broken, and that, by pleading guilty, he had clearly recognized his error. The judge even said that it should have been explained to the victim that pressing charges would ruin the boy's life. He said he could see why Nossel was confused—the alcohol, the location, the darkness, Sydney's moans—and that he wasn't prepared to compromise a promising young man's life. Nossel got two years' probation and had to register as a sex offender, but neither of those things stop him continuing at college. It happened off campus and Sydney Brown wasn't a student. He never spent a single day in jail."

"What happened to Sydney?"

"What always happens. She left town. Got warned about ruining a football career and didn't get her job back at the bar—the owner said she was bad for business. She came back for the trial then vanished again."

The three of them sat there, thinking about Sydney Brown and the injustice of it all. Carly got up and went to her shelf of CDs. Unlike just about everyone else, she'd never made that trip to the thrift store.

"You think now's the time for music?" asked Kate.

"I'm capturing the atmosphere," said Carly cryptically. She put in a CD and forwarded to the right track. The sound of a guitar strumming started up.

"Oh, this is 'What's Up' by 4 Non Blondes!" said Kate. "*Exactly* what I needed to hear."

"A billion hits on YouTube," said Carly.

It had been one of their karaoke favorites in the 1990s when they reunited at home for summer, Thanksgiving, or the holidays, before heading back to college. The three of them jumped to their feet and sang along.

As the song wound down, they fell back into their chairs, feeling drained from thinking about Sydney Brown.

"Let's do it," said Carly. "Cooper and Sheldon. I mean it."

"The question," said Seyram, "is how?"

Kate looked thoughtful. "You know, the father of Giovanni—who owns the haberdashery downstairs—kept a firearms collection in the basement. He loved guns, but he left them there when he moved to the suburbs. They're all still down there. Giovanni has no interest, and his dad is ninety-two, has dementia, and probably doesn't even remember his collection. We could use one of them. I mean, we can't just line up the town's jocks and shove them all into Coates Ravine."

"Or beat them over the head with a golf club," retorted Seyram.

"Settle down, you two," said Carly. "Who do we know who can shoot a gun?"

Carly and Kate turned to look at Seyram.

"Why are you looking at me?"

"Er, you didn't use guns growing up?"

"In *Mossberg*? Um, do you know my family?"

"No, before you came to America. In Africa?"

Seyram processed the question. "Ohhh, you mean to defend myself from the lions?"

"Exactly!" said Carly.

"I was thinking more about the armed militias," said Kate.

Seyram started to quiver, and then to shake, with mirth. Kate and Carly were embarrassed.

"What?" asked Kate.

"Do you girls know me so little?" Seyram gasped for air. "Ghana is *miles* safer than America. No one owns a gun! There are children everywhere playing in the street, salesmen walk door-to-door, and the old people sit out the front of their houses sticking their nose into everyone's business. Women walk around alone at night! As a little kid, Ma used to send me to the corner store after dark to buy milk or eggs. The lions and elephants were in a national park 400 miles away." Seyram couldn't resist a dig. "And tell me, did your parents put you in raccoon-skin caps and give you muskets to keep away the grizzlies?"

"That's unfair," protested Carly. "Grizzlies live in the Rockies a thousand mi— OK, I get your point. Sorry."

"You never talked about Ghana as a kid," said Kate. "I thought you came because of war."

"That's why everyone worried about you when you started high school," added Carly.

"What do you mean 'everyone worried about me'?" Seyram was intrigued now.

"Remember Mrs. Hoover, the counselor? How she wanted you to go to therapy? She thought you had PTSD."

"From the lion attacks?"

"Yes! And Mr. Gardiner, the English teacher, wondered why you wrote about Katherine Johnson the NASA mathematician, instead of Nefertiti or Nelson Mandela, when we did that assignment about who inspires us. He thought you were suppressing your African heritage."

Seyram let out a guffaw. "How do you know this rubbish? And Katherine Johnson is a descendent of Africans anyway. I wrote about her because she's a math genius!"

"Mom was head of the PTA," said Carly. "She got all the gossip."

"So, you two befriended me as a charity?"

"Not me!" said Kate. "You were the only girl who liked science. And the snooty girls didn't like *you*, so that had to be a good thing."

"Not me either!" said Carly. "I mean, I thought bad things had happened to you in Africa, but you stood up to the boys and all those girls who stood around flicking their hair."

"Seriously," said Seyram, "I was fifteen when I came here, and I realized on day one at high school that I had to become American. I changed my accent and clothes—being friends with you two helped—and I stopped talking about Ghana. Being from Africa was just too weird."

Seyram hadn't realized she had told them so little about this early chapter of her life, and still couldn't believe they thought she knew how to handle a gun.

"It's only since Nana and Kofi were born that I'm getting back into everything Ghanaian. I want them to know their roots, but they think Ghana is boring. They want to go to Los Angeles. Felix and I talk about going back for a period so they get to know their culture, but that window is closing fast. Nana goes to high school in a couple of years." Seyram turned indignant, "But, by the way, have you ever known me to go to a shooting range? My parents wouldn't let me *near* a gun! My prep school in Ghana armed us with bibles. The principal told us 'The only weapon you'll ever need is the Lord's Word.'"

"There goes my plan to let you loose on the town." Kate wasn't smiling any more.

"I can do it," Carly piped up. "Seriously. Let's have dessert and then go see Giovanni's guns."

"I wasn't trying to put you on the spot, Carly," said Kate.

"Kate's right," Seyram added. "What happened, happened. It's not like we need to get a scalp each or anything."

"Don't try to protect me. I told you I was sick of being meek. Let's go see the basement."

THEY DROVE TO Kate's place later that afternoon. Kate went upstairs for the building keys, then led them down creaking internal stairs to a locked basement door, their way illuminated by naked light globes.

"Kate, this is totally creepy," said Carly, now feeling less confident. "Are you sure we're not going to find a skeleton or anything?"

"Well, there are only two keys—this one and Giovanni's— and there wasn't a skeleton last time I did my biweekly check. It's unlikely anyone has stumbled into the cellar and been eaten by rats since."

"Eew!" said Seyram. "Are there really rats down here?"

"Girls, relax. There are no rats because my job is to set traps, block up holes, and kill the critters, and there are no skeletons because Giovanni's dad's armory is a locked room. No one can get in without a key."

Kate approached a nondescript door, unlocked it, and flicked a switch. An assortment of firearms rested on gleaming rows of wall-mounted brackets.

"Holy Cow! There must be over two hundred guns here!" exclaimed Seyram. "What's that? He's got three of them." Seyram pointed to something with a short barrel and two grips.

Kate peered at the label. "It's a Beretta M12 submachine gun. Italian."

"Does he have ammunition?" asked Carly, remembering why they were there.

"It's all in there," Kate indicated two metal cabinets. "Boxes and boxes of the stuff."

Carly looked around and said flatly, "This isn't going to work. When I was fourteen, I shot a gun at a can on a stump twenty feet away. I missed. There's no way I could pick off Hanson and Nossel at a distance. And if I approach them holding a gun, they're going to figure out pretty quickly what's going on. They're two big guys; they'll overpower me. I'd need to get up close and I'd still need a big target."

"Get them in their car," said Seyram, ever logical. "You hide in the back seat of my car—it's got shaded windows. Then you can get up close."

"I would still need to aim straight. That's the problem."

"Destroy the entire car," advised Kate.

"With what?"

Kate surveyed the walls. "This." She pulled a strange-looking contraption off the wall. It had a stubby barrel and no stock.

"Is that even a gun?"

"It's a grenade launcher. You attach it under the barrel of rifle and use the rifle sight to aim. It takes one round at a time, and you don't load any ammunition into the rifle. Fire the grenade close to anything and you'll vaporize it."

Kate unlocked the metal cabinets and looked for ammunition. "Here." She handed Carly a box labeled *M203 Grenade Launcher Ammunition*.

Carly weighed it tentatively in her palm and cautiously opened the box. "The shells look dangerous, and they're heavy for such small things."

"Isn't someone going to miss the launcher or the ammo?" asked Seyram.

"Like I said, Giovanni has no idea what's here and his dad can't remember a thing. You can see there are about twenty or thirty empty brackets and who knows if they once held guns. We can take the launcher and the ammo, Carly can use some shells as practice, and keep the others for the hit. There'll be another inexplicably empty set of brackets on the wall."

"What about ballistics?" asked Seyram. "If they find the grenade launcher, they'll be able to test to see if it launched the round that hit the car."

"That's where the mighty Mossberg River comes in handy." Carly was back to feeling confident. "Afterward, I throw it in the river along with the box with any leftover shells."

They walked back upstairs, and Kate poured Carly and herself a whisky—and made chamomile tea for Seyram.

"That's the weapon taken care of," said Seyram, "but what about the location? Kate, I know you suggested a drive-by, but we couldn't possibly do that on Main Street. It'd disrupt shopkeepers and frighten bystanders."

"Seyram, we're trying to assassinate them, not keep in the good books with the townsfolk," said Kate. "And you're the one who said you don't want to be good anymore. What's a little disruption?"

"It could hurt others," said Seyram. "And, on a practical note, we could get caught."

"Get them out of town, on the gravel road to Daineton," said Carly. "Past that intersection for the highway bypass that was never built. No one lives around there once the road gets into the hills. We blow up their car there and disappear from the scene."

"I can make a reservation at the Daineton Pizzeria," said Kate. "In case we're questioned, we can say that's why we were driving that way."

"How do we get them there?" asked Seyram.

"Lure them." Carly visualized the scene. "Hanson and Nossel are twenty. It's a safe bet they think with their dicks.

While I'm in the back of the car waiting, you, Kate, entice them to follow our car out of town."

"I haven't had a twenty-year-old boy interested in me since I was twenty. How do you suppose I 'entice' them?" Kate made exaggerated quote marks in the air.

"We've got a blond wig in our dress-up box at home. Wear that and some lipstick. Trust me, with that and a bit of playing hard to get, it's all you'll need."

"Now you're really confusing me. If I liked someone, I just went for them. I've never played 'hard to get' in my life." More air quotes.

"Kate," Carly gave a deep sigh. "Ask them where you can get a drink. Tell them they're *so* handsome. And, most importantly, tell them you like their car. Bat your eyelashes and there you go."

"What about this one?" said Kate, poking Seyram. "Is she supposed to be my driver?"

Carly gave another sigh. "Seyram, wear a low-cut top and show those boobs. If you can give the guys a good look at your cleavage, you won't need to do anything else."

"I don't own a low-cut top!"

"I'll get you one from TJ Maxx. We've got a few wigs in the dress-up box, so I'll find one for you too. Trust me. It'll work."

15

WYATT HAD BEEN so busy with work that he'd almost forgotten his planned visit to Grace at Sisterhood House. The stories Henry Konig insisted on printing about the deaths of Branson Vanburg and Preston Brock reminded him of the unanswered questions he had about whether Branson's death really had been an accident, as well as his questions about what might motivate someone to kill football players.

Grace, ever the patient community organizer, waited for Wyatt to arrive. She didn't think much of the *Gazette*, especially with its editor's insistence on maintaining a "Women's Page" focusing on cooking, fashion, and religion. However, she had hope for a reporter who was curious enough to visit Sisterhood House—the first ever from the *Gazette* to do so—and remembered that he had covered Mossberg's first march in support of the #MeToo movement.

She gave Wyatt a tour of the premises and introduced him to a couple of volunteers who were boxing up food supplies for distribution. Then they sat in the lounge area to talk.

"I can offer you a coffee, but we only have instant."

"Thanks, that'd be great. Cream, no sugar."

Wyatt's spoon clinked as he stirred his coffee and gathered his thoughts.

"So, how can I help?" asked Grace. "Do you want to do a story on Sisterhood House?"

"I'm not exactly sure yet, but I think I'd like to write something broader. About how women in Mossberg feel about … about men like Branson Vanburg and Preston Brock. In general, I mean. Just to plunge right in, is there a part of the feminist movement that thinks violence is part of the solution for stopping sexual assault?"

Grace studied Wyatt. He was evidently clueless, although not embarrassed to ask questions and at least recognized feminism as something potentially motivating enough to inspire violence. It wasn't a *bad* start.

"First of all, I don't represent all feminists. We're a diverse bunch. Second, some supporters of Sisterhood House wouldn't even call themselves feminists."

Grace stopped. She now realized where the conversation was likely heading. "Wait a minute. You're wondering if a woman—a feminist—is behind these two deaths? Is that what Henry Konig thinks?"

"No, Henry doesn't know I'm here. He's convinced a woman is incapable of killing a young man. I'm not so sure about that, and it makes me wonder whether there might be a story about motivation." Wyatt stopped, then added hastily, "I don't think *you* did it!"

Grace smiled. "That's a relief. But let me reassure you, a woman is plenty capable of killing those men."

"I want to do an investigative piece. Different to the rest of the *Gazette*'s coverage. Something that explains what women in our community think: whether they're angry enough, afraid enough, or fed up enough, to do this kind of thing."

"Women already know what women think about sexual violence. We don't like it. You need to write something that makes *men* realize what women think. But about feminism, and whether there's a part that believes in violence ..." Grace was thoughtful. "Baby boomers became feminists when the anti-war movement was flourishing. They marched for women's rights, but also marched against the Vietnam War, then campaigned against nuclear disarmament, so you're going to find very few older feminists who think violence is a useful tool for change. They thought feminism could change the world peacefully. On the other hand, Gen Xers like me saw its successes and failures. We also saw women enter the military and police—where women are armed and have authority to control men. Again, I wouldn't say they *believe* in violence, but they're open to the idea that countering violence may require violence."

"What are the successes of feminism?" asked Wyatt.

"Off the top of my head: more control over bodies; easier to leave relationships; not getting fired for getting married or getting pregnant; careers and promotions in hundreds of professions previously closed to women; leadership positions—twenty-odd countries have had a female head of state; higher wages; state- and employer-funded childcare; more girls getting an education and going to university."

"And the failures?"

"Feminism didn't change men much and didn't equip men to deal with the changes it brought; attitudes—especially in towns like Mossberg—haven't kept pace with legal changes; there's still a wage gap ..." Grace ticked off the points on her fingers. "... parents don't mind if their daughters have narrower lives than their sons; courts, churches, and police drag their feet around holding men accountable for abuse. Look at the judge's statements in the Preston Brock case, and before that—before you joined the *Gazette*—the judge's comments in a rape case involving a young woman called Sydney Brown. Or, last month in Canada, that man who pleaded *guilty* to sexual assault, but the judge decided there should be no conviction because it would have hurt the man's career. Women are tired of this *shit*." Grace caught herself and took a breath.

"Do you think the murderer could be a younger woman? I mean, Gen Xers are moms!"

"Listen, Wyatt, a long time ago I worked in a prison. It was full of moms who murdered a man because they were fed up with the status quo. You know how I said older feminists got some things wrong? Another thing they got wrong is they thought women shared the same priorities. This was never true. Black and Native American women were always just as interested in racial equality as in women's rights; working class women were always more interested in jobs and better pay than in getting Betty Friedan onto college curricula; Catholic feminists have little interest in abortion; and feminists in Saudi Arabia are probably more interested in being allowed to drive than in ditching the headscarf. But you know the one thing all women agree on? We don't like being sexually assaulted, including by our bosses, colleagues, movie producers, coaches, doctors, billionaires, princes, politicians, or strangers, and we also don't like it when they suffer no consequences." Grace paused, then continued in a quiet voice. "I could easily believe that a woman—not just someone who calls herself a feminist—would be sufficiently motivated to murder a rapist."

Wyatt had had no idea. He was sure there was a story to be written, but wasn't sure if he could write it, or even if he should be the one writing it, or what the local angle was. He knew that many Mossbergers thought the young men who died were heroes. Trying to explain *why* a woman might want men like them dead would be a minefield. And Konig would never publish it.

For another half-hour he asked about the #MeToo movement and how it worked, and whether Grace knew any victims of sexual harassment and violence who might be willing to speak to him. That, he concluded, had to be the angle, at least for an initial story: the scale and scope of sexual violence in Mossberg and what that meant for the way women lived their lives—without men ever realizing. It was his best chance of getting a story published.

Grace watched Wyatt get into his car and drive off. She liked him but wondered if he could ever make headway in an organization like the *Gazette*. She half-smiled, imagining the headlines for any exposé it might publish: "Shock Reveal: Women Don't Like Rape!" or "Gazette Exclusive: Women Don't Feel Safe at Night!"

16

COOPER HANSON AND Sheldon Nossel spent every Saturday night the same way. After the game, they'd get Coach Grossman's summary of how it went and how they played, get massages from the cute team physio and try to pinch her ass, and then just hang with the team. Once back at home and in fresh clothes, Cooper would take as many beers from his dad's basement fridge as he thought wouldn't be noticed, then drive to Sheldon's place where they'd steal more beer from Sheldon's dad's stash in the garage—they were still too young to buy liquor. They'd then cruise Mossberg in Cooper's red pickup truck, music loud on the radio, drinking and throwing the empties at young men they saw on foot or at any army boys. The army boys faced a lot of trouble back on base if they got into fights, so they usually restrained themselves. It was one of the local boys' favorite sports: seeing if they could provoke soldiers into a fight.

The early evening was spent cruising Mossberg: texting plans to get drunk and get laid, cramming friends into the back seat and then later in the evening picking up their current girlfriends. That was the real start of their evening. Because they were town celebrities—Cooper the college football captain and Sheldon, his notorious friend—they had no chance of sneaking into a club; every bouncer knew them.

They usually ended up at a frat house back on campus once they'd stirred up the town.

This Saturday night it was still early, but Cooper and Sheldon had already knocked back half a dozen beers each and were discussing which buddies and girls to pick up. Teammates were usually top of the list, but they could only fit a total of three people in the back. George Ezra's "Shotgun" came on the radio. "Woohoo!" yelled Sheldon. It was the hit of summer.

Sheldon was living his dream, just like the guy riding shotgun in the song, only he wasn't just "feeling like someone," he *was* someone: sailing through college; quarterback on the football team; his best buddy the team captain, who happened to have one of the coolest cars in town—and he was the passenger. A warm summer breeze blew in through the windows. Sheldon had never felt more in the moment. Overcome with happiness, he turned and gave Coop a punch. "Living the dream, bud!"

"Love you, bro!" said Cooper, turning up the radio to sing along.

"THERE IT IS," said Kate, spotting Cooper's pickup parked to the side, up ahead. "Seyram, drive by slowly and I'll check they're the ones in it."

Seyram pulled past the truck, which had its windows down and the song "Shotgun" blaring out. Kate turned quickly to look. "Yes, they're both there."

Seyram turned and drove around the block to come back alongside Cooper and Sheldon again. This time, she crawled past and lowered Kate's passenger-side window in anticipation of an exchange.

"Kate, you're on," whispered Carly, out of sight in the backseat. "Get their attention. You're the bait."

Grimacing, Kate turned back to Cooper who was just five feet away in the truck's driver seat. "Hey, boys, can you recommend a bar? We're *really* thirsty." She clumsily combed her fingers through her wig.

"Ho-la, Missy La-ti-na," said Cooper with an exaggerated accent. "You've come to the right man."

Sheldon leaned across so he could check out Kate through Cooper's window. "You girls want to suck on a beer ... or something else?"

Turning to Seyram and Carly, Kate hissed, "Can't we do it now?"

"We're on Main Street, for Pete's sake," muttered Seyram. Improvising, she called through Kate's open window, "Love your *big truck*, boys," and slowly drove off. It was the only time in Seyram's life she had used sexual innuendo.

Looking in her rearview mirror, Seyram saw Cooper pull out to follow them, then move into the center lane so they were now right alongside. Both cars drove slowly, front windows down. "We've hooked them," said Seyram under her breath.

"Hey there, chicky-poo," called Sheldon to Seyram.

Kate sat up. "Did he just call you chicky-poo? *Please*, Carly, do it now."

Seyram had never had time for flirting but she knew how it worked. She grasped the steering wheel with both hands and used her elbows to lever up her cleavage. Turning to Sheldon, she batted her false lashes and stuck her tongue out a quarter inch.

"Oh, you want it," called out Sheldon. "See that Coop? These chicks want us."

Both cars came to a stop side by side at a red light.

"Let's play with these guys," said Kate. "Stick it in neutral and rev it up."

Seyram revved loudly and roared off as the lights turned green.

The truck caught up to them at the next lights, Sheldon calling through the passenger window. "Think you're faster than us?" Silence from Seyram. "Not talking now?" More silence. The light changed to green and again Seyram sped off, beating the truck off the mark. One more traffic light to go before they could head out of town.

At the final light on Main Street, Cooper screeched to a stop beside the chicks' car. He and Sheldon were now pissed. Sheldon leaned out the window, "What's wrong with you? Think you're too good for us? Suck my *dick!*"

The chick in the other car looked at Sheldon and called back, "There's a nice bush a couple of miles outside town. Why don't you come find it?"

Sheldon and Cooper were infuriated. These women were toying with them. "These bitches think they can play us," muttered Sheldon.

The light changed to green and again the chicks' car zoomed ahead. Cooper was so angry he'd forgotten to get the jump on them at the lights. "They're heading to the pass. I'll force them to pull over, then we'll see who's boss." He banged his fist against the dashboard and accelerated after the car as it disappeared around a bend. "Hold that black one down for me when I slap her around," he told Sheldon. "That Latina isn't going to be much trouble."

"You got it, bro," Sheldon replied grimly. They bumped fists.

Seyram drove for another mile, the truck crossing into the oncoming lane and driving up alongside. The two men had worked themselves into a frenzy, yelling insults, and Sheldon throwing beer cans.

Mossberg had a fifth set of traffic lights, at an intersection outside town in a forested area that had been installed for a planned highway bypass. The traffic light operated—although most drivers jumped the red because they could never be bothered waiting—but the bypass still hadn't been built. Seyram pulled to a stop and the truck screeched to a halt, on the wrong side of the road but now separated from them by a concrete median strip.

"You fucking sluts! You drive off and don't even talk to us!"

That word, *slut*. In the back seat, Carly had a flashback to middle school. She lived in a world of friends, a happy home, the family dog, and her art and crafts. She had been carefree as a young teen and naive about boys. They didn't have a TV, so she read: the Famous Five, the Hardy Boys, Trixie Belden, *Black Beauty*, *Anne of Green Gables*, *The Little House on the Prairie*, Roald Dahl, *The Diary of Anne Frank*, *Little Women*, *Pride and Prejudice*, *Wuthering Heights*, *Jane Eyre* … books with nothing overt about sex. She remembered going on a date and the boy clumsily attempting to kiss her at the end of the night. It wasn't unpleasant, just totally unexpected. Kate and Seyram laughed when she told them afterward. Kate had kissed a boy months before and, although Seyram never had, they both said, "Didn't you expect that on a date?" Being carefree and naive made Carly a target.

Carly avoided the harassment, mostly, but a couple of times a week coming home from school a group of older boys would target her relentlessly until she turned into her street. They resented that she was so clueless about their needs and wants. "Show us your tits! Show us your pussy!" Carly was fourteen. "Suck our dick!" It was always plural: us, our. *How did boys learn so young to make group sexual demands and to think they had a collective dick?* "Come on, *slut!*"

"Come on, *slut!*" Carly moved her hand to the back seat door and pressed the button to lower her window, the guys hollering as they saw the back passenger window descend slowly.

"Coop, Coop, there are three of them. *Three sluts!*" Sheldon shrieked. "There's one in the back!"

In one swift move, Carly picked up the grenade launcher, swiveled back, rested the barrel on the open window, and pulled the trigger.

The grenade exploded the truck on impact, the boom rocking Seyram's car. Luckily Seyram's window was up and Carly, unprepared for the launcher's recoil, had been knocked backward away from her open window. The truck was a ball of fire.

"You could have warned us you were going to do that!" exclaimed Seyram. "Weren't we going to wait until we were further from town?"

"I didn't know I was. I just ... I just looked at them foaming at the mouth and thought, *I want to blow your brains out.* So I did."

"Are you OK?"

"*OK?* I feel like fucking *Gaia!*" whooped Carly. She pumped her fist in the air.

"Settle down," said Kate. "Half of Mossberg just heard that. You were supposed to do it on the pass. Seyram, go straight and turn right into North Hollow Road. Follow it for two miles to loop the back way to my place. We can drive into our underground parking so no one sees us. Then let's change into our normal clothes and go to one of those shitty bars and get a drink." Kate's mind was going a million miles an hour as the light turned green and Seyram accelerated. "And we need to get rid of this grenade launcher. No, wait. We need an alibi. Do what I said; loop around back to my place. When we cross Stowe Creek, toss the grenade launcher into the water—we can't risk keeping it until we have the chance to dump it in the Mossberg River as originally planned. Then we get changed, but then continue on by going down Third Avenue and filling up at the Shell gas station on Main Street. It'll get us on its CCTV. Drive back out this way again and I'll call the pizza place in Daineton—where I made the reservation—and tell them we can see a fire blocking the road so we have to cancel. Then let's go to Pizza Hut."

"Pizza Hut!" Seyram complained.

"Jesus, Seyram, I'm trying to create an alibi. We wanted to go to Daineton because it has the best pizza, then we saw the road was blocked, so we settled for Pizza Hut in Mossberg. CCTV from there and the Shell gas station will show us cool, calm, and collected. Got it?"

"Got it." Seyram looked at Carly in the rear vision mirror. "Seyram to Gaia, still OK?"

"Better endorphins than backbends in yoga," said Carly, sprawled against the seat.

SUMMER 2018

17

AGENT TED FINCHER of the FBI's Pittsburg branch had only been in Mossberg two days and already missed his wife and children. He had reluctantly returned to Mossberg after Chief Delaney of the Mossberg police called the FBI for assistance in investigating the deaths of Cooper Hanson and Sheldon Nossel.

During his first visit back in April, he had investigated reports of violent hate speech about women and girls being posted on the *Mossberg Gazette*'s website. He had worked on a number of cases involving hate crimes, either committed or planned, against Muslims, Jews, Asians, Blacks, Spanish-speakers, women, and gays. Perpetrators were usually white Christians, but there were a few ISIS supporters out there trying to kill anyone and everyone. It was the *hate* that got to him. At least with homicides the perp could be locked up, but with hate crimes the source of the motivation—the hate—seemed endless. After all, Fincher figured, hate doesn't occur in a vacuum; it is learned somewhere.

In the *Gazette*'s case, initial IT forensic analysis had traced messages left on its webpage to an establishment that appeared to be a part of Mossberg College. Fincher's meeting with the *Gazette*'s editor in chief, Henry Konig, had been unproductive, however. Konig had reacted defensively the minute dark-haired Fincher, tall and trim in a tailored suit, walked into Konig's office and showed his FBI badge. Konig had wanted to argue about the First Amendment, complained about interfering government, and asked what was wrong with not liking certain kinds of people. Fincher had patiently explained the crime was to post threats to commit violence.

His appointment with Mossberg College's new president, Dr. Susan Gutmann, was more enlightening. "Our IT forensics have traced some of the messages to an establishment called Opus Steel House, just outside of Mossberg," he said. "It appears they use different servers to Mossberg College, but I understand it is a part of the college. I wonder if you could start by describing the relationship between the college and this residence?"

"Yes, Opus Steel is an all-male residence. It's a huge old mansion out of town on the former estate of a nineteenth-century steel baron. It has an odd status within the college. I barely knew about it until I commissioned a property inventory just after I arrived here, which put it on my radar. Then I got your call and did further research. A benefactor bequeathed the property to Mossberg College in 1925, with the condition that we don't take full control for 100 years, which meant no one had a reason to pay it any attention until the property inventory. The bequest pays for maintenance, so financially it's been no imposition on the college. But reportedly it houses a group of incels—those odious men who believe they have the right to have sex with women. We can't get rid of them, and we have no idea how to find out what they're doing, but I don't like it. You mentioned their IT infrastructure and you're correct: it is completely independent of the college's, and we have no way of controlling it. Between you and me, this is not our only problem when it comes to female safety on campus. We have several fraternities that run riot, one in particular that houses a bunch of young jocks into all kinds of sports."

As Gutmann spoke, Fincher noted phrases like "cultural change" and "new era," as well as "legacy," "donors," "town fathers," and "cash-strapped." In other words, the college was a financial hostage.

"Dr. Gutmann, do I understand correctly that Opus Steel House and these fraternities have basically had free rein? It seems they've been allowed to do much as they please for generations—on campus and in town."

"In a nutshell. My guess is regular fraternity members are less likely to post comments on the local paper's website than the incels, but they're all part of a continuum of systemic harassment and sometimes outright assault in this town."

In the end, Fincher conducted an inconclusive investigation that left everyone dissatisfied. Nasty comments were now mostly being intercepted and deleted, a positive outcome, but insufficient evidence had been found to charge, let alone convict, anyone.

Now Fincher was back and having to deal with the same local police, although he was hoping to avoid the offices of the *Gazette* and its editor in chief.

In a meeting with Mayor Konig, Chief Delaney, Detective Schultz, and Trooper Chase, Fincher put aside memories of his previous visit and what he'd learned about how power was wielded in Mossberg, and forced himself to focus on the matter at hand. "We know Preston Brock died from blunt force trauma, and forensics show that Cooper Hanson and Sheldon Nossel died from a projectile hitting their car—most likely a grenade launcher, which I imagine is unusual anywhere outside a war zone. There were also scuff marks on the path above where Branson Vanburg was found. So, while these deaths could be unrelated, the profile of the individuals is close to identical: young white men. They were all also sporting figures in local teams, although we don't yet know the significance of this. Our working hypothesis should be the deaths are related."

Everyone was quiet as they absorbed this news.

"The deaths didn't happen at a highway rest stop outside of town or in a back alley in the center of town," Fincher continued. "They were all at locations I'm guessing only locals know: Coates Ravine, River Flats Golf Course, and Hills Pass Road through to Daineton. The killer, or killers, is here. He's in Mossberg."

"But we have no leads," protested Detective Schultz. "We know three ladies were walking in Coates Ravine about the time Branson Vanburg was there, but they saw nothing. With Preston Brock's death, we have the ladies who found him and a couple of other players, but they saw no one suspicious on the golf course. And we have a burnt-out car with two bodies and not a single witness or any surveillance footage.

Fincher looked at Schultz. "You said three women were in Coates Ravine at about the same time as Vanburg?"

"Yup. They called us up when they heard someone died."

"And how many women found Preston Brock on the golf course?"

"Three."

Fincher looked around the room, wondering whether he was the only person seeing a possible connection. "Are they the same three women?"

"Yup. But ... what's the connection?"

Fincher pinched the top of his nose. "Do we know for sure they are the same three women?"

"Sure. Seyram Boateng, Kate Bajwa, and Carly Schumer."

"You didn't think to tell me this before?"

"Ohhh, I see where you're going with this. No, no, no, no, no. They're three local ladies. Old."

"Did you interview them? Separately?"

"Well, no. I didn't see any reason. I got a statement from the churchy one—Mrs. Boateng. She's black. Couldn't hurt a fly."

"Did she sign it under oath?"

"Yes."

"And the other two?"

"There's Carly Schumer, a blonde. She's a flake. The third, Bajwa, runs Downtown Hardware on Main. Dresses like a man. I don't trust her."

"Did you seize their golf clubs?"

"It's not what you think!" Schultz was losing patience. "Bajwa's the only golfer."

"So, you didn't?" Fincher was incredulous. "Forensics could have examined it."

Schultz was angry at being spoken to like this in front of the mayor, Chief Delaney and Trooper Chase, a junior officer. "Agent Fincher, we're talking about a lady golfer here. It's like saying you can put a … a … chainsaw in the hands of a woman and she's going to do a Texas Chainsaw Massacre."

Fincher was having none of it. "Can you give me their addresses? I'd like to talk to them."

Schultz looked at Fincher, his contempt for know-it-all, out-of-town, federal agents plainly on display. "Sure. Trooper Chase can go with you. You know, two people doing the interview—just in case one of the ladies jumps you when your back is turned." He guffawed, turning to the chief so he could join in the laughter. Schultz was not in the mood to let the matter drop. "You're the FBI. You developed serial killer profiles. You know: serial killers tend not to kill outside their racial group; serial killers are pretty much always men. The victims here were all young white men. Surely that means we're looking for a white male perp?"

Mayor Konig couldn't contain himself any longer. "You've just said 'serial killer' three times. If word gets out that is what this is, it's going to be a catastrophe—politically, for Mossberg's reputation, for me, for the sanity of families who have sons. And then there are the victims' families." Konig shared Detective Schultz's prejudices toward out-of-towners, but also thought it prudent to have the FBI on board. He wondered how much a large investigation would cost, and what federal support might be available. He asked Fincher, "Can't we do something to draw the killer out? Into a public event where we scrutinize everyone, note down car license plates. Something he'd *want* to participate in. Isn't that what the FBI did in Atlanta when they tried to catch the killer behind the child murders there? They organized a march as a way of getting the man to show himself in public."

"The problem," responded Fincher, "is that in Atlanta, the theory was the killer was toying with the police, using media coverage of their investigation to mess with their heads. So, yes, the FBI thought the march was a way of getting him to show himself. The difference here is that whoever is killing these young men has not left a trace, at least not anything you've identified. They aren't playing with the police, they aren't moving bodies and leaving them in conspicuous places, and they aren't leaving any clues. Whether that's intentional or not."

Agent Fincher was fed up with these local men who ran a fiefdom and thought "local knowledge" was a substitute for detached analysis. On his first morning back in Mossberg he'd been sent with Trooper Chase to the place in Coates Ravine where Branson Vanburg went over the edge, then to the golf course where Preston Brock was found. He was relieved it was Chase, not Schultz, who would accompany him to interview Bajwa and Schumer.

"The thing that puzzles me," said Fincher thinking out loud, "is that unless the killer just *happened* to come across Hanson and Nossel at the intersection out of town—which is unlikely, given the nature of their deaths—it means they were followed. Yet you say there isn't a single piece of surveillance footage of Hanson's car or any subsequent vehicle after they passed the Shell gas station on Main. Not because they aren't in the footage, but because there is no footage. There is no CCTV the entire length of Main Street leading out to that intersection after the Shell gas station, but there is CCTV at multiple other locations."

Detective Schultz guffawed again. "Fincher, you've got to learn you're in a small town! Sure, we get rapes, but little real crime, like property theft. Nothing bad enough to make the town or anyone else spend thousands on surveillance cameras."

Fincher glared at Schultz. "It's *Agent* Fincher."

Mayor Konig cleared his throat—he'd gone to conferences on law and order in small towns. "I must correct you there, Detective Schultz. We had those vandalism incidents in the parking lots a few years back." Turning to Fincher, he added,

"You'll be pleased to know, Agent Fincher, that we put in a whole heap of cameras. The fellas were real upset about damage to their vehicles."

Fincher looked at the room in stony silence. "My point is this: the killer might have known there were no cameras that end of Main Street, and therefore also known that following Hanson and Nossel along Main Street to get out of town was a safe bet. So, who in Mossberg would have this kind of information? Who installs security cameras?"

"The council just bought some from the hardware store. They recommend a contractor who does the installation," said the mayor.

"Is this the same hardware store run by the woman who was in Coates Ravine and wields a golf club? The one you"—Fincher gestured to Schultz—"didn't interview?"

"That's the one," confirmed Schultz with a broad smile.

Fincher wondered what he had done in a past life to end up in this office with these people. He continued, "This intersection where they were killed. Is it a kind of lovers' lane? Do people go there to have sex? Could the boys have followed someone there for that reason?"

Shultz snorted derisively. "And *my* point is this, *Agent* Fincher: about you not needing to do more interviews. Those boys were Mossberg prime beef. The only reason those three ladies would go near them would be to collect their laundry." Schultz wiped the tears from his eyes at the thought of a romantic tryst. The corners of Mayor Konig's and Trooper Chase's mouths also started to twitch.

Schultz was on a roll. "And what would be these girls' motivation? They're upset because a boy somewhere fucked a girl?"

"Detective Schultz, do you have daughters?" Fincher asked.

Schultz was not amused by this sudden focus on his personal life. "One," he said stiffly.

"So, what did you think when you heard the allegations of rape against Branson Vanburg, Cooper Hanson, and Sheldon Nossel?"

Schultz was sharp. "My daughter has enough motivation to avoid getting herself into compromising situations."

Fincher thought about his own daughters, both tweens, and how their zest for life would propel them into any situation that promised fun and meeting new people.

Mayor Konig, reading the tension in the room, attempted to change tack. "About holding a march. Is there any reason why we should *not* do it?"

"Probably not," said Fincher, "but what's the angle? What is going to draw the killer out?"

"It's pretty clear what the killer is against," said Schultz. "I mean, the victims were a type: young, talented, sporty, white, American men."

"You could add 'heterosexual' into that mix," said Trooper Chase.

Chief Delaney, who had said nothing up to this point, saw his opportunity to exert authority. "Why doesn't the council host an event that's the opposite of all that? Something involving people the killer's got to support. He's probably some kind of Dem, right? But not black—you'd agree, Agent Fincher—serial killers usually being the same race as their victims?"

"That's what the data suggests, sir."

"So, a march should spark his curiosity—along with everyone else in Mossberg. We should make it a rights march. All those folks who support equality. The killer will turn out for something like that. We can get everyone to park at the sports fields and record license plates as they come in and get someone to film the crowd."

Agent Fincher wondered aloud, "Could a march like that be organized in Mossberg?" It wasn't the presence of organizational skills he doubted, it was the suggestion there were hordes of progressives in Mossberg.

Mayor Konig slapped the table. "Arlene Childs and Betty Stewart. No one in America can organize a march as efficiently as they can. Leave it to them."

18

MAYOR KONIG WAS the opening speaker at the council's extraordinary meeting that he had called to address "Urgent Safety Issues in the Community," as the invitation had been titled. The decision to hold the meeting had been informed by discussions with Chief Delaney and the FBI, who told Konig that a typology of the victims suggested the deaths may be linked, and therefore the community should be warned and preventative action taken.

"We have an unprecedented crisis in our community," the mayor commenced. "Four young men have died, and it seems they may have been targeted because of their youth and their sex."

The entire chamber sat up at this news. *Four murders? Preston Brock? Yes. Cooper Hanson and Sheldon Nossel? Clearly. But who was the first?* The realization hit everyone at the same time: *Branson Vanburg had been murdered!* A woman at the back of the room let out a small scream.

Mayor Konig, oblivious to the sensation he'd unintentionally unleashed, continued. "This is an unprecedented attack on the fabric of our community and is cause for alarm for all families. We need to take urgent action: upgrade the lights in the parking lots to protect the cars—they are a means of escape for our boys if threatened—as well as the lights around the football field, the hockey rink, and the sidewalks linking them to the school and the college. We need more parking spaces for parents to wait for their boys to finish games, and most of all we need extra security—overtime for police to make night-time patrols—and a taskforce to solve these murders. We'll set up a system of volunteers to patrol the sports fields and to ride shotgun with the boys on their way to and from sports practice. We can install CCTV in key places around town, including on Main Street where the bars are, and have a rapid reaction team that monitors the footage in real time and intervenes when they see something wrong. We also need to work with the Pennsylvania Office of the Attorney General to create a special court to fast-track cases of violence or harassment against our young men in a way that doesn't retraumatize them. And we need to lobby the legislature in Harrisburg to pass tougher state laws against harassment and violence. I'm asking for $10 million over three years to be reallocated from other city programs to this initiative."

The audience sat in stunned silence, absorbing the threat and the proposed scale of the response.

Someone in the crowd, their mind going into top gear to think of additional preventive measures, called out, "Shouldn't we think about how our young men should protect themselves? We could impose a curfew, so they don't put themselves in danger. Or give them training in self-defense, or teach them how to be more streetwise. Encourage them to go out together, in groups, and not drink too much."

"No, no, no, no, *no!*" the mayor insisted. "Our young men shouldn't need to be *streetwise!* They should be able to walk around in freedom. In safety. This is America!" He pushed back his chair and rose to his feet. "When I'm downtown on Friday and Saturday nights and see a young man stumbling drunk out of a bar or walking home alone, I don't *judge* him. I don't think *Oooh, that boy should be careful.* I thank *God* I live in a country where young men are free to go out and meet people and, goddammit, free to get drunk and walk home alone!" He banged the table. "Who wants to live in a country where young men are too afraid to walk around at night? What kind of society is that? I'm all for making the streets safer for our boys, but we shouldn't ask them to change their lives. They should be *free.* We need a curfew on the potential *murderers.*"

A woman at the back spoke up. "We all want them to feel safe, but there must be things young men can change, like women do when they go out."

"Like *women?*" Mayor Konig was apoplectic. "*You* can stop wearing lipstick, short skirts, high heels, sexy blouses, showing your breasts, looking at men, drinking alcohol, and wandering around at night like a bunch of I-don't-know-whats! What could young men possibly change?"

"Not wearing sweaty T-shirts over perky nipples and bulging biceps," called out a septuagenarian, grasping her cane with sudden intensity. "That's enough to provoke anyone."

MAYOR KONIG HAD been nervous before this meeting. Possibly the most important in the history of the council. He knew the money for safety upgrades was needed but wasn't sure his pitch was going to be enough. He confided in his wife Jenny, and she came up with a brainwave. "Why not get one of the students from the college to say something? I mean, they're the ones being targeted." She shot him a look. "Like when Sisterhood House invited those three students to speak in support of its budget pitch. I thought they were very convincing about the need for extra money."

Mayor Konig jumped on the phone to coach Grossman at the college, who had personally known Cooper and Sheldon. "Grossman. Konig. I'm making a pitch this Thursday night at the council for a special town security budget in response to the murders. I need a student who can speak in support of the motion. Not one of the players; someone who can string a sentence together. Someone who can persuade the council. Can you browse the cheerleaders and pick me one?"

Grossman didn't hesitate. "Tulip Sorensen. There's no one like her."

Tulip was the princess royale of Mossberg Hills. She was possibly the most beautiful woman Mossberg had ever known: a honey blonde with sparkling brown eyes, long, long legs, and a formidable competitive spirit. In addition to being a cheerleading captain every year since middle school, she was crowned Miss Teen Mossberg in her first year of college—she raised $150,000 for the Junior League. Now a sophomore,

Tulip was doing a self-directed study program on leadership across business, media, and cheerleading. She chose her professors carefully: Mr. Schmidt, Mr. Greene, Mr. Miyazaki, Mr. Rockman, Mr. Carter, and Mr. Ortez.

For assessments, Tulip always asked to give presentations on aspects of leadership, and her professors never said no. As part of her leadership initiative, she had created a wonderful support team to help with presentations: a gay boy, a mousy girl, a fat girl, and a mousy fat girl, all devoted to her. They wrote and submitted the paperwork, and she presented it. Tulip liked to sit herself on a table opposite the professor's desk while she spoke, turning alternately to address the professor, then the other students, occasionally leaning back with a toss of her head for dramatic effect. The only bad grade she'd ever had was when a female professor took over Mr. Rockman's classes. "Get off the table and stand," she'd snapped. "And stop flicking your hair."

Tulip's ambition was to be a news anchor or an influencer on social media. She already had 40,000 followers on Instagram and 30,000 on TikTok.

AT THE BACK of the council chamber, Tulip was waiting in her cheerleading uniform—Mayor Konig had specifically asked her to wear it—when she heard, "I think now is a good time to give the floor to Tulip Sorensen, one of our accomplished students from Mossberg College." Inhaling deeply and closing her eyes to focus, she paused, then stepped down the aisle, channeling Beyoncé, between the rows of people slouched in the uncomfortable chairs. The only convenient table to sit on was where the council minute-taker was, so Tulip perched on that, presenting her profile to the room, her back arched so that a cloud of honey-blond hair flowed over the minute-taker. She turned to the audience, now keenly erect in their seats. Whatever she said had to grab their attention immediately.

"Branson. Preston. Cooper. Sheldon. I'm too young to know what it is like to be dead, but I'll bet right now none of them are happy. They were my future husbands. The future fathers of my children. Young men in this community are being murdered and *we need to keep them alive!* Imagine if the people murdering and scaring young men in Mossberg said they were part of a terrorist network that said it wanted to destroy the freedom of America's youth. *We'd be outraged!*" Tulip clutched her chest and let out a sob. "I implore you to pass this special budget prepared by Mayor Konig, so that we can *save our jocks*." She walked over to Mayor Konig, who stood at the lectern, wrapped her arms around his belly, kicked up a heel, and snuggled a cheek against his shoulder. Looking out at the audience through her long lashes, she breathed, "This man keeps us safe. Vote Mayor Konig. Pass the budget. God bless America."

Mayor Konig flushed bright pink. The crowd erupted in cheers. Applause. Wolf whistles. "Go Konig!" came from the floor.

"Hug *me*, Tulip!" called another.

"U-S-A! U-S-A! U-S-A!" chanted a group at the back.

The special measure that became known as the Mossberg Save Our Jocks Spending Bill was passed unanimously.

19

MAYOR KONIG WAS the glummest he'd ever felt in his life. His victory in getting a special budget passed for town safety was bittersweet. Yes, he had the money to improve safety, but the meeting had set off alarm bells in the community. And he was still faced with the fact that there were four unsolved deaths in his town—all first-class sportsmen, the cream of the crop. He wondered if Mossberg could ever make the playoffs again.

The Konigs had been in Mossberg for nine generations. His grandfather was mayor in the sixties, his great-grandfather during World War I. Mayor Konig was in his sixth year and loved the job. He knew many of the families, loved the hilly area and the languid neighborhoods beside the river, and got a sense of satisfaction knowing that Mossberg's diverse economy offered many jobs. It was a regional shopping destination—one of the few places that still had a thriving central shopping precinct; there were IT and white-collar professional businesses; it had the army base, the college, and several poultry farms outside of town; it was surrounded by farms on the river flats; and it had a couple of quarries nearby. It was a town to be proud of, and he loved it. But Mossberg was changing.

Instead of waving their sons goodbye with a cheerful "Drive safely!", mothers clutched their sons to their bosom and chided them for wanting to go out, implored them to give up sports and to stay at home and watch TV—or to help prepare meals and do housework. The Mossberg Mothers Facebook page posted tips for home crafts that might entice boys to stay at home. Fathers encouraged their sons to take up woodwork and furniture upholstery in the safety of the basement, or to tinker with cars in the garage. Churches and schools issued whistles to young men to blow if they felt afraid. Parents organized car shares and convoys to and from school and sports practice, and few boys could be seen walking anywhere anymore. The sons themselves were crazy with boredom: stuck at home, car keys often confiscated, playing endless computer games and needing parental permission to drive three or four in a car under strict curfews. *It wasn't fair!*

Even soldiers at Fort Byrd had been advised to travel in groups, and night curfews had been imposed. In fact, many in Mossberg suspected the murderer may be someone from the army base, such as a soldier jealous of the town jocks and their prowess on the sporting field and with girls.

From the perspective of some, the changes in town were not all bad. Sexual assaults and other public violence dramatically decreased as men absented themselves from public spaces. The vast majority of early morning joggers and walkers were now young and middle-aged women, who were no longer afraid to exercise alone.

Males, on the other hand, felt uncertain about being unaccompanied in public, and several false alarms contributed to them feeling this way. A carload of young men driving around town on a Friday evening—getting a breath of fresh air after being cooped up night after night—noticed two young women taking photos. Panicked that they were being recorded as future prey, the men called the police, who interrogated the women, who turned out to be students from the college fine arts program doing a photography project on Mossberg's nineteenth-century architecture. Other young men crossed the street when a stranger walked toward them on the sidewalk. Four baseball players who had risked walking home in a group after practice rounded a corner and came face-to-face with a six-foot-six drag queen heading to Mossberg's nascent gay scene. Everyone froze. The drag queen gave the merest flutter of lashes … and the baseball players threw down their kit and hightailed it. "Boys, come back," she called. "I just want to say hi!"

Feeling depressed about what he might find, Mayor Konig rarely went downtown anymore in the evening. On this particular night, he felt compelled to survey the damage the "events" were causing his community. In anticipation of empty streets and depressing conversations with bar and store owners, he brought along Scottie, his little white terrier, for company. Konig always made sure to circulate on foot and say hello to business owners, who all loved Scottie.

Turning into Main Street, Konig was confused to see lights and action, and music thumping from several bars. A minibus pulled up outside a club and twenty five young women spilled out. A trio of drag queens—not previously sighted in Mossberg before 2018—burst out of the same bar, laughing and lighting up cigarettes. All he could see looking down Main were groups of two, three, four, or more young women: outside the cafés, bars, and restaurants. For a second, he wondered whether the past few months had been a dream. He got out to speak to Moh Habib, the proprietor of Moh's Kebabs. "Moh, what's going on? There are people everywhere. I thought Main Street would be dead."

"Didn't you hear? Main Street businesses were trying to think of ways to bring back customers, and they posted on Facebook a few days ago that Main has been proclaimed a safe space. Things went crazy! There are none of the regular boys …" Moh cast an eye at the smokers "… but the young ladies, they are coming here in their hundreds."

"But … who buys them dinner?"

"Some of them don't even need men," said Moh, lowering his voice. "Tonight, I've got an order for sixty halloumi vegetarian kebabs for a busload of lesbians coming from New York City for the weekend. Many different sauces."

Konig felt faint. "We could start by banning drag shows," he mused aloud.

"No, Mayor! Look around you: people are happy, business is booming. You know Moose Bar, where the college boys used to try to bait the army boys into a fight? It's going to have a gay night three times a week. That's where the lesbians are going after they've enjoyed my kebabs. But you go there now, and you'll see it is already full. I never knew Mossberg had so many homosexuals. The wonderful pink dollar!"

As Moh spoke, a conga line of men wearing shirts patterned with toucans and tropical fruit, each clasping the bouncing hips of the one in front, appeared from around the corner. "We. Are. Fam-il-y," sang the conga as it crossed the street and disappeared into a tavern.

Scottie tugged at his leash to follow.

"That's not all," continued Moh. "Tomorrow the *Sports Bar*—can you believe it!—is hosting a Lindy Hop dance competition for African Americans. People coming from Cleveland, Philly, DC, and Baltimore by the carload. The wonderful Black dollar!" Moh wore a beatific smile.

Mayor Konig remembered being a small child and watching a Disney cartoon where the master of the house had gone out, his three cats had fallen asleep, and two dozen mice came out to play—darting in and out of their holes, jumping onto the dining table, rifling through the kitchen cabinets, and racing around the sleeping cats. Panicked by the loss of order, Konig had shouted at the TV for the cats to wake up.

He rushed to his car and slowly drove the length of Main Street, did a U-turn, and drove back. Lines of young women were waiting to get into the French bistro, Burgers-on-Main, Moose Bar, the Tavern, Pizza Hut, Starbucks, and a dozen other venues. He was aghast. All these carefree, laughing, going-about-their-business young women—and *others*—not giving a damn that half the young population was staying at home worrying about being assaulted or murdered. With a screech of tires, he turned toward home.

20

"ASSHOLE!" SHOUTED EMILY as the car coming toward hers did an abrupt U-turn before heading back into town.

"I had no idea downtown was going to be this busy," muttered Wyatt as his girlfriend, Emily, parked. "Are you sure I'm safe?"

Emily stifled a laugh. "Wyatt, I love you because you remind me of Clark Kent. An assassin with a penchant for jocks isn't going to target you."

Wyatt pouted. "I'll take that as a compliment."

Curious at what they'd heard about a transformed downtown, Wyatt and Emily had come to see for themselves. Like Mayor Konig minutes before them, they discovered it was jumping.

They joined the line to get into a bar, and overheard the whispered conversation between the two male college students in front:

"Dude, this was a mistake," said the first, glancing anxiously around. "The bar's going to be full of chicks and gays. Any one of them could be the killer. We should get out of here."

"We're never going to get laid if that's our attitude," whispered the second. "We can't look at porn our whole life.

Besides, we're going to wait an hour if we try to get a cab now, and there's no way I'm walking home in the dark."

"Call your mom."

"She lives in Pittsburgh."

"Call 911."

"And say what? That we don't feel safe?"

"Yes!"

"Wait. I'm sure my roommate said his sister was coming here tonight. I'll text him and get her number."

The reply came in seconds.

"He says she's here. Her name's Sissy. She's real nice. I'll text her to come out."

Minutes later a petite young woman with curly blond hair emerged from the bar wearing a spangly black dress and heels.

"Over here!" the first college student called out. He took off his cap and mopped his forehead in relief. "Thank God, Sissy, can we come in and sit with you?"

Sissy took them by their elbows and dragged them to the front of the line. "They're with me," she said to the bouncer, who checked their ID and let them through the rope. "Stay close and you'll be OK," Sissy told them.

A few minutes later, Wyatt and Emily were also allowed in. Nudging their way through the packed room, Emily and Wyatt spotted two empty stools at the end of an otherwise crowded table.

"Let's grab those stools while we have the chance," called Wyatt above the noise.

"Check out the crowd. Nearly all women and most of the guys look gay," Emily shouted back.

As they settled on the stools, the woman next to them lent over to Emily. "Are you in the Public Health Master's? I'm sure I've seen you before."

"Yes, I am." Emily smiled. "I didn't recognize you out of context! What's your name again?"

"I'm Beth. These are my friends, Tanisha and Bao."

"I'm Emily. This is Wyatt."

Shouting above the din, the five of them discussed the downtown atmosphere, until the conversation came around to the cause.

"I'm glad those guys' deaths scared the shit out of straight men and made women feel safe," said Tanisha. "That's why tonight is so packed."

"Let's drink to that!" yelled Bao.

The five of them clinked glasses and bottles.

"Wyatt's writing a story on the murders," shouted Emily, dragging him into the conversation. "He thinks the killer might be a woman."

"*Really?*" Tanisha, Beth, and Bao sat up.

"I can't be sure," said Wyatt, continuing above the noise, "but there's evidence of women at two of the crime scenes. I did an interview with the woman who runs Sisterhood House—do you know that place? I asked if she thought there was anything in feminism that might support violence against men."

"You mean Grace?" asked Beth. "We all know her. We do volunteer work with Sisterhood House."

Another clinking of glasses and bottles.

Wyatt, who could never resist canvassing people's opinions about his latest story, asked, "Do you think it's unlikely it's a woman? You all seemed surprised when I said that. Grace thought most feminists were against violence. She said the women's movement was connected to the peace movement in the sixties and seventies."

"You've got to remember she's talking about a different generation," shouted Tanisha. "I call myself a feminist, but people my age are different."

"Older feminists are really black-and-white about things," said Beth. "You're a man or a woman; straight or gay."

"Even Grace told me once that although in practice she was straight, philosophically she was bisexual," said Tanisha.

"Bisexual!" exclaimed Emily, Beth, and Bao, rolling their eyes.

"What's wrong with being bisexual?" asked Wyatt.

"Oh, Wyatt," said Emily. "Nobody says that anymore. It's *pansexual*. Bisexual buys into the whole binary thing."

"It's *so* last semester," said Bao. "It's like they don't believe in variation outside a few limited categories, or in movement between them."

"We're way more fluid about sexuality," continued Beth, "and more conscious of race. More into individual expression. Feminism is one of many other things important for us, like being a savvy consumer, being environmentally aware, or being a vegetarian. My grandmother is a feminist," added Beth, "but she says that the way my generation thinks makes her head spin."

"My grandmother is a feminist too," said Tanisha, "but she wouldn't agree with Grace on violence. She was an activist back in the sixties when the Black Power movement was around and there was a backlash against civil rights to be countered, along with anti-colonial wars in Africa. I'm not saying she *believed* in violence, but she definitely thought a violent response was sometimes the only thing to make already violent societies sit up and take notice."

"So, you think a woman could have killed those guys?"

"I can imagine women being fed up enough to *want* to," shouted Tanisha. "I'm sure you saw coverage on TV of Black Lives Matter, Occupy Wall Street, and Antifa demonstrations. There were loads of young women involved. It's not just men who attack police and burn down buildings."

"What did Grace think?" asked Bao.

"She said she used to work in a prison full of moms who'd murdered men because they were fed up with the status quo."

Bao laughed. "So that's your answer."

Wyatt felt a sudden pang of homesickness. How had he ended up in a bar like this, having conversations with people who seemed to think it was *normal* that a woman might want to physically attack a man? It made him miss the daily certainties of the family farm.

The taut opening notes of Camila Cabello's "Havana" came over the sound system and the entire room cheered and jumped to its feet as one.

"Let's dance!" shouted Beth.

Leaning in close to Wyatt's ear, Emily asked, "Want to get out of here? I've got to finish a paper tomorrow." Wyatt nodded.

"We'll see you around!" called Emily as Beth, Tanisha, and Bao headed to the dance floor.

A FEW WEEKS LATER, Wyatt drove Emily to an aged care facility run by a Black church where Emily was doing a project on seniors. As he sat in the reception waiting for Emily to finish interviews, a tiny, wizened, African American woman on a walker slowly rounded the corner. She must have been at least ninety. As he watched her cross the carpet, his conversation with Tanisha came back to him and, wide-eyed, he saw the elderly woman morph into someone else: straight-backed, gun holsters on both hips, spurs clinking, bandoliers of bullets across her breast, and a monumental Afro; Clint Eastwood meets the Black Panthers. He never looked at little old ladies the same way again.

21

SEYRAM WAS SCHEDULED to visit her parents that evening but had given her apologies, pleading a tiring week and the need for a relaxed evening with her friends. Felix, the kids, and her parents got on like a house on fire—and Felix, Kofi, and her father all shared a love for storytelling and laughter—so she knew everyone would finish the evening in high spirits.

There was a flurry of sounds and footsteps as Kate and Carly arrived with pizza, salad, and garlic bread for dinner, along with Kate's Coronas and Carly's sauvignon blanc. Seyram had already done everything she needed, which was setting out plates, cutlery, and napkins.

"Hi, gals! Come in." Seyram stayed sitting at her table, from where she could see her back door, and waved Carly and Kate to come through.

"You really have had a tiring week," said Carly, kissing her on the cheek. "When Seyram Boateng doesn't get up, that means she's out of gas."

"A tough week in the lab. I had these orders to fill, but one of our machines broke down on Monday morning and we couldn't get it repaired for three days. We worked to midnight last night, and I was there from five this morning."

"Did you get the orders done?"

"Yes, thank goodness. But I'm exhausted."

"You should have canceled," said Kate. "We could have come around next week."

"No, no. This is exactly what I feel like: getting together with friends and sharing a meal. Sorry I broke our rule by not cooking and asking you to bring the food!"

Carly and Kate put the food on the table and poured themselves drinks. They noticed an unfamiliar gold liquid in Seyram's glass, in place of the usual fruit mocktail. Seyram saw them looking.

"Alright, confession: I opened one of Felix's beers." She gave a tired smile.

"This will cheer you up some more: we picked up the pizzas downtown, and it's remarkable," said Kate. "Few men around, but young women everywhere. Looks like a big queer crowd too."

"You know it's us that's done this, don't you?" said Carly. "We've literally made half the population of the town feel safer."

"And made the other half feel like the rest of us used to feel," added Kate.

"It makes me feel satisfied," said Seyram. "And bad. But, if I'm totally honest, I feel good about feeling bad. This town has been shocked into some sort of recalibration."

"Maybe we should scale up," joked Kate. "Go for statewide change."

"You know," said Carly, "I've got a cousin in North Dakota, where the nukes are. Maybe we could steal one of those and blow up the intercollege football tournament in December? We could take out every jock on the Eastern seaboard."

"That's not a bad idea," said Seyram thoughtfully. "We could steal one of those missile launcher tractor trailers and hide it in the forest reserve outside Mossberg."

"So, let me get this clear," said Kate straight-faced. "We steal the missile from its silo in North Dakota, put it on a tractor trailer launcher, which we also steal, then drive incognito down the I-90 through Chicago, take the Mossberg exit, drive into the Forest Reserve, and hide out there for a few days. Do I have that right?"

"*Yes.* You're reading my mind."

Kate and Carly looked at each other. Carly opened her hand and mimed drinking from an imaginary glass. 'Ohhh,' mouthed Kate. Seyram's annual beer had gone to her head.

Seyram caught the exchange and threw a piece of garlic bread at Kate, hitting her on the nose.

"Lucky this isn't Mom's food," said Kate in mock objection. "My parents would never forgive such disrespect." The three of them broke into laughter.

"Can I ask you both something?" said Carly. "It's been bothering me about … what we're doing."

"Sweetie, you can ask us anything," said Seyram. "You know that."

"Well, speaking of your parents, what *would* your parents think?"

"Of what?"

"Of what we've done. What you say isn't going to change how I feel, but I guess I wonder whether my parents would think me a terrible person."

"So, why don't you start? What would Mr. and Mrs. Schumer think?"

"Now you've put me on the spot, I have to think about it," said Carly. She poured another glass of wine and gazed out the kitchen window while Seyram and Kate waited for her to speak.

"They both marched against the Vietnam War, but I think they were more against certain types of men than violence itself. Like President Johnson, who was obsessed with his dick, or military guys who are gung-ho about war. Dad once told me he'd never been bored in his life except in a bar full of Top Gun 'Maverick' types. As for Mom, she surrounded herself with women in fiction where a basic theme was how to survive and thrive in a world controlled by men. I think they would find our actions extreme, but forgivable. It wouldn't stop them loving me ... but as for me personally? I'm feeling pretty conflicted. I know we had just talked about taking action, and Vanburg's and Brock's deaths weren't premeditated, but the fact is they're dead. I don't regret that they're dead; I just regret we had a hand in it. Kate, what about you?"

Kate gave a short laugh. "My parents have plenty of other reasons not to love me. I'm not saying they *don't* love me, but I don't think what we've done would influence their opinion. They have a strange attitude toward violence. Our family was exposed to a lot of communal violence when Pakistan and India split, and I would guess that all my aunties were beaten at some stage by my uncles. They might talk about the community upheaval and chaos, but they would never talk about sexual violence. They see it as something unpleasant, but also think it's more important to get on with life and not make things worse by open discussion. If my family found out what we'd done, they'd probably say 'Oh, there goes Kate again. Creating problems for the family and killing off every chance she has of getting a husband.' It's as though the problem with violence is that it's inconvenient for the family, rather than immoral."

"What about *you*?" asked Carly. "Do you think killing people is immoral? I really need to know."

"I've never been against the death penalty. I jumped for joy when our military got Osama Bin Laden. I don't have a problem with targeted killings."

"No conflicted feelings there, evidently," said Carly drily. She turned to Seyram. "What about you? What about your mom and dad? I honestly have no idea what they would say."

Seyram pursed her lips. "Ghana is very peaceful, and the second there's any kind of fisticuffs in the street, bystanders get involved and try to stop it. Culturally, it's really important for Ghanaians to resolve conflict through talking. So, in that respect, they'd be horrified. But the Catholic Church also has a doctrine allowing 'just wars,' and most Catholics would feel strongly that violent aggressors should be stopped. The question is who gets to stop them, and who defines who is a violent aggressor? Ma also used to rail against the subordination of women, even though she's never been anything but a dutiful wife to Dad. I think she would understand our motivation but wouldn't think it was our place to act, whereas Dad would be clueless about the motivation and be amazed that women could act like we did." Seyram took a sip of beer. "Anyway, I'm not my parents, and as far as I'm concerned the anger we're feeling is righteous."

"Would they still love you?"

"They'd pray for me, but they wouldn't abandon me."

"What about your kids?"

"We made the fatal mistake of buying Kofi a pet rabbit for his birthday, so now he's against killing anything. He wouldn't approve. He's also confused about young men being targeted. He thinks he's still a child, which he is, but he's aware that others sometimes see and treat him as a teenager, and he's really puzzled about how young men are supposed to behave toward women. That's partly about being an uncertain tween, but also about the confusing signals boys get about girls in the current climate: they're desirable, but untouchable—except sometimes they like being touched. You should be nice to them, but talking to them could annoy them—but sometimes they want you to talk to them. The world is a pretty confusing place for boys."

"And Nana?"

"Nana would say 'There you go again, Mom, being *bothered* about everything!' So she wouldn't approve, because she'd think it wasn't a chill thing to do."

"And Felix?"

"Felix is opposed to the death penalty, so he'd be against what we're doing for sure. Thankfully for me he's also opposed to divorce, so at least he'd visit me in prison." Seyram gave a pained half-laugh. "What about Summer? What would she say?"

"Summer is totally self-focused at the moment," said Carly. "She's really, *really*, into boys, but gets mad against anyone who impinges on her *rights*, as she describes everything she does, including her right *not* to put her clothes in the washing basket or set the table. She'd probably want me to take a bazooka to school and do away with any teacher who made her do homework and any classmates who had crossed her during the school year."

22

Seyram, Kate, and Carly were not the only people in Mossberg reflecting on motivations for murder. The same evening on the other side of town, Mayor Konig was giving Arlene Childs and Betty Stewart—his nominated march organizers—a briefing on the kind of parade he wanted.

Arlene was a stalwart of the local Republican Party and could organize anything. She had six children and was proud to be one of those "deplorables" who stayed at home and baked cookies—and the one hundred and one other things entailed in running a household. She and her best friend, Betty, had run bake sales for fifty-seven years, raising money for the school library, Christian summer camps, repairs to their church roof, people whose houses had burned down, the local sports teams, fundraising drives for the firefighters, and a myriad of other good causes. Together they had organized anti-abortion marches across ten states and held fundraisers for both of Ronald Reagan's election campaigns. Back in the early seventies they had worked with Phyllis Schlafly to oppose ratification of the Equal Rights Amendment. Arlene and Betty were possibly the most driven people in Mossberg, and the most fulfilled.

"It's possible, isn't it," mulled Betty, "that the shooter is not just against men, but also anti-white? What we know is that all four victims were young men, played sport, and were white. We need this parade to be pro-equality for the sexes *and* the races."

"I can throw in a couple of Black Lives Matter signs," said Arlene. "We should get them to chant something too. They can't just march in silence."

"Yesss," said Betty slowly. "Signs and slogans are both good ideas, but I'm seeing a pattern among these boys. Dated half the girls in Mossberg, from what I hear. We need to cover our bases. This march needs to be everything the murderer most likely believes in. Equality. Between the sexes. The races. The religions. Homosexuals. To draw him out so the police can scan the crowd, isolate him, and catch him."

Betty pulled out her phone and posted a message on her various Facebook groups asking for volunteers to make signs. Later that evening, researching online, she stumbled over a puzzling string of letters, numbers and signs one of her Facebook friends had sent her: LGBTQIA2S+. Fortunately, Arlene had a nephew who was known in the family to be artistic. She gave him a call and was impressed at his ability to decipher it.

Arlene googled slogans to chant. She recited three she thought would grab people's attention, and by that she meant the killer's:

"Women's rights are human rights and human rights are women's rights."

Betty snorted. "Rights, rights, rights. Who said that?"

"Hillary."

"Trust a Democrat to come up with something like that. What else did you find?"

"I will not be lectured about sexism and misogyny from this man." and "We should all be feminists."

"We should all be feminists? Good Lord! Who said *that*?"

"A girl from Nigeria. Chima—Chima … something."

Betty had a sharp intake of breath. "Do people know Nigerian girls are saying this kind of thing? We should tell someone."

"It's perfect," Arlene reassured her. "Like you said, the march is to appeal to the killer. Engage with him. We want the marchers to say equal rights things that will entice him to the parade."

Arlene and Betty concluded they needed a name for the march, something to give it focus and to advertise its purpose, but they were in a bind. They didn't want anything about diversity, because the name was going to be recorded for posterity, and Betty cautioned, "Who knows what *officially* encouraging diversity could lead to?" At the same time, they wanted *non-regular* folks to turn up to make the killer feel at home. In the end, they proposed "America's Finest Celebrate Their Town!" as a kind of non-committal banner headline that could guarantee a crowd. When they explained their proposal to Mayor Konig, he could see the sense in packaging the event that way. He already imagined himself under the banner—

right beneath the word "Finest"—while photographers from near and far took his picture.

"We also need parents involved in the march," said Arlene to Betty. "Especially the dads, so everyone knows families support the young people targeted by violence: dads and grandpas walking in support of their sons. Mayor Konig says the media are going to come—TV stations from Philly and Pittsburgh. That's going to be real powerful imagery. And the whole thing is going to be safe for children. He says the FBI warned him the march could stir up other troublemakers, so he's asked them to provide backup. There'll be sharpshooters on rooftops the length of the parade route, and armed police in civilian clothes will mingle with the marchers." Arlene lowered her voice. "And this isn't public knowledge, but Mayor Konig asked the NRA boys to stake out the crowd at different points. They're going to be in cars, and on corners, and in stores, watching and ready to respond with firepower if there's the least hint of violence. There are going to be guns *everywhere*. What could go wrong?"

23

AGENT FINCHER AND Trooper Chase pulled into the parking lot of Downtown Hardware, a nondescript building with windows filled with tools for fall: leaf blowers and snow blowers, along with electric drills and chainsaws. The store was crammed floor-to-ceiling with merchandise. The motto on its website was "We sell everything!" and this seemed to be true.

Its manager, Kate Bajwa, was first on Fincher's list of interviews. Fincher was dressed in a dark suit and Chase wore his police uniform. They were an incongruous pair amidst the workmen and do-it-yourselfers purchasing supplies.

"We're here to see Ms. Bajwa. Is she in?" Fincher asked the clerk, passing over his card.

The clerk scrutinized them, then picked up the phone. "Kate, the FBI's here."

Fincher and Chase were shown up to Kate's office on a mezzanine level at the back of the store. It held neatly organized shelves, filing cabinets, and a desk next to the internal windows looking over the shop floor. Paperwork was arranged into piles in front of Kate, who stood to shake hands.

"Take a seat." She indicated two chairs in front of her desk. "What can I do for you?"

"I'm Agent Fincher from the FBI, assisting Mossberg police with their investigations into recent deaths in the community.

I understand you were in the area when the first man died and were one of the people who found the second man. I have some follow-up questions I want to ask. I hope now is a good time?"

Kate sat back and gazed at them, not the slightest flicker of anxiety crossing her face. Agent Fincher had rarely met someone so cool when face-to-face with an FBI agent. He was immediately on alert.

"Sure. Detective Schultz got a statement from my friend who was with me when we found Preston Brock, but he never spoke to me."

"I've read the statement your friend Mrs. Boateng gave, so I'm aware of what she stated, but wondered if there may be something you had noticed that she had not. At Coates Ravine, where Branson Vanburg was found, I understand you saw no one else. Is that correct?"

"Correct."

"And at the parking lot, no one else was parked there?"

"Well, we were on our walk for about forty minutes. Someone may have come and gone while we were walking, but there were no other cars there when we arrived or when we left, other than the truck that I assume was Branson Vanburg's."

"I understand you turned around on your walk. Why was that?

"Seyram got blisters. I think her shoes were new. They were causing her pain, so we turned back."

"The shoes you wore, do you still have them?"

"Well, it happened back in April, months ago, but I'm pretty sure I haven't thrown out any shoes since then."

"The police found prints of several different shoes on the path. We'd like to eliminate the prints of anyone with an alibi." This was a lie. Fincher had been livid when he found out Mossberg police had neither photographed nor created molds of any footprints at the point of the path where Vanburg presumably went into the ravine. Four months later, any trace had been washed away. "Do you remember where you turned around on your walk?"

"Not exactly. But it was on the long straight stretch on the other side of the ravine."

"If you recreated the walk, do you think you could find the turnaround point?"

"Perhaps, but the path looks a lot the same that side of the ravine."

"Do you recall the wooden railing that runs along the path where it is right next to the ravine?"

"Yes."

"Do you recall if it was broken anywhere?"

"No. I mean, it may have been and we just walked past it, but I don't remember noticing that it was broken."

"And you and your friends didn't do anything to break a rail?"

Kate looked at Fincher. "No, Agent Fincher. We did not."

Fincher didn't pause. "Turning to Preston Brock's murder, you were golfing with your friends when you found him. Is that correct?"

"Yes."

"What happened?"

Kate puffed her cheeks and visibly gathered her thoughts. "I was golfing. I couldn't get a four—four players—so my friends came along to caddy and to keep me company. They don't golf. It was just a round for practice, really. We rounded the thicket that's just after the eleventh hole, before the tee box of the twelfth, and we saw him lying there on the green. We didn't know who it was, but we could tell something was wrong. We went up to check and realized he was dead. Then Carly ran to get help from the players behind us and someone called 911, and I called the clubhouse. The manager came out to wait with us for the ambulance."

"How far were you from him when you first saw him?"

"Twenty or thirty yards. We couldn't see him beforehand because of the bushes."

"Who went up to him first?"

"Me. I'm the golfer; it's my course. Seyram and Carly's job was to be my caddies, so they trail behind. Eventually all of us went up to him, but we were in shock."

"You're sure it was you who went up to him first?"

"Yes."

"Did any of you try to help him?"

"No, he was dead. We all know first aid, but we didn't even think to check for a pulse."

"How did you know he was dead?"

"He was motionless on his back on the green, with his mouth open, and a dent the size of an apple in the side of his head."

"I see."

Fincher wanted to rattle this woman who looked at him so quizzically. "Ms. Bajwa, do you happen to have the golf clubs you played with that day?"

"Of course, I use them every weekend. If you want to inspect them, I can drop them around to the station for you."

"No, that's fine."

"So, why did you ask?"

"Excuse me?"

"Why did you ask if I have my clubs if you don't want to see them?"

Kate wasn't about to be intimidated.

"We may want to see the clubs at some stage. I wanted to know if they were available."

Fincher was still in disbelief that Detective Schultz had not seized the clubs and had them forensically examined the day of Preston Brock's death. It was far too late now to hope that any DNA would be found—that is, if Bajwa had anything to do with it.

"Let's move on to Cooper Hanson and Sheldon Nossel. Where were you the evening they died?"

Now Kate was in a bind. She knew CCTV from Pizza Hut and the Shell gas station would have captured images of her, Seyram, and Carly—that was a planned part of their alibi. What she didn't know was whether CCTV had captured images of Seyram's car on Main Street before they got to the stretch where there *were* no surveillance cameras. She could lie and say they were never on Main Street, but Fincher may already know they had been there and would therefore know she was lying. It was a potential trap. *Better to tell part of the truth.* Kate took a breath.

"I was with my friends, Seyram and Carly. We were in Seyram's car. We had reservations at the pizza place in Daineton, that's the next town over, across the range. We were on our way out of town when we saw a fire on the road up ahead. Afterward, we assumed that what we saw had been Cooper and Sheldon's car after the explosion, although we didn't know that at the time. We turned back when we saw the fire, thinking the road to Daineton was blocked."

Fincher reflected on Kate's words. "So … this was a second time the three of you turned back?"

"What do you mean?"

"Well, the three of you turned back on your walk in Coates Ravine, and you turned back again on your drive to Daineton."

"I guess we did." Kate was inscrutable.

"Daineton seems like a long way to go for pizza."

"It's spring. We wanted to get out of town and go somewhere else for a change. The drive through the hills is beautiful."

"Sounds like a winding road," said Fincher. "Trooper Chase, you must know it. Is it surfaced? It doesn't sound like a very pleasant drive."

"It's gravel," said Kate and Chase at the same time.

"Outside of winter when it's sometimes closed," Kate continued, "that's the way every local goes to Daineton. Seyram's SUV manages a road like that just fine—and it saves thirty minutes each way, otherwise it's not worth going the long way around for a night out. We called the Daineton restaurant to cancel and ended up eating at the Mossberg Pizza Hut."

"After you saw the fire up ahead and you turned back to town, did you return the way you came?"

"The same way we came."

"Did you call 911?

"No. We heard a siren and assumed it was coming out to the scene. We kept out of the way of first responders."

"How long after you saw the fire did you hear the siren?"

"A few minutes. We stopped on the side of the road trying to decide if it was safe to continue. We didn't think it was safe to go too close."

"Thank you, Ms. Bajwa. I don't have any more questions."

Fincher and Chase stood to leave, when on a whim Fincher turned and asked, "Ms. Bajwa, does this store sell surveillance cameras?"

"Yes."

"Do you install them?"

"No. We recommend a few different contractors, but that's the customer's decision."

"Are there other businesses that sell CCTV systems?"

"Most of the hardware stores in Mossberg sell them, but we have the biggest range. Loads of people buy them online or in neighboring towns, and then come to us for installation—which we don't do."

"Would you say you know which businesses have surveillance cameras? Where there is CCTV in Mossberg?"

Kate sensed another trap. She paused. "I don't have a map or anything, but I could look up our records and tell you our clients' addresses. Do you want to know about a specific location?"

"I was just curious. Apparently, there's no surveillance footage of the two boys who died driving out of town to the location where they were found, because there is no CCTV anywhere along that route after the Shell gas station on Main Street."

"They were men."

"Pardon?"

"You said the 'two boys who died.' They weren't boys, they were men."

It was Fincher's turn to pause. "Does that change the way you feel about their deaths—that they were men and not boys?"

"It's always a little more tragic when a child dies, don't you think?" Kate smiled sweetly. "Perhaps that's just the softie in us women."

Fincher's eyes were drawn to a framed photo of Kate on the wall behind her. She was wearing a tank top, jeans, and a hardhat, standing astride a huge tree blocking a road, wielding a red chainsaw. His eyes flicked back to her.

"Thank you for your time, Ms. Bajwa."

"DID YOU SEE THAT photo on the wall behind her?" said Trooper Chase after they got back into the police cruiser. "I'll bet that was taken after the tornado came through a few years back. The hardware store couldn't supply enough chainsaws during the cleanup, so the staff got out there with the demonstration models, sawing up fallen trees. She's one capable lady."

"Yes, but capable of what?" mused Fincher. "Is she well known around town?"

"Everyone knows her. The store's got everything and if it doesn't, Bajwa orders it in."

"What do people think of her?"

"I don't know if she has many friends, but people respect her. She's a local, you know. She was a few years behind my parents in high school." Chase turned to Fincher. "Do you really think she's involved in these deaths?"

"There's something she's not telling us. Protecting one of her friends, maybe."

Chase looked knowingly at Fincher. "You may not have realized this ..." He lowered his voice. "...but word is she's a *lesbian*." He mouthed the word. "If that's true, I'd keep to myself too. It can't be easy being gay in this town."

Fincher looked at Chase. "Maybe just being a woman in Mossberg isn't easy."

"You got me there!" Chase chuckled. "What do we do now? Interview Carly Schumer?"

"What time do you finish your shift tonight?"

"In three hours—at eight p.m."

"Let's do it tomorrow morning when we're fresh." Fincher changed topic. "Do you have access to an unmarked police vehicle?"

"Yes ... is there something I can do?" Chase was thrilled to be working with the FBI but was torn between Detective Schultz's conviction that women could not possibly have committed the murders and Fincher's logic that suggested this line of enquiry should not be dismissed.

"The hardware store closes at six thirty," said Fincher. "Follow Ms. Bajwa when she leaves. Make sure she doesn't see you. I'd like to know where she goes, especially if she pays a visit to Schumer or Boateng."

"Sure thing, Fincher." He hastily corrected himself. "*Agent* Fincher."

24

A LITTLE BEFORE six p.m., Carly and Seyram saw the text at the same time: *Do either of you have a large roasting pan?*

I do, Seyram texted. *I'm seeing Carly at the café at 6:45. Meet us there. I'll bring the pan.*

Carly and Seyram sat at a corner table in the café of the Whole Foods Market as Kate pulled into the parking lot.

Kate walked in, her face hard to read. "Hello, you two. I'll just get a coffee."

"Here's the pan," said Seyram passing over a bag to Kate after she had sat down. "Better take it out and wave it around a bit in case anyone is watching."

Carly lowered her voice. "Is that a joke? You think it's not safe to talk here?"

Seyram was reassuring. "I deliberately didn't say which café. So even if our phones are bugged, they wouldn't have known where we were going or where to install a listening device—but I knew you and Kate would know it was the usual place."

Carly looked around cautiously. "No one has come in after you, but do you think the customers are undercover cops?"

"Well," said Kate, "that's Garth Olsen sitting over there. He's an electrician, and he's with Garth Finkler. He's a carpenter. I'm pretty sure neither one is undercover."

"And that's Mrs. Grantham, Kofi's friend's mom." Seyram waved to a figure over by the checkout. "She's being served by Rashida, who came to Mossberg last year as a refugee from Syria. I'm pretty sure neither of them is undercover."

"So … what's up?" Carly asked Kate. "Why did you 'need the roasting pan'?"

"An FBI agent came to the store today and interviewed me. He was with that young cop from the Mossberg police."

Seyram nearly fell off her chair.

Carly looked ashen. "The FBI?"

"Shhh! Lower your voices! They might not be undercover," Kate indicated the other customers with her head, "but we don't want to attract attention."

The three of them leaned in toward each other.

"Tell us what happened."

"They were in my office for about twenty-five minutes. Asked me questions about when we were in Coates Ravine and on the golf course, then where we were the night Cooper Hanson and Sheldon Nossel died. The FBI agent—Agent Fincher—did all the talking. He was fixated on certain details. Probably trying to catch me out with some inconsistency. Seyram, he said he'd read your statement to Detective Schultz."

"Shit." Carly broke into a sweat. "I can't go to jail. Who would look after Summer?"

"Carly, we're not going to jail," said Kate in a firm, low voice. "We've got to keep our cool."

"Easy for you to say. You don't have kids!"

"What's that supposed to mean? Jail's OK for me?"

"Stop it!" Seyram hissed. "Kate, Carly's just freaking out because she's a mom. That's what moms do. Don't take it personally. And Carly, I have no intention of going to jail. I want to be there for my kids too. We're going to outsmart these cops."

"I'm sorry," muttered Carly. "I did freak out."

"No, I'm sorry. I shouldn't have snapped," said Kate. "Look, the interview was stressful—he had me on my toes—but Fincher's probably going to pay you a visit, so be prepared. We've gone over the details of the story we're going to tell. Don't deviate from that. It's like we're back in the car in the snowbank: trust each other and we'll get through this."

Carly swallowed. "I'm glad you let me know. If they'd just turned up at home without warning, I probably would have blurted everything out. I don't want us to go to jail."

"Or do a Thelma and Louise," added Kate.

"What's the FBI agent like?" asked Carly. "Is he intimidating?"

"Tall, dark and handsome type. Very professional. Wore a suit."

"Sounds like a male version of you," said Seyram, "except for the suit."

"I didn't ask for his Tinder profile," said Carly.

"Don't be silly!" Kate blushed. "Can we stay focused?"

"If we stick to our story, we'll be fine." Seyram was firm. "I already gave that statement to Schultz, and it's exactly what we'd agreed."

Carly nodded her head and got up from the table. "I have to go. I've got to pick up Summer from baseball practice. Thanks for the heads-up, Kate."

"Me too, I have to pick up dinner," added Seyram. "Stay cool, Carly."

"If you're interviewed," added Kate, "send a message on WhatsApp asking me how I went with the cooking—you know, using the roasting pan. It'll tell us they paid you a visit."

25

WHEN TROOPER CHASE parked out the front of Carly's house, the entire street was immediately aware that a police car had arrived. "Remind me what happened last night when you followed Kate Bajwa to Whole Foods," said Fincher to Chase.

"I could see them clearly through the store window. Schumer and Boateng were waiting in the café area when Bajwa went in. They seemed pretty relaxed. Boateng handed over what looked like a big cooking dish to Bajwa."

"A cooking dish?"

"That's what it looked like. I couldn't hear what they were saying, but they leaned in toward each other, like they were discussing a dinner recipe. Schumer appeared upset at one stage, like Bajwa was getting the ingredients wrong, then Bajwa got mad at her, but it looked like Boateng reassured them both. It made me hungry wondering what they were cooking up!" Chase was pleased with his account of his surveillance.

Fincher wasn't convinced. "In between the cooking tips, I'm guessing Bajwa told Schumer to expect us. The element of surprise is probably gone, but let's see what we can find out."

Summer opened the door to Fincher's knock. "Are you after Mom? She's in the studio in the back," she explained. "You can walk around the side to get there."

Carly had spent hours, months, years of her life working in her studio, a delightful space lined by drying cabinets, with large windows reaching almost to the ground bordered by flower beds in summer and snow in winter. The kiln firings meant it was often warm, and in the summer months Carly opened the front double doors to let cool air in. Year-round she could work in a T-shirt, light pants, and a pottery apron, losing herself in the texture of the clay and the hum of the wheel.

When she was starting out as a potter full-time, Carly used to run the studio as a private gallery, working while customers came and browsed. As her reputation grew, she found she could make a living from commissions and no longer needed a visiting public. Her specialties were one-off themed collections of glazed jugs, massive bowls, and five-piece dinner sets for twenty people. Several calendars had featured babies curled up, sleeping, or standing in her bowls, and her dinner sets retailed for $9,950 in upmarket boutiques in the Hamptons, on Martha's Vineyard, and in Aspen.

Engrossed in shaping a bowl, Carly had forgotten she should expect a visit from the FBI. She didn't notice Fincher's knocking on the studio door until he stuck his head inside and loudly called, "Ms. Schumer? Do you have a minute? I'm from the FBI."

Despite all the encouragement from Seyram and Kate the day before, Carly felt a familiar draining of confidence in the face of male authority. *If only I could start shaping a new bowl …*

To her surprise, however, she heard her own voice calling out firmly, "Give me two minutes, will you? I'm almost finished this bowl and then I'm yours."

It bought Carly time to think, and Fincher time to observe.

With her back to them, Carly put the bowl in the drying cabinet, collected her thoughts and wiped her hands on her apron. Taking a breath, she turned, "Hello, Officer Chase." Carly knew everyone. "Sorry about that. I've got an exhibition coming up and I'm trying to finish off the pieces. What can I do for you?"

"Ms. Schumer, I'm Agent Fincher from the FBI," said Fincher. "I'd like to ask you some questions, if you don't mind, about your recollections of finding Preston Brock on the golf course and your walk in Coates Ravine the day Branson Vanburg was found deceased." Fincher took in Carly: sweaty blond hair, clay-spattered clothes, laugh lines on her open face. He sensed a weak link and decided to go for it.

Carly forcibly quelled her panic, remaining motionless for a few seconds. Oddly, the clay flecks on her face and her work clothes gave her strength. Memories of firing the grenade launcher came back to her. She lifted her chin.

"Ms. Schumer? Ms. Schumer? Are you OK?"

"Sorry," Carly shook her head. "I have to do a bisque firing and was just trying to figure out when I need to start the kiln."

"Pardon?"

"A bisque firing. When you glaze ceramics you do an initial firing, called a bisque firing, before applying the glaze and then firing it again. What's your name again, sorry?"

"Agent Fincher."

"And what is it that you want, exactly? I've got to do more bowls this afternoon."

The conversation was not going to be as easy as Fincher anticipated.

"Ms. Schumer, I've read the statement your friend Ms. Boateng made to Detective Schultz. We want to follow up a couple of things to see if the people who were with her, such as yourself, might remember additional details."

"Have you spoken to Kate? Kate Bajwa?"

"Yes."

"Well, I probably won't have more to add, but go ahead."

"On the day Branson Vanburg was found in Coates Ravine, I understand you turned around on your walk. Why was that?"

"Seyram got blisters and it was too painful for her to continue."

"Do you remember where you turned around on your walk?"

"We were on the other side of the ravine and we'd walked about twenty or twenty-five minutes. I don't remember exactly, but that part of the path looks pretty similar."

"So the answer is no?"

"Correct."

"Do you still have the shoes you wore? There were footprints of other people where Branson Vanburg appears to have gone over the edge. We're interested in eliminating people who were *not* at that location on the path." Fincher wondered if Carly would show alarm at this suggestion of physical evidence, albeit invented.

"I have about five pairs of shoes I use for walking, but I haven't thrown any out. I'll bag them up for you." She coolly looked at Fincher.

"That's not necessary. We'll send someone if we need them. If we can turn to the day you found Preston Brock, tell me about when you first saw him. Where were you, personally, standing?"

"I was right there when it happened. The three of us were together."

"When what happened, Ms. Schumer?"

"Excuse me?"

"You said you were right there when 'it' happened. As though an event happened. What was the thing that happened?"

Carly swallowed and looked nervously from Fincher to Chase and back. "When we *saw* him, Agent Fincher. When we saw Preston Brock. We were following Kate on the green and walked around some bushes just before the twelfth hole, and then it *happened*. We saw him lying on the ground. It's pretty confronting seeing a dead person."

"Who went up to him first?"

"Kate."

"And then what happened?"

"We freaked out." Carly was now recalling the actual truth. "I started crying and ran to the players behind us for help. Then someone—I forgot who—called 911, and I think Kate called the clubhouse. Then the manager came out and waited with us until the ambulance arrived."

"Did you try to help Preston?"

"No. He was dead."

"How could you tell?"

"His head was smushed."

"Alright. Moving on to the day Cooper Hanson and Sheldon Nossel were found dead, where were you that evening?"

"The three of us had a reservation at the pizzeria in Daineton. When we saw a fire on the road up ahead, we turned back. We called the restaurant to cancel because we figured the road was blocked and we didn't want to drive the long way around. We ended up at the Pizza Hut in Mossberg."

Fincher looked at Carly for the longest time, noting that she wasn't surprised to be asked about Hanson and Nossel— which could mean Bajwa tipped her off, or could mean she thought she *should* be asked about them. Carly looked right back at Fincher.

"Thank you for your time, Ms. Schumer. We'll let you get back to the firing."

Carly showed them around the side of the house to the front, where she said goodbye. Curtains in two neighboring houses across the road swung back into position, let go by the people peeking through them.

"She didn't seem to know much," said Chase. "You know she's won loads of prizes for her pottery. One of her bowls is on display in the State Capital Building in Harrisburg."

Fincher shook his head. "These women are hiding something. Did you hear the way she told us about calling the Daineton pizzeria to cancel because they didn't want to drive the long away around, and then eating in Pizza Hut? They're planting an alibi. She and Bajwa used almost the same words. And, when she was talking about Brock, she definitely said when 'it' happened—as though his death happened in front of her. She also wasn't surprised I asked about Hanson and Nossel and immediately mentioned seeing the fire on the road up ahead, even though I hadn't presented her with anything suggesting she was near the scene. There's something she's not telling us."

"What do we do now?" asked Chase. "Interview Ms. Boateng?"

"Not yet. We wait until we're sure we can catch Boateng out on a lie in her statement, and then we interrogate her until she breaks."

FALL 2018

26

THE LEAD MARCHERS assembled for Mossberg's inaugural "America's Finest Celebrate Their Town!" parade, were nervous. It was a beautiful fall day: color everywhere in the trees that lined Main Street, the sky blue, and the air crisp and clean. The forests and fields around Mossberg were peaceful, but there was agitation among the lead row of marchers: a chattering of teeth, a clattering of sports gear, and a shivering of bodies. This wasn't from any early fall chill, but from fear. An unknown number of assailants lurked in the community, apparently intent on wiping out the town's jocks. The lead marchers felt like sitting ducks. The soccer team captain Angel Fernandez, carrying a large plus sign, the "+" in LGBTQIA2S+, was trembling so much he kept hitting himself in the face with his placard.

Tulip Sorensen had volunteered the entire college cheerleading team to participate in the parade. Mayor Konig asked them to lead it, their twirling batons, short skirts, and high kicks always crowd-pleasers, but Tulip wasn't having a bar of that. "What, so if the killer attacks we get shot first?" she snorted. The organizers caved. They knew it was important to have as many people as possible participate, so after negotiations with Tulip it was decided the cheer team would walk behind the initial row of marchers, with batons twirling high above and the occasional somersaulting girl. In front would be a row of Mossberg's surviving jocks, dressed in their sports gear to demonstrate solidarity with the fallen.

The march nearly foundered over who would carry each element in LGBTQIA2S+. Nine placards had been made, and chief organizer Arlene had planned for a row of nine young men, each in his sports gear, to carry a placard to form the LGBTQIA2S+, in that order from left to right at the head of the march. She'd tipped off the *Gazette*'s photographer to be ready to capture the nine placards and nine young men in the parade's front line.

Allocating the placards, a week before the parade, had not been straightforward. The new Mossberg River High School football captain, thinking the S was for straight, yelled, "Give me the S! I'm straight!" But Arlene's nephew—the artistic one, who had been roped in to help with the craftwork—explained that the S went with the 2 and stood for "two-spirits," which had its roots in Native American traditions ... inspiring the college swim team captain to a whoop, "I'm a Kansas City Chiefs fan! I'm carrying the 2S!" The nephew then explained that the tradition was of certain Native Americans having both masculine and feminine spirits, at which the team captain tried to backpedal, "I'm no freakin' two-spirits!" But it was too late, and he was stuck with 2S.

The college hockey team captain said that as a Christian— he was a member of one of Mossberg's numerous Pentecostal churches—carrying any letter representing unbiblical lifestyles was against his faith. He could, however, carry the +, as Jesus himself had died on a cross.

The new Mossberg Hills High School football captain said he could be bi, but there was no way he was going to be queer. "All my buddies are going to be watching!"

Betty tried to give Q to the high school field hockey captain, who muttered "I ain't no queer" and grabbed for the L, for lesbian, at the same time as the college athletics captain. They nearly came to blows over who got to be lesbian, but athletics won and field hockey went queer after all.

The T was unclaimed until the new college football team captain, in a kind of religious one-upmanship with the Pentecostal, said *his* Lord loved everyone including transpeople, and he would carry the T with pride. (He was a Unitarian).

Betty had thought asexual would get snapped up, thinking it to be neutral, but she'd forgotten that for young people being sex*less* was a fate worse than death. As Angel Fernandez was late, the basketball team captain and swim team captain battled it out over asexual, gay and intersex. In the end, basketball went gay and swimming went intersex, which left Angel asexual.

Just as the dust had settled, one of Betty's friends loudly remarked, "Oh my, but doesn't that itty bitty cross look just like a target out on the shooting range?" She was referring to the plus sign. Everyone was hyperaware of the possibility of a shooter or shooters lying in wait for the parade. Literally a second later Angel arrived, prompting the Pentecostal to abandon the cross and leap for A before Angel got to it ... leaving Angel with the + and, one week later, standing in the front row with teeth rattling in fear.

CARLY HAD KNOWN as soon as she heard about the march, that she would attend. "If I don't go, Grace Schmidt and all my friends will find it so strange it could make them suspicious. I want to go, and I have to go." Her announcement that "Tulip Sorenson's going to be there" was enough to guarantee Summer's participation as well.

Kate, however, needed persuading. "It's another attempt by Mayor Konig to divert attention from the real issue: that Mossberg is run by the boneheads for the boneheads."

Seyram disagreed. "Sure, Konig wants it to be some kind of symbol of defiance against *the man attacking Mossberg* as he keeps telling the media, but everyone I know—including at church—thinks it's more about the community coming together and showing unity. The kids' catechism class is attending, along with half the parents—including me."

"Showing unity against the killers?" said Kate. "Ironic if we attend, don't you think?"

"Everyone at church knows those four men were predators and rapists. Going to the march means we're unified against such attitudes and actions. And, personally, I *am* against them."

On the day, Seyram's Catholic group had the parade's most eclectic signs, calling for more support for poor people, an embracing of family values, tolerance of diverse political opinion, an end to all forms of violence, the renunciation of materialism in favor of spiritualism, and a return to kindness in daily life—and a whole bunch walked with their dogs to celebrate the recent feast day of St. Francis of Assisi.

Carly's planned group fell apart completely. She had posted on Facebook and Instagram for anyone to join her under the slogan 'Feminists Together, Fighting Together!' However, when transwomen turned up, a group of ciswomen walked out; nonbinaries left when a feminist muttered, "Why don't you make up your minds!"; a group of older white women left when a young Black woman looked them up and down and said, "What is this? The Martha fucking Stewart Show?"; gay men left when a woman pulled a face and asked, "Are we allowing men?"; an argument broke out between women who said they should march as Jewish lesbians and others who said they should march as lesbian Jews; others walked out saying the group felt hierarchical and not sufficiently grassroots; and Feminists for Decoloniality departed when they realized the idea originated from Carly—"You're demanding we internalize white initiative as natural authority!" The final straw came when Mossberg's Women in Business turned up with free hotdogs for everyone: "We thought this was a meat-free zone!" "You may as well ask us to chop down the

Amazon!" "The bread rolls aren't even organic!" "You're a Trojan horse for global capitalism!"

Carly and two others were the last ones standing, including the young woman who had made the Martha Stewart comment. She fixed Carly with a glare, declaring, "This group is offensive on so many levels," and stormed off.

Carly shook her head in despair and started to laugh, looking at the other person remaining—a college student—to include her in the comedy-drama.

The student's bottom lip started to tremble. "Would you mind not doing that? Humor is a trigger for me."

"*What?*" Carly was dumbfounded.

"I was bullied in school … It's the laughter …"

"Go fuck yourself!" Carly said, and walked off.

Arlene spotted Carly, alone and forlorn. They knew each other from school bake sales, Arlene's granddaughter being in the same year as Summer. "You look like you need a pal," said Arlene, giving her a hug.

"I don't know how you and Betty do it," said Carly. "If only you could work your magic on my crowd."

"They didn't turn up?"

"They *all* turned up," sighed Carly. "That was the problem."

In the end, Carly and Summer marched with the contingent from Sisterhood House. Seyram had invited Kate to join the Catholics ("Are you kidding?") and Carly had asked her to walk with Sisterhood House ("So Grace can hit me up for a corporate donation?"). Finally, Kate carried a sign saying *Enforce Title IX*, and walked with the female sports coaches from Mossberg College.

There had been a moment of tension before Seyram, Kate, and Carly headed off to their various groups, when they bumped into Agent Fincher. Fincher thought his attendance was a waste of time—it wasn't as though the killer was going to carry a sign saying *I'm here!*—but it was an all-hands-on-deck affair for the Mossberg Police Department, so he felt obliged. Feeling out of place in his suit among the rainbow flags and peace signs, he made his way around a group of cheerleaders limbering up, and found himself face-to-face with Seyram, Kate, and Carly. They all stopped in their tracks.

Kate spoke first. "Hello, Agent Fincher. I guess you're here on police business?"

"The law never rests, Ms. Bajwa." Fincher nodded to Carly and Seyram. "But in the end, we always get our man. Or woman."

They stared at each other.

"We'd better join the march," said Carly breaking the standoff. "We're hoping it'll bring justice to Mossberg."

"Me too," said Fincher. "Have a good day."

MAYOR KONIG STROLLED among the crowd, eyeing the cheerleaders and trying to get into the frame of every photographer's shot. He was distracted by a *"Psst!"*

It came again. *"Psst! Mayor Konig, over here."* It was the Mossberg Hills football team captain. "Mayor, the bros are scared. We don't want to do this march." The team captains pressed in a scrum around Konig.

Konig knew a pullout would be a disaster. He thought quickly. "Boys, you've got to man up. This is *your time*. It's like Iwo Jima: you've got to raise the flag and keep the enemy at bay."

"But she's already here!"

"She's among us!"

"We can't see her!"

"This is freakin' scary, Mayor."

Konig tried to keep his voice calm and looked around for inspiration. He caught sight of Tulip in her knee-high boots, assembling the cheer squad into a row behind the team captains. "You can't let Tulip see you like this," he said in desperation. "Think of her behind you—she's got your backs—and let her words inspire you!"

Tulip, who was a genius at turning any word, any assemblage of letters, any slogan into an inspirational chant, had wasted no time training her team in LGBTQIA2S+. And, at that moment, precisely when Mayor Konig needed her, she gave her call to arms. "Pom-pomzz … zzzup!"

The cheer squad shook their pom-poms in the air—the jocks swallowed, took deep breaths and fell into line—and then loudly, grandly, and initially slowly, Tulip called out:

"Gimme an L! Gimme a G! Gimme a B, T, Q. Gimme an I! Gimme an A! Gimme that Two S! And heeeeeeeere's Plus!"

Pom-poms shook overhead with each letter and batons were thrown high into the air after each "Plus!".

In the days leading up to the march Tulip had worked with the team captains on the slogans. "Remember," she instructed them, "you can't just have the people behind you chanting slogans. It makes more of an impression if you chant too."

She had trained them to work through the slogans together, looking to the next person as though handing over the words:

Athletics started: "Women's rights …"

"… are human rights," intoned basketball.

"And human rights …" followed Hills football.

"… are women's rights!" called college football triumphantly.

"We should all be feminists!" Field hockey punched the air.

The captains and cheerleaders then started up, singsong fashion:

"I will not, be lectured about …"

"Sexism and mis-og-y-ny …"

"By. This. *Man!*"

From there it became a musical free-for-all, with cries of "We should all be feminists!", punctuated by "I will not be lectured about sexism and misogyny!" and "Women's rights are human rights!" coming from the length and breadth of the march. The parade had begun.

To be frank, the parade had been organized on a flawed premise on the part of Chief Delaney and Mayor Konig: that assembling conservative political groups in faux support of liberal progressives with whom a suspected serial killer of jocks presumably identified was a way to lure the killer into public view so that he—or she—could be captured. Yet because its purpose was so amorphous, because of Arlene and Betty's magnificent organizational efforts, and because of media reports of the first row of marchers carrying LGBTQIA2S+ (each team captain had been interviewed on local TV), Mossberg turned out in all its diversity—much to the surprise of the many townspeople who thought it had none.

Participants were, however, startled to find that each person had quite different ideas of what the march was about. Wyatt Bell, covering the day for the *Gazette*, heard marchers tell him they were there to support LGBTQIA2S+ rights, women's rights, Donald Trump, family values, Christian values, American values, Black Lives Matter, the Aryan Nation, immigrants, illegal immigrants, no immigrants, no war in Syria, Free Palestine, Friends of Israel, the Republicans, the Democrats, sports programs, young men, Title IX, the #MeToo movement, incels, animal rights, vegetarianism, the Proud Boys, gun rights, environmentalists, net zero carbon, pro-lifers, pro-choicers, the US military, and #FreeBritney. Wyatt got a headache.

One reason for the high turnout was the way the parade had been explained to different groups as a response to the *new atmosphere in town*, as it was being called. The council, at the behest of Mayor Konig, ran advertisements in the *Gazette* stating the parade would be a safe space for young men to assert support for their "American freedoms." This message was instantly retweeted, Instagrammed, and Facebooked throughout every sports team and fraternity in town as a rally to "Save Our Manhood." It was then repurposed as a call to "Save America" by Aryan Nation, the Proud Boys, and the NRA, which flooded Mossberg with recruiters.

To liberals, on the other hand, the *new atmosphere in town* had created an opportunity—the first in Mossberg's 280-year history—to publicly demonstrate values, identities, and causes. Notwithstanding doubts about a march led by nine jocks carrying LGBTQIA2S+ signs, assembling en masse for a single day felt like it could be the shove needed to topple a statue or oust a dictatorship.

At the back of everyone's mind, regardless of their reason for marching, was the knowledge that someone in Mossberg was targeting jocks. Although the police had never officially stated they were looking for a female suspect, nor had the *Gazette* ever run a story to that effect, word had gotten around that the perpetrator might—just *might*—be a woman. These two pieces of information—the apparent profile of intended victims, coupled with the possible profile of the (female!) killer—caused a great unsettling. It became a point of masculine honor to many men, especially old white Republicans, to turn up that day to defy the Killer Lady.

Mayor Konig knew it was an unprecedented event for Mossberg. He wanted to record it for posterity, as well as for future electoral campaigns, investment promotion videos, tourism videos, or even as part of a montage of "Mayor Konig Accomplishments" for that distant day when he retired. To this end, the council contracted a media firm to film the march using a drone. Of course, there was also a chance the drone could capture images of a killer lurking around the parade. A livestream had been arranged to computers in a van where FBI analysts would scrutinize footage in real time for suspicious movements and run database searches on every face captured.

The drone captured Mossberg in all its glory, a throng of *thousands* of citizens walking the two miles from the sports fields complex to City Hall. It also caught Dan and Dylan, students in a fraternity known mostly for its stoners, letting off firecrackers from their resting place in a side alley.

"Dude, do it now!"

"Nah, bro, after the cheerleaders pass us, that's when we should do it."

"Let's scare the girls!"

"Awesome!"

"Sweet!"

"Duuude."

"Brooo."

Dan lit the match, while Dylan held the string of firecrackers then threw them toward the crowd.

A burst of firecrackers sounds like a burst of automatic gunfire. If people are already primed to think they are targets of assassination, their response is guaranteed. From above, the drone captured the moment: for a fire-crackling second, everyone froze. Then, half the marchers—men, white men, straight men, jocks—*stampeded*. Ducking and weaving to avoid bullets, flapping their hands and shrieking, they ran the three blocks south and jumped into the Mossberg River, or ran to the wooded peaks in the north and hid behind trees, or bolted into stores to cower behind bra racks and lipstick counters. Boys, seeing the fear in their fathers, uncles, and brothers, took their cue and fled after them a half-second later.

As the yelping gurgled into the river, a tremor ran through the remaining crowd. There was a collective calculation as to whether they fitted the victim profile, and should therefore make a break for it, or stand firm … until brought back to life by a call:

"Pompomzz … zzzup! Gimme an L! Gimme a G! Gimme a B, T, Q …"

Tulip, never one to leave a leadership vacuum unfilled, did a cartwheel and forward handspring over MAGA caps and NRA signs to take the place of the nine leading jocks, who had all fled. She gave a shrill blast of her whistle, the cheer team shook their pom-poms overhead and threw their batons in the air, and the march continued.

27

SUMMER THOUGHT THE parade was the most fun day she'd ever had. All of her friends were there, and they circulated through the crowd, joining and leaving groups, swapping signs, singing the chants, yelling "We love Hillary!" at anyone in a MAGA cap, and trying to get a selfie with Tulip Sorenson in the background. The change had been subtle, but among Mossberg's teenage girls there was a new fearlessness, a sense of entitlement to participate in the public sphere, which they viewed as their space too. What's more, boys their age seemed to agree.

Carly and Summer returned home tired but happy, voices hoarse.

The *Gazette* already had its lead headline on its website and Facebook page, which Summer read out to her mother.

"'NRA holds fire as liberals invade Mossberg.' Mom, are we liberals?"

"I guess we are," said Carly.

"Why would the NRA want to shoot us?"

"I'm not sure how seriously the *Gazette* intended that headline, but the NRA thinks everyone should be free to have whatever guns they like. Liberals think there should be rules controlling who has access to guns and the type of guns they can have."

"What do you think?"

"Guns aren't for everyone. But if used ... responsibly ... by the right people ... on the right targets ... they have a place." Carly changed the subject, adding quickly, "The other reason the NRA doesn't like liberals is that we don't believe America is perfect just the way it is. We think it can always be improved, and that America's willingness to evolve is what *makes* it great."

"How do you know when reform is needed?"

Carly sighed inwardly and settled in mentally in for a long conversation. "Sometimes issues get ignored for a long time, like climate change, or Native Americans having their land stolen, or discrimination against African Americans or against women. Either the affected people stand up and protest, or people who are not directly affected realize that something is not right and do something about it."

"You mean like girls being treated badly?"

"Yes, honey, like that. I think women and girls should stand up and call it out, but I want men to stand up for us too."

"That's what the MeToo movement is about, isn't it? That girls should speak out when they're harassed or when someone is violent to them?"

"Exactly. It started because women were tired of their complaints being ignored. One of them, a young woman, started an online platform where we would feel supported to report—where we could say 'It happened to me too.' Women wanted to say it publicly, loudly, and in numbers, to support each other, but also so we couldn't be ignored."

"Like, if I heard about something bad happening to girls, is that where I should report it?"

So this is where the conversation is heading, thought Carly.

Carly adopted the most neutral tone she could and, without looking at Summer, answered carefully. "Yes, you could send a tweet, but you and your friends can also always tell me anything. If you want to go to someone else, you could go to one of the teachers at school, or to the school counselor, or Grace at Sisterhood House, or another parent. Or to Aunt Kate or Aunt Seyram. We'll all listen, and we'll all support you."

"What if it's not really something bad, but something creepy?"

"You mean creepy like fun-scary in a movie, or something that makes you feel weird?"

"Weird."

"If it's something that makes you feel uncomfortable, you should trust your gut instinct and tell someone. If you're wrong, no harm done for raising it."

Summer pondered this information as though she could have been thinking about what to watch on TV or whether to ask for a snack, then continued. "There's this boy at school, Ashton. He keeps asking girls to go to his brother's parties. Like, really pestering them to go."

"How old is his brother?"

"Really old. At least twenty. He's in Chi Omicron Kappa at college."

Carly furrowed her brow, wondering where she had heard about this fraternity.

"Apparently, it has parties every weekend," added Summer.

Carly remembered. "Isn't it the fraternity that Cooper Hanson was in? And Beatriz—the young woman who stayed with us that night—mentioned it. She said it was guys from there who tried to force her to go with them."

"That's what Ashton does. He tries to get girls from school to go to their parties, but he only ever wants one of us. Everyone says he does it for his brother."

"What are these parties? You're saying he only wants one girl to go—to hang out with all those boys?"

"They're just parties. At the frat house."

"Has he asked you?"

"Yes! He's asked everyone, but he never wants us to bring our friends, so we think that's weird."

"And you're pretty sure Ashton is not after a date?"

"It doesn't sound like a date."

"Well, you're way too young to go to a fraternity party."

Summer pulled a face. "Mom, I'm *fifteen!*"

"Have any girls from school gone to the parties?"

"Two."

"What did they say about it?"

Summer avoided looking at her mom. "One switched to a high school in Daineton and ghosted everyone from

Mossberg. The other one never says anything about it and just keeps to herself.”

“Have they told anyone? Do the kids talk about it?”

“That’s why I asked about the MeToo movement. Someone at school saw anonymous posts about the parties, saying the frat guys get a single girl to come and then treat her badly. They try to get her there by ten p.m. We wonder whether it’s the girl who switched to Daineton High who’s making the posts.” Summer stretched out on the sofa. “Can I have a snack?”

“Dinner will be ready in an hour, but heat up one of Aunt Kate’s mom’s samosas. Put it in the oven so it doesn’t go soggy.”

“What should I do about Ashton?”

Carly drummed her fingers on the kitchen table. “Leave it with me.”

28

"I NEED ANOTHER drink," said Carly. "Give me a sec and I'll make a margarita."

"What's up with Carly?" Seyram asked Kate, when Carly went to her studio to pick fresh limes from the tree she kept there in a pot. "Is Summer OK?"

"She seemed fine when I arrived."

Carly came back with margaritas for her and Kate.

"Spit it out, Carly," said Seyram. "I can read you like a book."

Carly took a deep breath. "You know how we were going to have a break from … the jocks … because of the FBI and everything? The fact is, we've let the genie out of the bottle—we've let *us* out of the bottle."

Seyram and Kate raised their eyebrows.

"OK, you know the Chi Omicron Kappa fraternity on campus? Summer was telling me that every Saturday they have a keg party. About twenty guys live in the frat house and they trick a girl into going there, then they all have sex with her. Apparently one of the frat guys uses his brother, who's in Summer's year, to try to get girls to go."

"You mean *prostitutes?*" Seyram couldn't quite believe what she was hearing.

"No. One of the guys gets a girl—often an underage girl—to come to the house. They get her drunk, or don't even bother doing that, and they rape her."

"But what if she doesn't want to? It can't possibly work like that!"

"Seyram, a bunch of twenty drunk guys intimidate a girl—who thinks she's come along to a friend's party, who has probably been told there are other girls there and has also probably been given booze or drugs the second she walked in the door—into having sex with them. They force her to do it. *That's* how it works. It's probably some kind of perverse bonding ritual. And remember how that traumatized young woman stayed with me earlier in the year because Sisterhood House had run out of emergency accommodation? The woman, Beatriz, said the guys who tried to force her to go with them were all from Chi Omicron Kappa. I want to blow up that frat house and everyone in it! It makes me want Summer to never go to college."

"What about the girl? We can't kill her."

"Apparently the girl is brought in after ten p.m. We do it before she arrives."

"I'm not against the idea, but here's a practical question," said Seyram. "How do we get in? We only found one grenade launcher in Giovanni's basement. It's not like we can get another and launch a grenade through the window."

"The basement," Kate interrupted. "Those big houses have huge oil heating systems and the oil tank is usually right near the heating system. Create an explosion next to the oil tank and the whole thing will go up in flames."

"I should have asked the question another way: how do we get past the frat guys? Wearing wigs and make-up isn't going to cut it at a frat party. It's an invitation for *too much* attention," said Seyram. "How do three middle-aged women go unseen in a group of twenty-year-old men?"

The realization dawned on Carly, Seyram, and Kate simultaneously. "We're invisible!"

Carly half-grimaced and half-laughed. "I was downtown the other day, walking straight toward a bunch of guys, all in their twenties, and one of them who was literally looking at me, walked right into me. Like, we bumped chests! He said 'Sorry. I didn't see you.'"

"Try being a *Black woman* in her fifties," said Seyram. "I've had white customers come into the lab and ring the desk bell right in front of me. When I ask if I can help, they look around reception and say 'Is anyone here?' like I was a voice that came over a loudspeaker. I'm literally standing in front of them— and it's *my* laboratory."

"So what are we proposing?" asked Kate. "We go into the frat house, find the basement, set it alight, then walk out? This seems deceptively simple. And ... somewhat reckless."

"Summer said it was a keg party," said Carly. "So, let's take them a keg. That's how we get in."

"What if the keg doesn't match what they're drinking?" asked Seyram.

"Seyram, they're guys having a key party at a frat house." Carly laughed. "Do you think if two people walk in delivering more alcohol in a nonmatching keg they're going to object?"

"OK. So we have a keg. Then what?"

"Fill it with gasoline," said Carly. "Put it in their basement, open it up, go back up the stairs, and throw a Molotov cocktail down the stairs, and walk out."

"How do you know about Molotov cocktails?" Kate was impressed.

"Mom's dad was from Finland. Ukki threw them at Russian tanks during the war."

"Isn't that going to create a huge explosion?" cautioned Seyram. "Someone is going to have to clean up that mess. Can't we do one of those precision detonations where everything collapses into a nice pile?"

Kate rolled her eyes. "Seyram, we're going to have a beer keg full of gasoline and Molotov cocktails. Lower your standards for tidiness."

"Here's another question," said Seyram, miffed. "Where do we get a beer keg?"

"Brewery and Co. on 22nd Street sells kegs direct to the public," said Carly. Drive behind it on a Sunday night and you'll see all the empties stacked out the back from parties the night before. If you buy one, you need to show ID. We should go after dark and swipe an empty.

"I'm not going to steal property!" Seyram was indignant.

"I'll steal it for us," said Kate.

"Can't we leave fifty dollars in an envelope?"

"With fingerprints and a signed thank-you note?"

Seyram wasn't happy but could see she had lost the argument. "I just want you to know I'm not a thief."

"You told us you were tired of being good."

"Not being good doesn't make me a thief."

"We've got another problem," said Kate. "I can steal the keg, but I don't think I can get away with walking into the frat house. Frat boys come into the store all the time wanting advice about hardware, and there was someone yesterday wanting a CCTV system. I've got no idea which fraternity he's from, but it's too risky."

"Seyram and I can do it." Carly was firm. "Kate, you get us the keg and give us coveralls and caps from the store so we all look the same. We just need a getaway car."

"The store keeps an unregistered jalopy in the yard," said Kate. "We could use that, then dump it."

"What about Mr. Smith, the store owner?" asked Seyram. "Won't he notice it missing?"

"He lives in Florida and stopped paying registration years ago," replied Kate. "He probably doesn't even remember it exists."

With their minds made up, over the next few days they planned the attack. Carly checked Google Maps to identify the best place for Kate to park and wait. She noticed the property's driveway ran through to the back lane—perfect for approaching the property from behind, where fewer eyes would see them. Summer's story about Chi Omicron Kappa filled the three of them with a determination to close down the fraternity's "parties" definitively.

<h1 style="text-align:center">29</h1>

Chi Omicron Kappa was appearing on the radar of other people too. Sitting at his hotel room desk, Agent Fincher stared at his laptop and wondered how he could describe the status of the investigation to his boss.

Mossberg's Hampton Inn felt like a second home to him now: reception knew his preferred room, and the cleaning and restaurant staff knew his name—and he knew theirs. Previously Fincher had managed to return home to Pittsburg every Friday, but the march the previous weekend had kept him in town. After almost twelve days in Mossberg, he was looking forward to time with his family.

What a screw-up the march had been, Fincher thought. There had been chaos when half the crowd stampeded at the sound of "gunfire." Police officers had drawn their weapons and citizens had suddenly produced theirs—including about thirty NRA members who had appointed themselves as vigilante security for the day. Meanwhile half the crowd had continued marching as though there was no threat at all. Mossberg had been lucky to escape an almighty gunfight that could have caused scores of friendly-fire deaths. *At least the police arrested and charged those douchebags who set off the fireworks.*

Before and after the march, the police and FBI called for tips from the public about the deaths of Vanburg, Brock,

Hanson, and Nossel. Fincher's insistence on the inclusion of Vanburg in the notices had caused a storm. Both Mayor Konig and Chief Delaney had opposed it, arguing there was no evidence Vanburg's death was a homicide or in any way related to the other three. Chief Delaney also realized that including Vanburg suggested the Mossberg police had missed something during their initial investigation. Fincher could feel the hostility in the room every time he met with them.

The public had come forward with hundreds of pieces of information, all of which had to be analyzed. It was overwhelming and frustrating given the high probability of most tips producing little useful information. However, without clear evidence connecting the killings and showing a serial killer was at work, the FBI was not going to allocate more resources to the case. Fincher worried that spending effort on filtering these tips would distract him from signals of an impending murder.

Late one night, after another fruitless day following up the public's emails and calls, Fincher mulled the lack of anything definitive connecting the deaths—although, as unlikely as it seemed to everyone else, Fincher *knew* those three women were somehow involved. Background profiles of Boateng's husband and Schumer's ex-husband had yielded nothing, with no evidence of motivation, capability, or even opportunity to commit murder, and Bajwa appeared to have no partner and few other associates.

Fincher revisited the profile of the four dead: young, sporty, jocks. "Where else have I heard these words?" he said out loud. Finch was sure someone else, talking about something else, had said these same words ... he ran over past interviews, then reached for his notes. Finally, he found it: his first meeting with Dr. Gutmann at Mossberg College. She had spoken about a fraternity whose members were sporty young men, alluding to them being a danger to female safety on campus.

A Google search brought up a list of fraternities at Mossberg College. Another search, of police databases, found a tiny number of actual investigations that was completely disproportionate to the number of reported complaints about one particular fraternity. Yet another search, this time of social media, found scores of online allegations and complaints about the same fraternity. Chi Omicron Kappa.

Once Fincher had made the initial connection, the similarities were crystal clear between the four dead and members Chi Omicron Kappa. Cooper Hanson had even been a member of this fraternity. All its members were young sporty men, many with allegations of sexual assault against them. Fincher was hit with an intense feeling of unease that members of this fraternity were sitting ducks.

The next day, Friday, Fincher was due to return to Pittsburg. He sent a late-night email to his boss and Chief Delaney, suggesting a pause in the investigation to focus on immediate action to identify potential victims and warn them they could be targets, then to recommend measures for their security. Fincher added that their second priority should be background searches on everyone who had made allegations of sexual assault, to try to identify if she could be the perpetrator.

Chief Delaney, tossing and turning in bed next to his snoring wife, and also wondering how to proceed with the investigation, responded within minutes. He would arrange a meeting with the mayor and the council for Monday morning.

WYATT BELL HAD also been doing research. He had been trawling the internet for stories about sexual assault in Mossberg—court records, media articles (few in the *Gazette*), and social media—when a tweet caught his eye under the hashtag #MeToo. He knew of the #MeToo movement from the tweets and allegations about Harvey Weinstein that had gone viral the year before, but it had been remote from his first job writing agricultural stories in Iowa and the new job in Mossberg, and he had paid it little attention. He read the tweet, then clicked on more, then more, and then more.

There were dozens, *hundreds*, of tweets from women alleging sexual harassment or assault by one of the members of one fraternity at Mossberg College: Chi Omicron Kappa. It wasn't just its Mossberg chapter that was implicated, but chapters on campuses across the nation: in Florida, Georgia, New York, Massachusetts, Michigan, Arkansas, Texas, California, Washington, Colorado; the list went on and on. Wyatt created an Excel spreadsheet to keep track of the data—

nearly all members of Chi Omicron Kappa in Mossberg had an online allegation of sexual harassment or assault against him, largely because several women alleged they had been brought to the frat house under the pretext of going to a party and had been raped by every guy present. He counted eleven women who said they'd made reports to the Mossberg police and twenty-three who had made reports to campus security. The college had given a couple of guys warnings, but all the other complainants said no action was ever taken. The harshest criticism was kept for the Mossberg police, which had not laid a single charge.

Emily was woken by Wyatt clattering in the kitchen making a coffee. "Wyatt, it's the middle of the night! Come to bed."

"I think I'm onto a big story here, Em."

Emily groaned. "Don't tell me: your serial killer again?"

"Yeah. I was researching reports of sexual assault in Mossberg and there are all these tweets about it and how Chi Omicron Kappa has 'rape parties.' Seriously, there are dozens of women who allege they were assaulted by its members."

Emily was still half asleep. "You didn't know that?"

"You *knew* that?"

Emily propped herself up on an elbow. "During my very first week on campus a girl warned me to stay away from those parties. Everyone says they prey on freshman girls because they're unsuspecting and are impressed by all that jock garbage."

"Girls talk about that kind of thing?"

"Jesus, Wyatt, of course we do. Girls learn as teenagers to exchange information about boys so we can find the good ones and stay away from the bad ones. Well, a bit bad is OK if we want to aggravate our parents, but good enough to treat us right. It's sociology 101." Emily giggled. "Girls who stuck around campus this summer had a great time going out, because those murders made loads of the *bad guys* mind their p's and q's and it kept others off the streets altogether. We felt safe. But it also meant the *good* guys were nowhere to be found." Emily laughed again. "Honestly, it's like every guy secretly thought he excelled at sports, had a six-pack, and was kind of dangerous—like he had a secret inner jock—and therefore was target for assassination. Girls don't mind nice guys. They could have gone out downtown! We just don't want to be harassed."

Wyatt reflected on the story about gender politics in Mossberg he wished he could write but knew his boss would never print. "So, what do the bad guys do now they're worried about being murdered? They can't all just be sitting at home looking at porn or playing computer games."

"Word has it they get a *nice guy* to trick girls into coming to parties they hold behind closed doors." Emily yawned. "I've got to sleep."

"Em, I know these guys aren't angels, but I think they might be in danger—of being murdered."

Emily yawned again. "See how that story goes down with your editor: *Football Stars Mossberg's Most Vulnerable*. Come to bed."

30

THE HARDWARE STORE had a rusted Dodge RAM pickup—single-cab with a bench seat—that was used to cart materials short distances and to jump-start customers' flat batteries. It was no longer registered and didn't even have license plates. Kate knew if they were stopped by the police—a near impossibility in Mossberg unless one had out-of-state plates—she could easily come up with an excuse and abort the mission.

"One more thing," said Kate to Carly and Seyram before starting the engine. "We should turn our phones off. Our calls will bounce from the phone tower nearest to the frat house. If we use our phones while we're on the way, or when we're there, the police will be able to see we were in the vicinity. If we get split up for some reason, wait until you're back home before using your phone."

The three of them were kitted up in generic coveralls and caps and sat three abreast in the cab, silent and grim. Seyram had the keg filled with gasoline between her feet, Carly clenched the Molotov cocktail between her knees, and, in an act of total recklessness, Kate trailed a cigarette out the window.

Kate drove through backstreets to get to the frat house, approaching it from the lane—not the street where CCTV on adjacent houses' front porches might record them. She reversed into the driveway beside the fraternity, the car facing into the lane for a quick escape, and turned to look at Seyram and Carly. "I'll keep the engine running. Any problem, don't talk to anyone, just exit, and we'll drive off. *Good luck.*"

AS SOON AS she walked in the door, Ana Vargas knew she had made a mistake. A group of tall half-drunk men turned to look at her. Not a girl in sight. She spun around to get reassurance from her friend Ashton, who had invited her to the party, and saw him high-fiving his brother Hunter, whom she'd met once before at Ashton's house.

"Ashton, what's going on? Where are we?"

"Party's about to start, Ana!" called out a man she'd never met.

"Come get a beer, Ashton!" called another.

In desperation, Ana announced, "I have to go the bathroom! Can someone tell me where it is?"

"Time for that later," a man snarled.

Thinking quickly, Ana turned to Ashton's brother, Hunter, and lowered her voice. "I'm on my period. Can you show me the bathroom?" She had no idea if the ruse would work, but figured her frankness would shock the men and buy her some time. Hunter and another man walked her toward a bathroom at the rear of the building. Ana heard the front door open, and more people come in, but it was too late to run.

CARLY AND SEYRAM took a deep breath and got out of the car. The *thump-thump* of music and raucous laughter sounded from inside the house as they pulled down their caps and held the keg at either end, walking sideways up to the front door. They turned the handle and walked straight in. To the left was a kitchen filled with guys swaying and talking loudly. Music was coming from an adjacent living area. To the right was what appeared to be a couple of bedrooms. Directly ahead there was a staircase with a flight going up, and another going down.

"Seyram, down the stairs." Carly tilted her head toward the staircase. "That's got to be it."

A drunk young man stumbled in front of them and looked at them puzzled. "Keeggg!" Seyram bellowed in a deep voice. The man stumbled on. From the kitchen they heard someone shout "More beer's arrived!", followed by cheering.

Sure enough, the staircase led downstairs to a games room, with a pool table, foosball table, and a bar area. Seyram spied a door beside the bar and tried the handle. A bathroom.

"The boiler room has got to be here somewhere!" Carly could feel a rising panic.

Seyram spotted another door next to the staircase and turned the handle. It swung open to reveal two boilers and a large oil storage tank, lit by fluorescent lights. *Bingo.* "This is it. We have ninety seconds."

They placed the keg on its side beside the oil heater and loosened the cap so that gasoline started to flow out. Carly took the Molotov cocktail from inside her coveralls and walked back toward the stairs, trickling gasoline as she went, all the way through the games room to the foot of the stairs. She then took a rag, presoaked in gasoline, out of a plastic bag and stuffed it into the neck of the bottle. They walked back up the stairs to a landing.

"You go to the top of the stairs," said Carly. "I'm going to light this and then throw it back to the bottom. The bottle will smash and the gasoline will catch fire and burn all the way to the oil tank. As soon as I've thrown it, *we need to run.*"

Carly fumbled with a lighter she'd taken from Kate, lit the cloth, and threw the bottle. As she came level with Seyram they heard a smash, then a dull woosh. They sprinted out of the front door, around the side of the building and dove into the car, whose engine Kate had kept idling. Within five seconds the car was in the lane. Five seconds later they were 100 yards away. Then, *kaboom.*

31

FINCHER RECEIVED THE call at midnight and was on the road thirty minutes later. He drove directly from Pittsburgh to the Chi Omicron Kappa frat house. On his instruction, the scene and vicinity were secured. He didn't want any basic errors as had occurred at Coates Ravine or the golf course, and in contrast to the interchange car attack he was determined that this time he would get hold of CCTV footage.

At five a.m. Fincher was in a meeting with Dr. Susan Gutmann at Mossberg College, getting background on the Chi Omicron Kappa fraternity. Privately he was kicking himself for not prioritizing an investigation into the fraternity, its activities, and its potential enemies—and not warning its members they might be the target of a killer. His realization that this group was likely both a perpetrator of violence and a potential target of a former victim—or someone else—had simply come too late.

"Dr. Gutmann, thank you for meeting me so early, I'm only sorry it is under these circumstances. I've just come from the fraternity house site and it is a grim scene. My condolences to you and the college."

"Thank you, Agent Fincher. I'm also sorry we're meeting like this. Chief Delaney has given me an update on the potential death toll. It is truly a terrible day for the college." Gutmann looked haggard and was still in her dressing gown.

"Dr. Gutmann, if I remember our last conversation correctly, although we focused on the incel residence out of town, the Chi Omicron Kappa fraternity is—had been—a problem organization on campus. Individual members were threatening to some of the student body, especially females."

"Yes. We had frequent complaints of harassment and sometimes actual assaults by the fraternity's members."

"Are there likely to be individuals on campus or in the community who may have wished harm on the fraternity?"

"After over a year in the job, I can definitely say yes."

"Has anything changed in the past few months, since I was last here, in the fraternity and the broader college community?"

"Cooper Hanson, one of the two young men who were murdered during summer, was a member of that fraternity. Nobody connected his death at the time to possible threats to other fraternity members or the frat house itself. However, the atmosphere in town and on campus changed dramatically. On-campus partying and drunkenness and harassment increased. Campus security said it has been almost exponential. Meanwhile, you've probably heard that the town center has almost been reborn as a ... I'm not sure what to call it, a female *space*; gay-friendly too. I couldn't tell you if this means someone was emboldened to actually attack them." Gutmann paused and studied Fincher. "So, you think this wasn't an accidental explosion of some kind, I take it? You think it was a targeted attack?"

"Well, we're not ruling that out. I'm going to the hospital now to speak to the survivors, if that's possible, to see what they can tell me about the evening. Thank you for filling me in."

FINCHER WALKED TOWARD the hospital room where the two male survivors were recuperating. He was keen to speak to them as soon as possible. Getting contemporaneous information on possible criminal events was the gold standard in policing.

A nurse with a Jamaican lilt showed him in. "It seems their biggest problem is a hangover," she said primly. "The doctor says you've got ten minutes."

The two men were sitting up in bed eating breakfast, looking remarkably well given the circumstances.

"I understand you're John and Hunter," said Fincher, reading their names from the charts at the end of their beds. "I'm Agent Fincher from the FBI. Do you feel well enough to answer a few questions about what happened?"

"The FBI? That is *cool!*" exclaimed Hunter.

"Awesome," added John. "Happy to answer!"

"Thank you. Can I ask you to recall the events of last night? I understand you were in the middle of a party. Was there anything strange? Did anyone unexpected come?"

"Well, it was a closed party for fraternity members. The only person we didn't know," said John, thinking out loud, "was the girl, but she was brought in just before the final keg was delivered."

Fincher made a mental note of the words *the girl … brought in*, but asked, "Before the *final* keg was delivered? Did you get several deliveries?"

"Apparently there was some mix-up. Hunt, do you remember?"

Hunter furrowed his brow in concentration. "Didn't those two people come through just before the explosion?"

Agent Fincher was alert. "Two people you didn't know came in?"

"Yeah, but they brought us beer."

Agent Fincher exhaled. "Let me get this clear. Two people you didn't know and weren't expecting came into the frat house in the night, and you think they brought you a keg. Is that right?"

"They said they had a keg for us, so we said 'Cool!'"

"Can you describe them?"

"They were kind of …" John waved his hands in the air to indicate nothingness.

"Like the ladies who come to clean," said Hunter.

"*Ladies?* How old were they?"

"Dude, at least a hundred."

"You're sure they were *women*? Two *older women*? Came into your fraternity on a Saturday night while you were having a party and brought you a keg of beer?"

"It's hard to recall. I mean, we'd drunk a bit and they weren't memorable in any way."

"What did they look like? Tall? Short? Fat? Thin?" Fincher tightened his grip on the bed rail. He had three very specific women in mind.

"I honestly couldn't tell you. Like Hunt said, we get ladies who come in to do stuff for us. I guess they looked like them. Ancient."

"Were they white? Black? South Asian?"

"They would have been white," added John. "There are no blacks in Mossberg."

"They were kind of … grayish." Hunter was trying to be helpful.

"And you think they delivered beer?"

"Yeah, someone said it was a keg. We were happy we got more beer."

John and Hunter did a fist bump across the space between the beds.

Fincher thought these were the dumbest people he'd ever interviewed. Collecting himself, he asked, "About what time was that?"

"Maybe nine thirty or so. We saw them when they walked in, then they disappeared somewhere. That's when we helped the girl go to the bathroom."

"She wasn't sure where it was," John added. "A minute later the house blew up. Just went *boom*."

Fincher pondered the information. "What was in the keg? Was it beer?"

"I don't know," said Hunter. "Everyone was drinking from the keg already set up in the kitchen."

"Who was the girl?"

A strange look passed between Hunter and John.

"Oh, we don't know. You know, a lot of chicks out there love frat parties. She was friends with one of the fellas, so he invited her along."

"We don't usually exchange names or anything."

"When you said earlier 'she was brought in,' you were talking about the girl. What did you mean by that? Which of the fellas brought her in?"

Hunter and John exchanged glances. Hunter said, "Oh, um, it's just whoever invited her to the party."

"Did she come alone? Were there other girls there?"

"Nooo, no other girls. Not that night. I guess she just wanted to party."

"Let me get this straight. There was one girl at your party, and she needed help to go to the bathroom, and she asked you, even though she'd never met you before." Fincher gave them a long, hard look. "Why did she need your help?"

Another glance was exchanged. "She got drunk real quick."

"But lucky for us, hey? The bathroom must have protected us from the blast, because I saw the medics talking to her when they took her to the ambulance."

"Lucky indeed." Fincher wondered if the girl's story would match theirs. "Who was her friend—the person who invited her to the party?"

Hunter looked pained, then answered, "Ashton Wade. Is he in another ward?"

Fincher never saw the point of being delicate about bad news. He figured the only way to deliver it was to be blunt. "Everyone else died. You two and the young woman are the only survivors." He watched them absorb this news.

"My brother's dead?" Hunter went pale in shock.

"*Everyone* else died?" exclaimed John, putting two and two together. "Hold on a minute, you're from the FBI. All those questions about the keg and who delivered it—you think it was a *bomb*?"

"Someone wanted to kill us?" Hunter was astonished.

"Who doesn't like us?" said John, wide-eyed. "We're like the princes of Mossberg!"

"Have you even heard of the American Revolution?" Fincher was sharp. Correcting his tone, he continued, "We're investigating the cause of the explosion and whether there are grounds for a criminal investigation. That's all I can tell you at the moment. I'm sorry your friends died."

The nurse came to Agent Fincher and whispered that the young woman, who had not yet been identified, had regained consciousness. The doctors had permitted Fincher five minutes.

Fincher nodded at the two men, "Gentlemen, if any details of the people who brought what you think was a keg come back to you, call me." He gave them his card.

In a private room nearby, Agent Fincher gazed down at a slip of a girl, surely not much older than his daughters. He mused on how panicked her parents would be when they found out she'd been caught up in the explosion.

His face creased in concern, he bent over the bed. "Miss, can you hear me? I'm Ted Fincher, a police officer. I'd like to ask you some questions about last night."

The girl opened her eyes. She struggled to sit up, only to be restrained by the bedding and tubes. She sank back with a groan. Despite her obvious pain, she was remarkably free of physical injuries.

"Miss, what's your name? We'd like to let your family know you're here in hospital."

Swallowing, she croaked, "Ana. Ana Vargas. I'm from Mossberg."

"What's your parents' phone number?"

Ana croaked out a phone number and Fincher scribbled it down.

He couldn't resist the question. "Ana, how old are you?"
"Fifteen."

How did a fifteen-year-old end up the only girl at a party in a frat house? Fincher was grim. *Most likely not by choice.*

Ana lay there, breathing heavily, and Fincher exchanged glances with the nurse. At least they could contact her family. He stood up to leave, but Ana opened her eyes again.

"What happened to the guys? The ones in the frat house?"

Fincher exchanged glances again with the nurse, who shook her head.

"You don't need to worry. The hospital is taking good care of them." He hesitated. "Did you have a boy— Was one of them a friend? Do you want me to pass on a message to the family?"

Ana had the strangest look on her face. "Yes, I have a message for Ashton Wade and his brother Hunter. I wish they'd been blown up." She faded back into unconsciousness.

"It's time to go, Agent Fincher." The nurse was curt and gestured to the door.

32

FINCHER RETURNED TO the police station and immediately walked into a meeting with Police Chief Delaney, Detective Schultz, and Trooper Chase who, again, had been assigned to accompany him.

The chief spoke first. "I'm going to throw all the resources I have at this, but we don't have a forensic fire investigator nor the kind of intelligence analysts we're going to need. Can I rely on the FBI to provide personnel?"

"Yes, sir. I can put in a call."

"Did you get much this morning?"

"The two surviving men said there was definitely an explosion before the fire. They heard and felt a boom. They were with a young woman in the bathroom, and it seems all the concrete protected them. They managed to get out and were taken by ambulance to the hospital. I couldn't get much out of the woman, but we know her name, age, and parents' phone number. We'll need to interview her again when she's recovered. Before we spoke to her, one of the two survivors, Hunter, told us she'd been invited to the party by another young man, Ashton Wade. However, Ana—the young woman—made a comment that she wished Ashton Wade and his brother Hunter—I'm assuming that is the Hunter in the hospital—had died during the explosion. It appears she was the only female at the party and was not there by choice.

"Another interesting thing is that both men are sure two individuals—who were not part of the fraternity—entered the house shortly before the explosion with a keg, or something that looked like a keg. They said that about one minute after they left, the explosion occurred." Fincher consulted his notepad. "This was about nine forty-five p.m. The 911 calls first came in at nine forty-seven."

The chief rubbed his chin. "You think this was some kind of bomb?"

"I'm not sure, but it should be a line of inquiry."

"Any description of the two men who carried it in?"

"John and Hunter were hazy on the details, but they seemed to think it was two women."

"*Women?!*" Delaney and Schultz exclaimed together.

"Chief, while their memories are fresh, I'd like to arrange a lineup. Tomorrow if possible."

The chief was surprised. "Normally we have suspects in lineups. Do we have any suspects?"

Fincher braced for derision. "They were fairly certain the two women were older. Middle-aged. I'd like to put those three women from the golf course in the lineup: Carly Schumer, Seyram Boateng and Kate Bajwa."

Detective Schultz looked at the floor in disgust. Trooper Chase gawped. Chief Delaney stared at Fincher for a long time.

"The black girl, the clerk, and the potter?" The chief had a pained look.

Schultz couldn't contain himself. "That can't be right. Black girls don't murder white men. It's the other way around! Think of all those whores and transvestites. White. Guys. Did. That." He jabbed the table with a sausage finger to punctuate each word, as though this was an accomplishment in which he shared.

"Fincher, may I remind you," said the chief, "that we found no physical evidence to tie those three to the scene at Coates Ravine, they gave convincing testimony about discovering the body of Preston Brock on the golf course, and all had alibis the night of the explosion that killed Cooper Hanson and Sheldon Nossel. There is no footage of them driving to the intersection. In fact, CCTV from Shell shows them filling up with gas, and CCTV from Pizza Hut shows them calmly eating herb bread."

This wasn't at all how Fincher would summarize the evidence. "It's a hunch." He could hear the pleading in his voice. "We have no other leads. I'd like to do this while their memories are fresh."

Finally, the chief replied. "OK, but it's on your head, Fincher. If the *Gazette* runs a story on this, I'm going to tell them it was the FBI's idea. Chase, organize the lineup."

33

It was Monday afternoon and Agent Fincher, Detective Schultz and John, the first of the two male survivors from the explosion, stood in front of a large one-way mirror. Schultz radioed Trooper Chase, who was waiting in another room. "Bring on the girls."

The lineup consisted of nine women, who filed in slowly and were instructed to turn and face the mirror. Six of them ranged in age from twenty to thirty-five, were white, and between five feet to about five-eight. Tulip Sorenson was on the far right and a redhead stood far left—Trooper Chase, in his haste and enthusiasm, had gone to campus to recruit volunteers. In the middle were Seyram, Carly, and Kate, all over fifty. Kate and Seyram were the only women of color, and they were both five foot ten. Carly was shorter at five-seven. The nine women looked straight ahead.

Fincher shot a glance at Chase: Don't you know the protocol for line-ups? You couldn't find six women more closely resembling our suspects?

John, who had been released from the hospital shortly after Fincher's visit, stood with Fincher and Schultz on the other side of the mirror.

"Take your time and look carefully at each individual," said Fincher to John.

After a minute, Fincher asked, "Do you recognize any of them?"

"Tulip Sorenson," said John.

"But was she the one who came into the frat house?" Fincher asked impatiently. "That's who I'm trying to get you to identify."

John scanned the line intently. "No."

"Are you sure? Look carefully and tell me what you see?"

John hesitated. "Six women. Tulip is one of them, and that hot redhead at the other end."

"*Six* women? Are you sure? You can't see more than that?"

John squinted intently through the mirror. "Oh, dude, you mean those three old ladies in the middle? I got sidetracked by the babes. I can see them now. You're right."

Agent Fincher had a pained look. "Do you recognize those three in the middle? Do they look like the people who came into the frat house two nights ago?"

"Honestly, I just couldn't tell you. Like I said, the two who came in, they looked like ... nothing."

Fincher's jaw muscles twitched. "Thank you. You can go."

Schulz accompanied John out and came back with Hunter.

"Hunter, take your time," said Fincher, "then let us know if you recognize any of them."

"Tulip Sorenson," said Hunter. "I'd recognize her anywhere."

"Aside from Tulip, do you recognize any of them?"

"Never seen any of them before."

"Are you sure? You're looking carefully at each of them, right? There are older and younger women, so look carefully at each of them."

"Where are the old ones? Oh, man!" Hunter recoiled. "There are three old ladies in the center."

"Middle-aged," said Fincher between clenched teeth. He was a year older than Kate, Carly and Seyram. "Do you recognize any of those three *middle-aged* women as the people who came into the frat house?"

"That one right in the middle, doesn't she run the hardware store?"

Fincher's pulse quickened. "Was she one of the two who came in?"

"Nah. I went into the store to ask about CCTV for the frat house. I spoke to her."

"What did she say?"

"She said she could sell us a system, but when I told her we wanted it installed ASAP, she said the person she recommends for installation was only free the following weekend."

"When did you want it installed?"

"This weekend. It would have been put in yesterday morning."

"So, if it had been installed when you wanted it, you would have had CCTV last night?"

"Yes, but"—Hunter looked confused—"are you connecting that to the explosion? How could she have anything to do with it?"

Detective Schultz couldn't resist another dig at Fincher. "Boy has a point there, Agent Fincher. Girls aren't killers; girls *get* killed. It's like a law of nature." Schultz was pleased with himself, as though he'd discovered a fundamental truth about the universe like $E = mc^2$.

Fincher looked at the ground as though experiencing pain. "Thank you, Detective Schultz. Hunter, the other two *middle-aged* women—do you recognize them?"

"I honestly couldn't tell you."

"So, let me ask you this: do any of the *young women* in the lineup resemble the people who came into the frat house?"

"No way. We'd remember them. They wouldn't have made it out alive."

34

WALKING DOWN THE stairs of the police station, Kate, Seyram, and Carly were each lost in thought. Despite beech, elm, and maple trees turning vibrant colors all around them, they felt cold and humiliated by the lineup. Although Trooper Chase was the only police officer they saw—and he seemed bewildered that they were even there—they sensed Agent Fincher somewhere nearby. The experience had shaken them.

"Do you two have time for a drink, or do you have to go home?" asked Kate.

"I can come. Summer's at a friend's place."

"I'll text Felix, but I'm sure it'll be OK."

"Let's go to the Sports Bar. It's a pretty friendly place now the downtown crowd has changed. And it's happy hour before six. There'll be hardly anyone there on a Monday evening."

"Why are you so perky?" said Seyram. "We've just been through a police process that could have seen us charged with a bombing and a whole lot of other crimes."

"We're going to fall apart if we don't talk about this." Kate was firm. "See you there in five."

The Sports Bar had only a dozen customers, so Seyram, Carly, and Kate easily found a corner table away from other patrons. They had just taken their first sip when every phone in the place started to ping and buzz. Even the landline beside the cash register rang.

Carly looked at her phone and put her hand to her mouth. "Oh my God!"

Kate looked around at the commotion. "Let me guess, the *Gazette* just updated its coverage on the frat house fire?"

Seyram read her text. "Felix says there are three survivors from the fire: two guys and a girl."

"A friend of Summer's posted that the girl is Ana Vargas," said Carly. "She's in Summer's year."

Seyram continued. "The two men are Hunter Wade and John Redleaf."

"Hunter Wade, he's on the college hockey team," said Carly. "He's Ashton Wade's brother. Summer says Ashton is in her and Ana's year. I feel terrible about this." She lowered her voice. "We could have killed Ana! I thought no girls came to the parties before ten. *Shit*." Along with several other patrons, all reacting to versions of the same messages or phone calls, Carly started to cry.

Kate scrolled through the story, then shook her head. "Carly, we just *saved* Ana. It's exactly like that soldier from Fort Byrd, Beatriz, told you when those guys tried to force her to go with them to campus that night, and what Summer confirmed: Chi Omicron Kappa have a party where one of the guys tricks a girl into coming. Can't you see that? Hunter got his brother, Ashton, to bring along Ana. *She* was the girl they were going to rape. She's fifteen. They just arrived too early."

The truth about the night dawned on them: they had got the timing wrong, which could have resulted in Ana's death, but they were right about the parties and the fate of the unlucky girl pressured, tricked, or 'invited' into coming.

Seyram was fierce. "I'm *glad* we did this. Poor Ana and what they were planning to do ..." Her voice trailed off.

35

IN THE DAYS after the explosion, the *Gazette* posted updates on the frat house fire every hour, including photographs of the scene and video of investigators at work. There were few details yet about the dead, who were still being officially identified and their next of kin notified—although social media was full of speculation about the victims. The *Gazette* warned Mossbergers to brace for casualties, and described how the authorities were assembling resources to deal with the aftermath. On Tuesday morning, names of the dead started to trickle out as families were formally notified or made posts online about their loss. Finally, at five twenty p.m. on the Tuesday, the *Gazette* posted a consolidated story: *COLLEGE EXPLOSION: Sports Stars Among Victims.*

Nineteen residents of the Chi Omicron Kappa fraternity had died, and the article named all of them. There were three survivors: one young woman so traumatized she had only just been identified—although her name had not been released— and two local men. All three had been in a room against the back wall; its concrete and proximity to the outside saved them.

It wasn't the article Wyatt Bell had wanted to write. He and Emily had been watching *Orange Is the New Black* on Netflix over a dinner of Chinese takeout and beer when his phone buzzed. "Son!" barked Henry Konig, who still called him that after a year. "There's been an explosion on campus. Get there ASAP and find out what you can. I want this online six a.m. tomorrow, updates all Sunday, and an in-depth for Monday."

Wyatt took photos of the scene: of fire engines, police cars, and ambulances taking away bodies and survivors, and of the building which was a burnt-out wreck. He heard firefighters mention that as an old building it was not up to code standards. The initial explosion, which fire-fighters surmised was linked to the oil tank in the basement, had blasted up through the interior of the building, the fire quickly spreading through the wooden floors, walls, and staircase.

Arriving home at one a.m., Wyatt went online into the small hours. He checked the fraternity's Facebook and Instagram pages, which gave him a list of names of likely victims—names he recognized from his previous research into the fraternity. From there he went to Twitter and back to Facebook, tracking down the individuals' friends and family members. Konig wanted profiles of each victim ready to print as soon as names were released, and without too much trouble Wyatt was able to find their ages and participation in college sports teams and clubs. The *Gazette* was planning an extensive article on the victims, and then another on the survivors.

Wyatt recalled his conversation with Emily about Chi Omicron Kappa, and how its members were potential targets of a killer. He also recalled the conversations he'd overheard from the scene. Bodies had been found and counted more or less in front of him as he stood behind the police tape, but he recalled both a medic and a firefighter saying "one girl only." Officials at the scene were talking about a college party that had been in progress, but *what college party has only one girl in attendance?* By midday Sunday, the *Gazette* had also learned that the three survivors had been in a bathroom against an external wall of the building. But *why were they in the bathroom together?*

None of this added up.

Wyatt's frustration had mounted during meetings with the team the *Gazette* had put together to cover the story going forward. He presented his background research: clearly there had been a tragedy, but the social media reports of violence at the fraternity's parties were equally important news—and something, apparently, known to just about every young woman in town. Wyatt described the tweets and described how the #MeToo movement had helped bring about the downfall of Hollywood mogul Harvey Weinstein. He mentioned the lack of headway women had had getting the Mossberg police or college to act on their complaints, and he tried to convince Henry Konig that what he had uncovered was systemic and newsworthy; part of a changing America.

Nothing he said could persuade Konig to make the story anything other than a tragedy about lost heroes. Wyatt hadn't even argued against such a story, simply proposing that they should run a second story, something along the lines of "Fraternity's Dark Secrets." He saw such a story as a hook for what he thought was the real story: *Was this a mass murder of young men?* Konig was dismissive to the point of being insulting. "There you go again with your killer girl theory. This was a tragic accident. Do profiles of the young men and prepare to cover the funerals over the next few days. I'll consider running a story on the risks of faulty basement oil tanks next week."

Wyatt wrote the story, but he was determined to get more information about the young woman survivor and what had led her to be at the fraternity.

The next day, Monday, at nine a.m. the police chief and Mayor Konig gave a press conference on the steps of the station to the assembled media. Every regional media outlet, every national newspaper, TV network and radio station, and even the foreign press, had sent reporters or camera crews to cover the story. Chief Delaney reassured the public a full investigation was underway and that experts from the FBI had arrived and were assisting. There was a deluge of questions from journalists:

"What was the cause of the explosion?"

"Where were the victims from?"

"How many survivors are there?"

"What is the condition of the survivors?"

"Do other college residences have faulty heating systems?"

"What message do you have for the community?"

Wyatt Bell, whom all the other journalists could tell was a cub reporter, had been elbowed to the back of the pack.

Valiantly he clawed his way to the front and managed to blurt out his question, "Was it murder?"

There was a collective inhalation as the pack realized Wyatt could be a step ahead, and then shouted a slew of new questions:

"Do you have suspects?"

"What was the motive?"

"Was this an assassination?"

"What is the town doing to prevent more killings?"

"How are you reassuring people?"

Mayor Konig's mouth tightened, and he looked disapprovingly at Wyatt. *I'm going to have to talk to my brother about this reporter.*

Chief Delaney replied they were investigating every angle, including the possibility of criminal conduct. There would be no further announcements until the arson forensic team had completed its site work. The police were, however, seeking two persons of interest, whom Delaney described in a prepared statement: "We understand two people entered the building shortly before the explosion. Based on descriptions from eyewitnesses, they are aged between forty and eighty, are possibly female and of grayish ethnicity, with indeterminate height."

This electrified the media:

"What do you mean 'possibly female'?"

"What is 'grayish ethnicity'?"

"Are they targeting young men?"

"Are *killer ladies* on the loose?"

And from Fox News, "Is this a continuation of America's genocide against white men?"

The hysteria went stratospheric. Within hours, every citizen of Mossberg knew that police were exploring the theory that one or more female serial killers was on the prowl, targeting jocks.

36

ON THE WEDNESDAY following the press conference, most of the Mossberg Police Department and the FBI team assisting it, were installed in the situation room that had been set up to deal with the rapidly evolving investigation.

Chief Delaney was feeling sheepish. He regretted speaking to the media and releasing the description of persons of interest. It took just hours before jokes appeared on Twitter and memes on Instagram of grayish people, possibly female, between forty and eighty, committing crimes. A demographer interviewed by NPR Pittsburgh said that if one were to apply a broad definition to "grayish ethnicity" and "possibly female," along with the forty to eighty age range, approximately 55 million Americans fit the description.

The FBI had deployed more personnel to Mossberg and the situation room was full of clacking keyboards and murmuring voices. Homicide detectives, arson investigators, intelligence analysts, forensic financial analysts, and telecoms experts requested and retrieved data, sifting through information looking for evidence of cause and for possible perpetrators, patterns, and connections. Now that it was crystal clear an unusually large number of young men in Mossberg were dying in suspicious circumstances, the investigation's focus broadened beyond the fraternity explosion to include the deaths of Vanburg, Brock, Hanson, and Nossel.

Chief Delaney, in conversation with Fincher, was distracted by the sound of running. The door to the situation room burst open and a young analyst entered.

"Sir, do you have a minute?" panted the analyst, trying to catch her breath. "This morning we visited a residence near the fraternity that had CCTV footage of a vehicle on the night of the explosion. We copied the image and sent it for analysis to Patty Bouvier at the Department of Motor Vehicles. We think we've got something." She flourished a USB.

"Stick it in the presentation laptop and project it onto the wall," ordered Delaney.

Everyone crowded around to inspect the image.

"The image shows a vehicle—no plates—moving along an alley in the direction of the frat house," explained the analyst. "You can see the time—nine forty-two. That's five minutes before the 911 calls came in, and we believe three to four minutes before the actual explosion. The time correlates with the probable speed of a vehicle traveling that distance and route to the fraternity. Because of the angle of the camera, the car is only in one part of the frame, but you can see there are two people in the cab, although their heads are obscured. One is wearing a baseball cap."

The analyst further enlarged the grainy image, and Fincher, Delaney, Schultz, Chase, and a dozen others studied it.

"What did Patty say?" asked Delaney.

"She said the vehicle is a 1979 Dodge RAM pickup. Single cab. There are fifty-seven of that model still registered in Pennsylvania, none in Mossberg. *But* they went back through historical records and there is a '79 Dodge pickup last registered in Mossberg twelve years ago to a Douglas Thornhill Smith. We ran checks on him, and a Douglas Thornhill Smith owns a business on Main Street."

"Oh, that's D.T. Smith!" said Trooper Chase. "He owns Downtown Hardware, which has this old car they use around their parking lot. I pulled it over once when I caught it out on the road. It's unregistered."

Fincher leaped to his feet. "Downtown Hardware? Where Kate Bajwa works? Christ, this is the connection we've been looking for!"

"Why are the two people sitting so close together?" asked Chase. "They aren't holding hands like a couple might if they were snuggled up."

"My guess," said Fincher, "is there's a third person out of frame—so three people abreast in the single cab—which means one person is in the middle squashed up to the driver. I think we can guess who those three people are." He clenched his fists on the table.

"Any intel on the cap or clothing?" Delaney asked the analyst.

"No, sir. We've enlarged it, and it's all generic and looks new. No embroidery, distinctive tears, or logos visible. These people knew what they were doing. You can see one inner wrist and palm, but there are no tattoos, and we can't make out any racial complexion. The skin is kind of grayish."

The analyst bit her lip as she realized what she'd said. Everyone avoided looking at the Chief.

Chief Delaney started barking out orders. "Schultz, prepare warrant applications to seize the vehicle, to search Bajwa's office and house, and to arrest her." This was a way for him to claw back some pride.

The room started buzzing with even more energy.

"Chase, the store will be open. I want you to go there immediately—use an unmarked car—and keep it under surveillance. If Bajwa leaves, follow her, don't lose her, and stay in radio contact. Agent Fincher, as soon as we've got the paperwork—that shouldn't take long—go there with Schultz and execute the warrants."

Delaney continued, his mind going a million miles an hour. "Fincher, can we get a chopper up from Pittsburgh? I'd like one overhead when you're at the store. We can have a sharpshooter on board and a couple of fellas ready to rappel down onto the store roof if there's a hostage situation."

"Yes, sir," replied Fincher. "I'll call HQ and put in the request."

Addressing the assembled officers, the chief barked more orders. "I need other teams in unmarked vehicles at the homes of Bajwa, Boateng, and Schumer, and another at Boateng's clinic. I want all four locations under 24-hour watch until we can make arrests."

"Yes, sir!" came the male chorus. The sound of pounding feet reverberated around the building. Outside the station, cars could be heard revving, then their sirens wailing into the distance.

Chief Delaney strode to the radio room and threw open the door. "Tell those *fucking* morons to turn off their sirens!" he yelled at the operator. "They're supposed to be undercover!"

Delaney spun around. "The rest of you, establish a perimeter around Downtown Hardware, and I want a bomb squad at Bajwa's residence—it could be booby-trapped. Then he bellowed into the next room, *"Dale!"*—Dale was the operations director—"Open the armory. I want everyone gunned up and in bulletproof vests. We have reason to believe this woman is armed and dangerous."

"GOODNESS, WHAT *IS* that thrumming?" Kate said to no one, getting up to peer from her mezzanine window into the store. Looking down, she saw Fincher and Schultz at the checkout counter speaking to the sales assistant. Her eyes narrowed and she sat down to wait.

Fincher and Schultz entered Kate's office without knocking, their right hands on their gun holsters. Kate wore the same inscrutable expression Fincher remembered from their first encounter. "Good morning, Agent Fincher—oh, and Detective Schultz. Come through. I didn't expect such personal service."

Fincher and Schultz were suddenly off guard.

"You were expecting us?" asked Schultz.

"I put in the call a few days ago. I figure you must have found it."

Doubt flickered across Fincher's face. "Found what?"

"Our stolen car. Isn't that why you're here?"

Fincher and Schultz looked at each other.

"What car?" Fincher asked.

"We had a pickup stolen from the yard last Saturday night. I called the station to report it." Kate looked from Fincher to Schultz.

Silence.

"Is there something wrong?" She had a look of the mildest surprise. "I mean, the car was a heap, but it was useful."

Fincher cleared his throat. "Ms. Bajwa, are you alleging that car was stolen?"

"Alleging? No, Agent Fincher, I'm telling you it was stolen. After I closed up the store last Saturday evening, I swung by around eight or eight thirty to check I'd locked everything properly and realized it was gone. I called the station to report the theft."

Silence.

"It was worth hardly anything, but I figured I should still report it. I mean, it wasn't registered ..." Kate hesitated. "Is that why you're here? Because it wasn't registered? It was kept on private property."

She's mocking us, thought Fincher.

She's so dumb, thought Schultz.

"Ms. Bajwa, you're alleging that car was not in your possession last Saturday evening, is that correct?"

"Yes. Sorry, can you tell me what is wrong?"

"Detective," Fincher turned to Schultz, "I wonder if you could confirm with the station that Ms. Bajwa reported a stolen vehicle at approximately eight thirty p.m. last Saturday." He turned back to Kate. "We'd like you to come to the station to make a statement—about your movements that evening and making the stolen vehicle report."

"Forgive me, but this seems overkill for a stolen old car," said Kate.

Schultz, inwardly cursing FBI agents and their "theories," wanted to find a way out of the situation. "It seems it may have been used in a crime, Miss. We're trying to establish the car's movements since it left your property."

"*Gosh.*" said Kate. "I can come now if you like."

"Yes, please. Let's do this," said Fincher. He beckoned for Kate to follow him out of the store.

Across the street, attracted by the thumping helicopter overhead, a crowd had gathered in anticipation of action. They barely paid attention as Kate and the two officers calmly exited and walking over to a police car.

Out of earshot of Kate, Fincher got on the phone to Delaney. "Chief, call off the chopper. We've got Bajwa with us. She says she reported the car stolen about an hour and a half before the explosion. We're bringing her to the station to make a statement. Looks like someone else may have used it." Fincher could feel a migraine coming on.

37

"YOU SHOULD HAVE seen their faces when I told them I'd reported the car stolen on Saturday evening!" Kate hooted with laughter.

"What I don't understand," said Seyram, "is how you knew to report it stolen, when it really *was* stolen, after you reported it."

Kate scoffed. "Local knowledge. There are thefts and attempted break-ins most weekends downtown—people stealing cars for joyrides, that kind of thing—although it's settled down since we made young men scared of the dark. When I returned the pickup to the parking lot, I left the keys in the ignition and parked in the corner of the yard that I know isn't covered by CCTV. There was a ninety-nine percent chance of it being stolen, and sure enough ..."

"So, you didn't *arrange* for someone to steal it?" asked Seyram.

"Nope. Just trusted my knowledge of shady weekend characters."

"Are we off the hook?" asked Carly.

"They can hardly say we led an attack on a frat house in a vehicle that wasn't in our possession. A defense attorney would have a field day with that argument."

"What if they find it?"

"What if they do? My DNA would be in it anyway because I've driven it a hundred times, and we can say the three of us sat in it a few times to have a girls' talk when you were crying."

"Why do I have to be the crier?" protested Carly.

"Have you ever seen me cry?"

"No."

"Have you ever seen Seyram cry?"

"With laughter."

"How often do we see you cry?"

"Umm, a few times per year ..."

"As I was saying ... It's a vague enough excuse for our DNA being in it. Let me assure you, I'm not going to be outwitted by those cops."

Later that week, Kate, Seyram, and Carly did appear to be off the hook, because the pickup was found in a wooded area five miles out of town, dumped and burnt-out.

38

FUNERALS OF YOUNG people have a large circle of potential attendees: immediate family, extended family, friends, friends of the family, classmates, teammates, people from church, and neighbors, all yet to be whittled down through age and death. In Mossberg, people had grappled with the suddenness of the deaths of Vanburg, Brock, Hanson, and Nossel, although many also felt secretly relieved about Brock. While highly talented at sport, he was such a dope many thought the US military had dodged a bullet in not having to accept him into its ranks.

These first four funerals were conventional in another way. Rumblings about the individuals who had died—the sexual assault allegations against them, the failed prosecutions, the light sentence for Nossel—were expressed in private: private outrage, grim satisfaction, and a lack of forgiveness. At the funerals and in church services there was a lot of delicately phrased "praying for souls."

"Because no one would pray for the assholes themselves," said Kate.

Of the Chi Omicron Kappa members who died in the explosion, three came from Mossberg, as did Ashton, Summer's fifteen-year-old classmate who had lured Ana to the party. They were all buried the same Saturday. A cortege of four hearses, each carrying a body, drove slowly up Main Street, before the vehicles peeled off in turn to go to different churches for the funeral services. The day came to be enshrined in Mossberg's history—not for collective grief, but for something quite unexpected.

Chi Omicron Kappa was never on the radar of the general community, but to teenage girls it had been a topic of conversation for months on social media, in the schoolyard and at sleepovers. After the explosion, the intensity of posts, chats, and whispering intensified, reaching a crescendo the week leading up to the funerals, when more and more girls tweeted how they had been approached by fraternity members to attend their parties and, in some cases, had attended—and suffered the consequences. Most girls hadn't reported it because they thought no adult would believe them. And indeed when a small number had tried to report it, they had not been believed.

No one quite remembered who first suggested it, but it was decided that action was needed to take attention away from the perpetrators' deaths and refocus it on what they had done in life. On the day of the funerals, 300 schoolgirls in small groups lined the route on both sides of Main Street, wearing coats—innocuous enough on a late fall day, but underneath, pinned to their backs, were signs. As the hearses approached, they took off their coats, and turned their backs to the coffins to reveal their slogans:

Rapists die!
No pity!
Rot in hell!
End sexual assault!
We hate you!
We survived!
#MeToo!

The local TV station, which had a camera crew filming the cortege from behind and above, captured the whole spectacle: girls turning their backs like a Mexican wave as the cars approached. The protest was an earthquake through Mossberg's social fabric. Families of the dead were aghast that anyone was prepared to comment so publicly about their sons. Adults generally were blindsided. Who had organized the protest? Why didn't anyone know about it? Frantic 911 calls reported hysterical girls out of control. Most outraged of all were the men who ran the town.

Much to Arlene Childs' chagrin, her own granddaughter Greta had participated in the demonstration. Arlene sat Greta down to explain the problem, taking a hard look at her scowling face and two blond plaits, and wondering where to start. After the shambles of the march, Arlene was feeling weary of organizing both the community and her family.

Greta was defiant. "But Grandma, those guys were creeps! At school we talked about how they tried to get us to go to their parties. We know what happened there. That's why we held those signs."

"Honey, the signs you girls held are just the start of the problem. Funerals are a sacred ritual, no matter who the person is."

"But—"

"Let me finish. Second, those expressions you wore. Three hundred young women scowling—just like you are now. It's unattractive."

Greta persisted. "But those guys did terrible things!"

"Aha. *This* is the real issue. Whatever they may have done, *you* spilled the beans and told everyone. Nobody likes being humiliated in that way."

These words from her beloved Grandma were like a blow to Greta's head. "We spoke up about a crime!" she sputtered.

"*Now* we're at the heart of the problem: your act of judgment. Fifteen-year-old girls presuming to hold men accountable. They are our providers and our protectors."

"But ... why can't we protect ourselves?"

"Then what would be the point of protectors?" Arlene replied impatiently. "All those young men in uniform."

Greta tried another tack. "Well, then who's the enemy?"

"There's *always* an enemy!" Arlene swept her arm in a wide arc. "Across that river and behind those hills, there are people biding their time to get into Mossberg. And I'm not just talking about Democrats ..." Arlene gave Greta a knowing look.

Greta had no idea what Arlene was talking about.

Arlene tried again in a gentler tone. "That demonstration humiliated the authorities by usurping their role. If we have rapists running around, *they* decide what should happen, not you. It was a violation."

Greta was genuinely confused. "A violation of what?"

"*Of social order!*" Arlene thundered. She'd had enough of her uncomprehending granddaughter. "I will *instruct* your parents to ground you for three months and"—Arlene paused to draw breath—"I will write to the *Gazette* to say that all God-fearing parents should do the same for any girl involved in your so-called demonstration. It was pure insolence."

39

As THEY HAD done after Preston Brock's death, Kate, Seyram, and Carly followed their regular routines after the Chi Omicron Kappa attack, to avoid raising suspicions. Confession again proved a psychological hurdle for Seyram until a turn of events meant she no longer needed to worry about this.

Keeping in mind the desire to maintain normalcy, Kate headed to Seyram's house around midday the day after the funerals, to return the roasting pan. She tucked it under her arm and rang the doorbell. Nana answered.

"Hello, Aunt Kate."

"Hello, sweetie. I like your new braids."

"Mom put them in for church this morning."

"How was church?"

"We quit."

This was the most improbable thing ever announced about the Boateng family.

"Quit?"

"Mom and Father O'Connor had an argument."

"Is she around?"

"She's in bed."

"Is she sick? Where's Daddy?"

"Mom said she's on strike, so Daddy and Kofi went to bring back lunch."

"What's happened?"

"Father O'Connor wanted us to pray for the souls of those men who died in the explosion, but after mass mom told him it was just as important to pray for victims of rape." Nana told the story deadpan. "Then Father O'Connor said to Mom, 'What business does a female have going into a fraternity house?' and Mom said, 'I've been asking myself that question when I walk into this church every Sunday.' Then Father O'Connor said equating the Church with a fraternity is blasphemous, so Mom said 'Good day, Father. We are leaving your church.' Mom says we're going to the Baptists because they accept lady priests."

Kate absorbed this information. "How do you feel about that?"

"Can lady priests wear braids?"

"I'm sure they can." Kate smiled, but she was thinking about Seyram. "Run upstairs and tell Mom I'm here. Say I'm coming up in two minutes whether she likes it or not."

Kate walked into the bedroom and perched on the edge of the bed. Seyram lay on her side, facing away. Kate rubbed Seyram's back. "I brought you back that roasting pan. I figured you'll need it for Thanksgiving."

Silence.

"Are you doing turkey again?"

"No," replied Seyram, not moving. "The kids have gone vegetarian."

"What?"

Seyram gave a sigh. "Nana wants to stop climate change, and after we bought Kofi that rabbit he's decided he's a vegetarian."

Kate suppressed a smile. "Nana told me what happened with Father O'Connor," she said in a gentle voice.

"What do you care?" said Seyram. "You don't even believe in God."

"I believe in you."

Seyram sat up. "After mass we greeted Father O'Connor as usual. I told him we should pray for the victims of rape, not just the souls of the rapists. Nana piped up and asked, 'What's rape?'—I guess I shouldn't have raised the subject in front of her, but I was so mad after his sermon. Then he *admonished* Nana and said 'Little girls should be quiet.' I guess he thought we were having an adults' theological conversation about forgiveness, but that comment made me see red. Girls are supposed to pray for the souls of perpetrators but can't even ask questions about what they did?!"

"Nana told me the rest. She said you equated the Church with a frat house." Kate chortled.

"It's not funny. I received confirmation in that church. I was supposed to be confirmed in Ghana, but we came to America. It was my family's first big community event here. I started going to that church thirty-six years ago."

"What does Felix think?"

"He wasn't Catholic as a kid, so it's different for him."

"Nana was excited to think that Baptist lady priests might wear braids."

"Is that what she said?" Seyram half-smiled. "That makes me feel a bit better."

"And," said Kate brightly, "you'll be able to wave your hands in the air."

Seyram shot her a look. "That's Pentecostals."

THE SAME MORNING that Kate pulled into Seyram's driveway, Wyatt Bell pulled into the Vargas family's driveway. He wasn't sure if he should be there: Ana Vargas was a minor, and how could she be anything else but traumatized after what had happened? But he knew he was onto a story about the underbelly of Mossberg—one that could change the town for good by telling its citizens the truth about Chi Omicron Kappa and the culture of impunity around sexual assault. It was a story that could make his career.

The *Gazette* knew Ana's name—its informants at the police station (Detective Schultz) and the hospital (the nurse caring for Ana) had confirmed it the day after the explosion—but the editors agreed to suppress her identity. The town fathers were keen that nothing undermined the narrative that the explosion was an awful tragedy for young college men with a brilliant future ahead of them.

Wyatt, having spent the week wading through social media sites, now realized it was all lies. He had reached out to some of the women who had posted on #MeToo, and they had tentatively agreed to speak to him. He had also managed to gain access to an incel chat room on the dark web, where he learned about a planned inaugural award night celebrating violence against women. This network and event appeared to have links to Mossberg College. However, the explosion had made him realize there was one witness whose account was needed to create a compelling alternative narrative about the Mossberg deaths.

Pulling his coat close against the gray skies and cold, he knocked on the Vargas's door. He mentally rehearsed his request to Ana's parents to let him speak to her. What had happened to her had happened to other girls, and this was an opportunity to stop it happening again. The door opened.

"Can I help you?" It was Ana.

Wyatt forgot his prepared speech. As he stood there silently, without apparent purpose, Ana became visibly nervous. He realized that to Ana, he must be like one of the frat boys: similar age, height, and race, just not as buff.

"Are your parents home?" he blurted out.

"They're at church."

"I'm sorry. I've come at a bad time." Wyatt knew he had to say something, anything, but could also tell his arrival had put Ana into a vulnerable position: alone at home, faced with a young man on her doorstep, two weeks after she'd escaped a gang rape and survived an explosion. He collected his thoughts. "My name's Wyatt. I'm a reporter. I know what the fraternity did ... what it was planning to do ..." He proffered his card. "If you ever want to talk, please call me. I want to write a story that will tell Mossberg the truth about itself. I hope you're healing ok. Thank you."

Wyatt turned and walked away. His timing had been wrong. The least he could do was not make the situation worse.

WINTER 2018

40

IT WAS SEVEN THIRTY a.m. on a chilly Sunday morning in December, and there was no longer denying winter was on its way. There was, however, a pre-holiday buzz in town as Christmas lights blinked and brightened the streets and stores.

Carly pulled into the curb opposite Kate's building, and she and Seyram unbuckled their seatbelts. The three of them were off for an early morning walk, a schedule they maintained as long as the paths stayed clear of snow. It was also part of following a regular schedule of activities to keep up appearances.

"We're early," said Seyram. "Kate's probably just getting ready. Let's wait until seven forty-five like we said." They pulled their coats tight and Seyram turned on the radio.

It was during the weather report—snow was on its way— that the sound of a door opening and closing distracted them. A figure emerged from the side door to Kate's building and walked toward the corner.

Seyram saw her first. "Who's that? That's not Kate."

"Kate's got a lover!" Carly exclaimed. "This is *fantastic*." She squinted through the windscreen trying to work out who it was, and a second later let out a gasp. "What the *fuck?!*"

As soon as the person disappeared around the corner, Carly and Seyram tumbled out of the car, ran across the street, raced up the stairs two at a time and burst into Kate's apartment. Kate was in her underwear in the middle of the living room, calmly buttoning up a white shirt.

Seyram and Carly stood like bouncers, arms crossed.

Kate looked like butter wouldn't melt in her mouth. "Oh, hello there. You're early."

Carly couldn't contain herself. "*Tulip Sorenson?!*"

Kate raised an eyebrow. "Already found out her name? I guess you introduced yourselves downstairs."

"You're getting it on with *Tulip Sorenson?*"

"You sound like you know her."

Carly and Seyram looked at each other.

"Don't you know who she is?" asked Seyram.

Kate tossed her head. "What are you talking about? She's not royalty."

"She's a *beauty queen!*" exclaimed Carly. "She was Homecoming Queen and Miss Teen Mossberg, and she's captain of the college cheer squad. She did a backflip on TV when the football team made the finals!"

"Tulip has 40,000 followers on Instagram, including Nana," added Seyram. "She's the most famous person in Mossberg."

Kate pulled on her jeans. "You both seem to know her pretty well," she said drily.

"Obviously not as well as *you*," retorted Carly. "Where did you meet? Have you been swiping right without telling us?"

Kate paused. "We met at the police lineup."

Seyram clutched her head. "You are the only person *on earth* who could meet someone at a police lineup."

"Wait a minute." Carly wagged her finger. "We were there with you, and Tulip was at the far end of the line."

"Oh, for Chrissake. I went to the bathroom. She was in the stall next to me and we came out at the same time."

"And that led to a Sunday morning walk of shame weeks later for Tulip?" Carly was in disbelief.

"To be fair to Tulip," Seyram corrected Carly, "it was hardly a walk of shame. She had rockstar hair and a spring in her step."

Carly was having none of it. "You owe us an explanation."

"We … washed our hands slowly, looking in the sink, then looking in the mirror, then looking at each other looking in the mirror …" Kate was enjoying their expressions. "Then we stopped moving altogether and just looked." Kate paused. "Then I undid the top button of my shirt, then Tulip undid her top button, then I undid another of my buttons. Then she undid another of her buttons. And then … I turned and grabbed her and gave her a kiss. The whole thing lasted two minutes and we didn't say a word." Kate zipped up her jeans and smoothed her shirt.

"You did it in the *bathroom?*" Seyram was shocked.

"Oh, Seyram," Kate inhaled and looked up at the ceiling. "*Unfortunately,* I had my two besties waiting for me, so I stopped and said, 'Come to Downtown Hardware on Main when it closes at six thirty tomorrow evening.' And she did."

"So, you've been—ahem—*together*, for a month?" Carly shook her head. "Kate Bajwa, you never, ever, cease to surprise me."

<h1 style="text-align:center">41</h1>

AGENT FINCHER WAS not in a good mood. He'd been warning Mossberg authorities for months that they may have a serial killer on their hands. No one had listened—no one had *wanted* to listen. This time he was going to tell it straight. He'd tried to have that meeting with Chief Delaney and the council about warning potential targets, but that had been derailed by the explosion at Chi Omicron Kappa. Now he had called a meeting with Chief Delaney and the mayor to lay out his concerns and to give them an ultimatum: either they take him seriously or they work with someone else.

"I'm not going to beat around the bush. If you look at the profile of every person who has died in Mossberg since Branson Vanburg in April, it is almost identical: young, white, male, excellent at sport. I could add other words, like cocky, entitled, and having a history of sexual assault. The only exception was the fifteen-year-old kid who died in the frat house explosion, and he was there because he brought the girl they were about to abuse."

Mayor Konig's face was crimson. "That's an insult—"

"Let me finish!" Fincher was in no mood for interruptions and knew he answered ultimately to the Pittsburgh FBI office and not the Mossberg Police, even though he had to get along with them for operational reasons. "I'm not saying they deserved to die, but I'm also not going to pretend they were angels. In fact, I would urge you to open an investigation into possible human trafficking related to parties that Chi Omicron Kappa held and girls they brought to those parties—but that is a decision for Chief Delaney. As far as the FBI is concerned, you have one or more serial killers in this town who seek out victims with a specific profile. They are not after young women, or old women, or any woman. They are after jocks. Stopping the serial killers is the FBI's business—in cooperation with the Mossberg authorities. Stopping whatever those men are doing to attract the attention of the serial killer or killers is *your* business."

Chief Delaney and Mayor Konig sat stunned at being spoken to like this; at the uncomfortable truth.

"What are you suggesting we do?" sputtered the mayor.

"We have a duty to warn people they may be in danger," said Fincher. "I'd start with that bunch of incels in the college residence out of town, as disgusting as they are. They're not jocks, but I'm sure that whoever is killing young men in this town would not approve of them."

"What am I supposed to tell the town?" asked Konig. "*Lock up your sons. There's a killer lady on the loose?*"

"More or less, yes. In particular, anyone who fits the profile of a jock or has a history of sexual assault."

"Politically, that is a nonstarter. This community will not accept that half their young people should be afraid to go out at night or to walk home alone. I'll get voted out of office and

Chief Delaney here will be forced to resign. There'll be a revolution."

"Maybe that's what this community needs." The words were out before Fincher could stop them, and he knew he had gone too far.

Silence.

"Thank you, Agent Fincher," said Mayor Konig stiffly.

"Yes, thank you, Agent Fincher," echoed Chief Delaney. "I think the Mossberg Police can handle it from this point going forward. If you think there are specific people in this community who need to be warned, you go ahead and do that. I think Mayor Konig will agree, however," Delaney looked at Konig, "that there is no need to issue a general notice of alarm to the public."

FINCHER DROVE UP to the gate and reached out of his window to press the buzzer. He'd navigated the security of plenty of homes, businesses, and other installations. *Usually a sign of wanting to hide or protect something,* he mused, which reminded him that this expedition to warn a bunch of contemptible college guys that they might be the target of an assassin was a good idea, regardless of what Mayor Konig and Chief Delaney thought.

Fincher had called his superior in Pittsburgh an hour earlier to say that his relationship with the local police had broken down and he could no longer contribute effectively to the investigation. His superior, familiar with fraught relationships between the FBI and local police, took it in his stride. "Should I assign someone else? With that many deaths, we've really got to keep boots on the ground."

"Yes, sir. The problem is me. I overstepped the mark this morning and they don't want my input anymore. You need to assign someone else to the investigation, although I'd also advise you to have the FBI take it over. My opinion of the local police is pretty low, and unfortunately they've become aware of that. I'm sorry I screwed up."

After this call, Fincher had driven to Mossberg College to have an urgent meeting with President Gutmann.

"Dr. Gutmann, I know that young men in this town have already started to modify their behavior, but I have grave concern for the safety of male students off campus, and possibly on campus too. In particular, I have concern that sporting types are being targeted by one or more murderers in this town. My advice to you is for the college to issue an unambiguous communiqué to all male students to exercise the utmost caution when outside of their homes or dorms. They should be personally aware of their surroundings at all times and take safety precautions. If traveling at night, they should travel in small groups in a vehicle."

Susan Gutmann received the message with alarm, but thanked Fincher for the warning.

Fincher continued, "Mossberg Police have a different understanding of the risks. However, given our previous meetings, I feel duty bound to tell you that I fear there may be more killings in this community. That said, I will no longer be working on this matter and am returning to Pittsburgh this afternoon." It was a relief to say those words.

THE WHIRRING OF a security camera as it moved to focus on him more directly brought Fincher back to the task at hand.

"This is private property," came a voice through the buzzer. "What do you want?"

Fincher recognized the voice of 'Cody,' the young man he'd met in May when he first came to Mossberg to investigate the origin of misogynistic hate speech being posted on the local newspaper website and social media.

"I'm Agent Ted Fincher from the Federal Bureau of Investigation in Pittsburgh. It's Cody, isn't it? I think we met back in May. I tried to call earlier but didn't get through to anyone. Are you available for a quick conversation?"

"I remember you, Agent Fincher. I'm not sure we have anything more to discuss."

Fincher kept a neutral expression, conscious he was being filmed. He despised these men. "I believe you and the other residents of this estate may be in danger. Can you come to the gate so I can explain? It won't take a minute."

"Wait there," said Cody.

Little shit, thought Fincher. He had done a background profile on Cody: twenty-four years old; doing a master's in engineering; some kind of leadership role at Opus Steel House; no links to organized crime or established hate groups; no prior convictions; no social media profile under his own name, but several Facebook and Instagram accounts under aliases and several more aliases on the dark web; a prolific poster on incel sites using pseudonyms. Fincher got out of the car, buttoning his coat against the chill, and paced the length of the ten-foot-high wrought iron gates. The security camera followed his movements.

A full ten minutes later, a thin hunched figure appeared in the distance, and Cody eventually sauntered up to the gate. He looked suspiciously at Fincher through the steel bars.

Fincher felt he was doing the residents a favor by simply being there and had no interest in playing games. "Cody, I'll make this brief. As you know, there have been many deaths of young men in this community, most recently the explosion at the Chi Omicron Kappa fraternity. I believe these were deliberately targeted killings, possibly by one or more female persons."

"You think female *persons* were behind this?" exclaimed Cody. Fincher's acknowledgement of women's personhood was all Cody needed to know that Fincher was on the other side. He'd already spied Fincher's wedding ring: a good-looking man selected by a woman for sex, reducing opportunities for Cody and other incels.

"You and I both know that many residents of Opus Steel are part of an incel group," continued Fincher. "It is likely that whoever is killing jocks in Mossberg does not … *appreciate* … your activities. You may be in danger. I can see you have a lot of security here, but you should increase measures around your personal safety when you leave the residence." Fincher watched Cody absorb these words. "That's all. I have no additional information."

Seething with victimhood, Cody gritted his teeth. "Thank you, Agent Fincher. Have a good drive back to your wife." He turned on his heel and walked up the driveway to the mansion when he was suddenly overcome by a realization. *Fincher put us in the same category as those fraternity jocks*, Cody thought. *Some killer is so impressed by us, they want to target us.* He reveled in the adrenalin rush.

42

FOR MONTHS CARLY had been working on a collection for her forthcoming exhibition, to be held at the campus art center. While her expensive dinner sets brought in the bread, exhibitions were where Carly let loose. This exhibition, titled "Vessel," featured sixty pitchers in fantastical shapes—human form, animals, trees, flowers, and one, to the perplexity of visitors, in the shape of a very large hand grenade—each with a distinctive glaze. It was to be a meditation on how form carries meaning.

As elsewhere, Mossberg's arts calendar got crowded when the weather became cold and people headed indoors. On this December night, there had been an extra vibe, as though life itself had become lighter for half the denizens of Mossberg, especially with the holidays so close. Entry to the official opening was by invitation only, and the venue was packed. Susan Gutmann gave the opening speech.

By nine o'clock, the evening started to wind up and Carly was exhausted. Her voice was hoarse from meeting and greeting, her back was sore from standing in heels, and her brain was tired from fielding questions about her technique and sources of inspiration. All she wanted to do was rest.

Kate and Seyram, who had been giving her space, loomed out of the crowd, carrying a glass of champagne and a glass of sparkling water respectively.

"*Thank* you!" Carly gulped down the water. "That's much better. Now give me the champagne." She took a sip, then a deep breath. "My impression is that it went pretty well. Am I being … overconfident?"

"Carly, it's a-*ma*-zing!" exclaimed Kate.

"You're amazing!" said Seyram.

"You know, Seyram, you were welcome to bring Felix. And, Kate, I was kind of hoping you'd bring Tulip." Carly's eyes twinkled.

"I'm not sure we're at that stage yet, Schumer."

"She might have done a cartwheel and smashed something," said Seyram.

"Nothing wrong with youthful exuberance, Boateng."

"Look out, you two," said Carly. "President Guttman's coming. I haven't had a proper chance to speak to her yet."

"Should we leave you alone while you talk?" asked Seyram.

"No!" Carly grabbed Seyram's arm. "Stay here. I'll try to make it short and introduce you."

Susan Gutmann walked over with a big smile and an extended hand. "Carly! We haven't had a chance to talk properly yet, but it's been wonderful to meet you in person. And your work is incredible! I'm so grateful you chose to hold your exhibition here."

Carly blushed. "Thanks, Susan, that's kind of you. I love doing the work, of course, but it's always gratifying when people like it. Have you met my friends? This is Seyram and this is Kate."

"Are you also artists? I'm discovering Mossberg has all these talented people tucked away and I'd love for the college to do more events like this."

"I run the hematology clinic in town," said Seyram.

"I manage Downtown Hardware on Main Street," said Kate. "We supply a lot of the tools for the college's fine arts program."

"Lovely to meet you both. You know, Carly," Gutmann continued, "one day we're going to have an even better exhibition space for you. This space is lovely, but its size limits how many can attend events such as these."

Carly's curiosity was piqued. "Are you planning to construct a new venue?" New college buildings cost a fortune and required years of planning, so she was surprised not to have heard this news before.

"No, in fact the college has this strange bequest, which I don't think is common knowledge. It's Opus Steel House, on a big estate just out of town built in 1885, which is on the National Register of Historic Places. It was never modified, so the original plan, structure, and fittings are intact. It was built by a steel baron as his summer getaway from Pittsburgh—like something out of *The Great Gatsby*. The Fine Arts, Theatre Arts, English, and Modern Languages Departments all tell me it's perfect for exhibitions, retreats, summer school, language intensives, and writers and artists in residence. It's even got a small amphitheater so we can do outdoor productions."

"I can't believe I've never heard of it," said Carly. "It sounds spectacular."

"The benefactor bequeathed it to Mossberg College in 1925, with the condition that the college doesn't take full control of it for one hundred years. The bequest pays for maintenance, so financially it's been no imposition on the college."

"Is it empty? What is it used for?"

"That's part of what makes it so strange. It's been a residence for 'gentlemen students'—I'm not kidding, that's how it advertises itself—who apply to the benefactor's trustees to get in. No females allowed in *at all*, even me. It's like the most backward kind of men's club. The college property manager, who dreads taking it over because of refurbishment costs, says visiting is like going back in time and finding dinosaurs, like in *Jurassic Park*."

"The problem, as I recall," said Seyram, who knew the movie well thanks to her children, "was that the dinosaurs escaped their island and terrorized the community."

"Funny you should say that," said Gutmann. "As part of my handover into the new job, I got an update from campus security. Apparently, there's a group of incels out there. The FBI traced threats and comments through a server to computers used there. Last May they sent out an agent to investigate."

"A cell of what?" asked Seyram.

"Incels. 'Involuntary celibates.' You haven't heard of them?"

"Never. What to do they do?"

"It's an online network of men, mostly young, who say they are involuntarily celibate because no woman wants to sleep with them, which is no surprise when you understand how they think. They operate on the dark web, and there's no organization as such, so it's difficult to understand them properly. But we know enough to know they believe women are property to be possessed and should have no choice deciding with whom they sleep—that's for men to decide. They think men have a right to sex, and they blame their own celibacy on women's standards for male attractiveness—standards that exclude them. It's the most perverse view of women and sexual relations imaginable."

"Wasn't it an incel guy behind that attack in Toronto earlier this year?" said Carly. "He drove a van along the sidewalk and mowed everyone down. He killed eleven people, including a ninety-four-year-old woman."

"Yes," said Gutmann, "and there was another attack in California in 2014 that killed six."

"What did the FBI agent find?" asked Kate.

"A bunch of misogynists, unfettered and probably encouraged by the alumni trustees, cyberstalking women, posting hate speech online, and downloading violent porn."

"The *New Yorker* had an article about incels recently," said Carly. "It had this shocking quote from one of their message boards, how women are just 'cum-dumpsters.' Our local newspaper employed an extra person to monitor comments posted to its stories, because every time there's an article about girls and women, especially anything with a photo of schoolgirls—gymnastics, soccer, girl scouts, you name it—horrible comments appear."

"But this is diabolical!" said Seyram, who was hearing this for the first time. "Haven't the police arrested anyone?"

"There's the rub." Gutmann grimaced. "The head of security tells me the FBI interviewed several people at the mansion. They found suspiciously good security—surveillance cameras everywhere along the driveway and around the house, as though they're trying hard to hide something or keep somebody out. Unfortunately, there wasn't enough evidence to press charges. Misogyny is not illegal, right?" said Gutmann. "As long as you don't harm anyone and there's no direct evidence you're inciting violence, there's little the college—or the police—can do about them. At least they know the FBI is now watching, although they've probably just gone even deeper into the web. It's an appalling legacy for any building and, if I had my way, I wouldn't let the residents—or the trustees—near the college community. But my hands are tied for now. Once we take control of the place, we can change the narrative."

"Where is this house, exactly?" Kate looked at the floor like she hadn't the slightest interest in the answer.

"You know the bridge before the *Welcome to Mossberg* sign as you're coming into town on the Mossberg River Road? There's a road between the bridge and the sign, that heads inland alongside a small tributary to the Mossberg River. The road leads into a private forest that backs onto Fort Byrd property. The building is right in the middle. It's a fifteen-minute drive from campus."

In a studiously calm tone, Seyram asked, "So, nobody else lives around it at all?"

"No, it's just the residents who've been allowed to live there by the trustees. The driveway is the only road in, other than an overgrown firebreak that connects to the Fort Byrd land behind it."

Kate, Seyram, and Carly flicked a glance at each other.

43

"I WISH THAT forest could come to life like something out of Narnia and strangle that goddamn mansion and everyone in it!" said Carly. They had headed back to Kate's place after the opening. "Stealing a nuke from North Dakota wasn't such a bad idea, Seyram."

"Did you hear what the trustees call the residents? *Gentlemen students!*" Seyram was equally enraged.

"And they're all just sitting out there planning how to hurt women and congratulating each other when they succeed. I wanted to smash every one of your vessels when Susan said there wasn't much that could be done." Kate spoke from the doorway to her balcony, already on her second cigarette.

"And they pick on girls," said Carly. "I want to destroy that mansion." The smell of coffee brewing wafted in from the kitchen, and she stood to bring back the mugs. "How do we do this?"

"As a note of caution, if we go after them, aren't we going beyond our terms of reference?" asked Seyram.

"Our *what?!*" said Kate and Carly.

"Our terms of reference. We agreed to go after jocks because we thought that was the quickest way to make men in this community change their behavior. Incels are the opposite of jocks. I can't stand these guys, but they're beyond our original remit."

"Seyram, you are such a nerd," said Kate. "We weren't replying to a tender notice advertising for 'Women to Attack Jocks.'"

"I just thought there might be better targets. Like that Detective Schultz. We could do a drive-by on Mossberg Police headquarters."

"But that might take out Trooper Chase too," said Carly. "He's okay."

Kate was impatient. "Forget the cops. We wanted to send a message, and we did. But online is where sexual harassers like incels continue to lurk—except when they're emboldened to commit mass murder in broad daylight. Attacking *them* will signal that using an alias on social media doesn't mean you're out of reach. Our message will go a whole lot further."

"I agree," said Carly. "Let's get 'em."

"I was just trying to be logical." Seyram was defensive. "But, in that case"—she pulled a pen and notepad from her purse—"what were Susan Gutmann's key points? She said there's loads of surveillance around the front entrance. No one else lives around. It's an isolated building in the middle of a forest. Trying to access the property by pretending we're delivering something like at Chi Omicron Kappa isn't going to cut it. They're too suspicious of strangers and they don't let women in."

"Susan mentioned a firebreak at the back."

"Leading from Fort Byrd," cautioned Kate, "which may as well be Fort Knox. It's got a checkpoint with armed guards at the entrance and a fifteen-foot fence around the perimeter. The mansion has its rear covered. They only need to guard the front. The only way in is to cut through the fence and go on foot through the forest. We're going to be vulnerable."

44

IN THE LEAD-UP to the holidays, the Mossberg community was washed by divergent tides of feeling. There was bereavement at the deaths of the Chi Omicron Kappa members, but stories circulated about their parties and what they'd done to the women and girls. Some families and individuals were in fear for their sons'—and their own—lives; a few even moved away. On the other hand, some households, especially those with teenage girls, but also single women and the LGBTQIA2S+ community, were experiencing a blossoming as harassment vanished from the streets and downtown establishments.

Henry Konig of the *Gazette* counseled his brother, Roger Konig, on the need for some kind of statement about where the community was heading. They decided Roger, as mayor, would do an interview on WMBG, Mossberg's Christian contemporary radio station, with its popular morning show presenter, Kevin Baumgartner. Baumgartner was known for his diverse guests and his ability to connect local happenings to trends in the wider world.

As advertisements played after the news, Mayor Konig was ushered into the studio and sat down in front of Baumgartner.

"… and that's the weather for this fine Friday. Remember, the long-range forecast tells us we can expect a white Christmas, but WMBG always keeps you company through rain, snow, or shine. Now, as promised, we bring you a very special guest who has steered us through what has been a tumultuous year. A man who needs no introduction. Welcome, Mayor Roger Konig."

"Thank you, Kevin, and hello listeners. It's a pleasure to be here again on Mossberg's own."

"Mayor, it's been a year of big and difficult emotions for Mossberg, with many deaths of young men. What message do you have as we approach Christmas?"

"Well, we support the families who have lost loved ones. If we stick to our American values of family and Christianity, and keep ourselves open to God's guidance, I believe we will come through this grief together and emerge stronger than ever in the New Year."

"There are many in our community—and I'm sure you've heard the stories—worried that these deaths weren't accidents," said Baumgartner. "People are saying there's an evildoer out there targeting innocent Mossbergers. Should we be afraid?"

"Kevin, I think you'll agree the battle against evil is constant. My job as mayor is to make sure Mossberg has all the resources it needs to keep families safe. I am working with the police to ensure this and, as you know, we have increased the town budget for security measures like CCTV and lighting. I am in constant communication with Police Chief Delaney, who has added extra patrols to keep us safe."

"Is there a reason the council isn't funding New Year's Eve fireworks this year? That sounds like you're worried."

"It was more a question of budget, given additional security expenses. And we didn't think it right to provide amusements after the adversities of the year."

"So, no killer on the loose in Mossberg. Is that the message?"

The interview wasn't going as Mayor Konig had planned.

"We … we are working closely with the authorities, including the FBI. Of course, I can't talk about ongoing investigations, and I encourage listeners to be prudent with their safety. However, I can assure you there is no cause for alarm over the holiday season or into the future. The situation is under control."

"There are some people, especially women, who have not always felt safe in our community. They tell me this sudden reversal of fear is a lesson for the menfolk. I'm sure you witnessed the protests during the Chi Omicron Kappa funerals. Many of those protestors attend local churches. What would you say to them?"

What the hell kind of question is that?! "Er, Kevin, I don't think we should gloat over the fear felt by others. I think that's not the message of Christmas. But—and I don't want to cast blame on anyone—it has been made clear to me that, in the past, young women have not always felt safe in Mossberg, something I may not have fully understood."

Mayor Konig was talking for his political life, but how this was happening on Christian radio he had no idea. Baumgartner, however, knew exactly what he was doing.

"In fact," continued Konig, "just last night my own wife Jenny and I spoke, and she said to me 'You have to think about this as a father. What would you want to happen if it were our girls who had been victims?' You know, Jenny has a way of clarifying things. Always has. And so, I've reflected on that overnight."

"And what did you conclude?"

"I hadn't fully appreciated that women who are ... *upset* at their interactions with men felt so strongly about it. But my wife gave me that gentle push to realize they are young women in need of a compassionate father. It made me realize I should listen harder. The Bible tells us Jesus himself was a wonderful listener, and he is an inspiration for me every day."

Mayor Konig finally came up for air, although through the studio glass the producer was glaring at Kevin and slicing a hand across his throat.

"Mayor Konig, surely you're not saying that people need to have children to have a conscience? I mean Jesus himself was never a father in the biological sense—and surely having children doesn't guarantee a conscience, anyway?"

The producer's throat-slicing became frantic.

Konig sputtered. "Ahh, err, Kevin ... well, umm, what I can say is ... parenthood ... parenthood ... makes us all *better people*. It reminds us of our American family values. Our Christian values." *Phew!*

"That's a wonderful note on which to end our morning interview with special guest, Mayor Konig: a philosophical question about morality and parenting. On WMBG Mornings we're not afraid of the heavy stuff! And, parents, you can buy your family Christmas ham and turkey from our sponsor, Gerrity's Supermarket, the home of wholesome family food …"

"What were you thinking?!" the producer asked Kevin once Konig had left the building. "The mayor is a friendly. We agreed you'd talk about all the good things the council is doing."

"The guy's a dinosaur. He pays lip service to Christian doctrine without reflecting on what it means in practice. Go to any youth camp and all they talk about is what the Bible can teach us about inequality, injustice, and global warming. They see their communities with X-ray vision and want change. Our radio show has to keep up."

Konig headed to the parking lot, feeling ambushed. He climbed into his SUV, where his dog Scottie waited, head cocked. Konig rubbed him behind the ears. "I know this is a bit scary and you don't always know what to say," said Konig to Scottie, "but Mossberg's a great town and you've got to get us through this." Scottie put his chin on Konig's lap as he started the engine to drive home.

45

FOUR HOURS LATER, in the offices of the *Gazette*, Henry Konig was thinking about his brother's interview. *How many times have I told him? You answer the questions you wished they'd asked, not the ones they actually asked!* He had, however, understood Baumgartner's message about the world changing, and pondered how the *Gazette* could respond.

"Son!" he shouted, the call reverberating down the corridor into the crammed space Wyatt shared with three other reporters. "I've got something you'll like."

Wyatt's colleagues looked at him and furrowed their brows. Wyatt shrugged in response. Everybody knew that *son*, especially when shouted, meant Wyatt. They also knew Konig never printed the stories Wyatt liked: about the community, its dynamics, and its underbelly. Wyatt valiantly kept pitching them, but he got assigned to veterans' reunions, Republican fundraisers, and fall duck and deer hunts. Wyatt knocked and entered the editor's office cautiously, wondering what *something you'll like* meant.

"Sit. We've got female troubles. That woman monitoring nasty comments about girls and ladies posted on our website, she's quitting. Says it's too disgusting. Comments are a part of our product. The community likes them, likes to post them,

305

and likes to read what everyone else posts. Not having them is a problem.”

“You going to assign that to me?” Wyatt was despondent. It wasn’t the kind of ‘something’ he wanted.

“Hell, no. You’re a reporter. You cost twice what we paid her. I want you to find out who’s posting them and why they’re posting them. An investigative piece. We’ll make it a story about how the *Gazette* is making moms and children safe.”

“What if it’s their husbands doing it?” Wyatt blurted out.

For the first time, Konig didn’t have a ready answer. “Hmm. We’ll think of something. Dads driven to evil by negligent wives. That kind of thing.”

“I’m sorry, Mr. Konig. I didn’t mean to be impertinent.” Wyatt was realizing the potential of this story. “I’d love to do it. I’m exactly the right person. What length are you looking at?”

“Well, let’s first see what you can get. But if it’s got legs, we could make it a feature piece.”

Wyatt’s heart raced. *This* is what I’ve been waiting for.

“Thank you, Mr. Konig. I won’t let you down. I’ll get on to it right away.”

“Hold your horses. There’s more. When those comments first started to appear, the FBI came to see me. They think there’s some kind of online network behind it, upsetting ladies all over the country. Involuntary celibates. Incels. Told me they traced many of the messages to that old Opus Steel estate out of town but couldn’t prove which individuals were responsible. I want you to go there, interview everyone, and find out what's going on—what they stand for. Show me what you get and we'll take it from there."

46

THE UPHEAVAL OF gender freedoms in Mossberg upset many people, some of whom had already put themselves under a self-imposed fear-driven curfew when it got dark. Online forums flourished, railing against women, LGBTQIA2S+ communities, Blacks, Democrats, Hillary, and feminists in particular.

Arriving at work early one morning, Kate was confronted by monster graffiti painted overnight on the storefront. She lit a cigarette and looked at it. Was it a threat? A challenge? An observation? Unable to decide, she went inside.

Her staff, arriving soon after, stopped in shock when they caught sight of the word. Walking into the store, they looked quickly up at Kate's office on the mezzanine, knowing she was there because her lights were on.

"What do we do? Should we just clean it off?" someone whispered.

"She'll tell us when she's ready," another whispered back.

At ten a.m., Juneeta, Kate's mom, who frequently brought refreshments for staff, arrived. Kate heard her panting up the stairs and braced in anticipation of a scene. The door opened and Juneeta, clutching a box of samosas and a thermos of chai, burst into her office.

"There's a terrible word painted on your storefront!"

Kate looked at Juneeta, then gave a hard exhalation. "Mom, the word is *dyke*. D-y-k-e."

"I know how to spell."

"It's another word for lesbian."

"I know that too."

"The technical term is homosexual."

"I also read the newspapers."

"Is it so terrible?"

"It's public!" Juneeta hissed. "You should erase it. What would the family think?"

"You're my family."

Juneeta softened. She calmed her breath, then poured chai from the thermos into a cup and pushed it over to Kate's side of the desk. "Katiya." Her voice quavered "I just want you to be happy."

Kate sat stone-faced, arms crossed. "What makes you think I'm not happy?"

"Sometimes you're not very ... welcoming. Like now."

"*Welcoming?*" Kate gave Juneeta a look that would kill a cat. "Mom, I'm fifty-one. I know how I want to live my life, and I think you do too. Thanks for the chai, but I've got work to do." Then it was Kate's turn to soften. "Sorry, I didn't mean it like that. Really, I love it when you drop by, and thanks again for the chai."

At lunchtime, Kate went outside and contemplated the graffiti, taking long slow drags on her cigarette. She pulled out her phone and made a call.

"It's Kate. How's Florida?"

"Hiya, Kate. Florida is paradise," came the reply. "How's Mossberg? I keep hearing about those murders."

"Well, silver lining, right? Every man stuck at home is repairing the kitchen cabinets, renovating the basement, or painting the house. We're selling tools and materials by the truckload. Started a delivery service too, for the fellas afraid to come downtown. The money's rolling in."

"So, what can I do for you? You after another pay rise for the staff?"

"We got graffitied last night," replied Kate. "Big letters."

"Nothing against Trump, I hope. I'm going to a fundraiser for him tonight. Can't you just clean it off?"

"I was thinking we may be able to use it in advertising. Are you happy for me to try something out?"

"Kate, in my experience you've got rock-solid judgement when it comes to business. Keep the profits coming and I'll stay happy in Florida."

"Thanks, D.T. I appreciate it."

Hardware stores are frequently staffed by tradesmen knowledgeable about products and techniques, but who no longer have the physical fitness to participate in their trade. Downtown Hardware was no different, and Kate had an encyclopedic knowledge of each employee's skills. She walked back inside and went to the paint counter, staffed by a former painter.

"Tully, I've got a job for you." She grabbed a selection of paint color cards and handed them to him. "I need about a gallon of exterior paint for brickwork in each of these colors, and"—she scribbled two words on a piece of paper—"I need you to incorporate the graffiti outside into this. Similar style, same size."

Tully gave her a quizzical expression, which Kate ignored.

Kate then went to the electrical section, where she found Jessie, a former electrician who had kept up his license. "Jess, I need strings of lights in these colors." She handed him another set of paint cards, then drew a sign with dimensions on a scrap of paper and gave it to him. She walked along the store's lights display aisle, which had a full selection thanks to the approaching holidays, and pulled off some more samples. "And I want enough strands of these samples to outline the whole thing."

"Katie, that's a shitload of lights!" said Jessie.

"Tully's going to prep the wall today, paint tomorrow, and then I want you to attach the lights the day after that. We'll need them on a timer, connected to outdoor speakers, with an extension cord to a computer so we can synchronize everything. Friday afternoon, we'll turn them on."

Kate next went to the crafts section. "Nelmy, I need to you to make me a music mix." Nelmy had a second job as a DJ. "I'll pay you extra." Kate scribbled yet another list and handed it over. "I want these specific songs, mixed with a selection from these genres, to synchronize with the lights Tully's going to hook up."

"Umm, Kate, this is a weird mix …" Nelmy called after Kate, who disappeared up the stairs back to her office.

That Friday, as December's early dusk set in, there was a buzz among staff and customers in the store. Intrigued by the working bee at the front of the store for the past few days, staff and customers had been asking each other what was going on, especially because the graffiti that had been so prominent on the storefront had been hidden by scaffolding and a tarp. The store's social media pages had told people to come at four p.m. for the unveiling of its new holiday light display, something Kate secretly hoped would be more of an advertisement. A fresh lights display was exactly the kind of family-themed story the *Gazette* wanted after the endless reporting on killings. It sent an intern reporter from its women's page to do a spread.

Juneeta, never one to miss a moment of family pride, had joined the crowd, although she noted that Kate seemed to avoid her. Juneeta regaled the journalist with stories of Kate's brothers' achievements at university, in business, and as family men.

Kate stood on a stepladder. "OK, folks!" she announced to the assembled crowd.

"That's my daughter!" Juneeta whispered to the reporter.

"Thank you all for coming. We wanted to do something different this year—something that picked up on the new atmosphere in town to help us celebrate the holidays. I hope you enjoy the show."

Kate turned to Tully and Nelmy. "Tully, pull down the tarp. Nelmy, hit the music."

The tarpaulin dropped as lights flashed to reveal the sign, ten feet high by twenty-five feet wide:

DYKES
WELCOME

The crowd's collective jaw dropped.

Each letter had been painted a different color of the rainbow—red, orange, yellow, green, blue, and violet—and edged in similarly colored fairy lights. The entire display was framed in a double border of crimson chili lights and marigold flower lights. And so the sign flashed:

DYKES—WELCOME
WELCOME—DYKES
DYKES—WELCOME—DYKES
WELCOME—WELCOME—WELCOME—DYKES—
DYKES —DYKES
WE—WELCOME—D—Y—K—E—S

Nelmy started the soundtrack: "Girls Just Wanna Have Fun," then "Thriller," then "Footloose," then a whole bunch of Bollywood hits, then Christmas classics like "Feliz

Navidad," "Silent Night," and "Jingle Bells," then a chaotic mix of eighties, Bollywood, and Christmas tunes. The flashing lights ebbed and flowed with the music, the chili and marigold border lights ran first in parallel, then in opposite directions, then burst into crazy flashes before everything stopped for thirty seconds at the end of the cycle.

"Call an ambulance!" shouted someone in the crowd. Juneeta had fainted.

47

EMILY SETTLED HERSELF into her chair and waited for the professor to arrive in the lecture hall. She was loving her Master of Public Health program, most of all because it attracted students from such diverse backgrounds. A woman she had vague recollections of meeting somewhere sat down a bit further along. Remembering her Midwest manners, Emily turned to greet her.

"Hi, I'm Emily. Are you a health major? I'm sure we've met before."

"I'm Beth. I'm in the Law & Society Program. I think we met at a bar downtown a few months ago. I was with my friends Tanisha and Bao."

"Now I remember! I'd forgotten you were in this course. Most of us have a nursing or health background."

"I'm doing my master's on how the women's movement has changed American institutions. I want to focus on health policy, and I found this class. What about you?"

"Geriatric care. Way more fun than it sounds."

"You from Pennsylvania?"

"No, Des Moines. Iowa."

"How are you settling in? I'm from New York so I found Mossberg pretty conservative, but I guess the Midwest is too."

"I'm loving it. I expected to like the health program because it has such a great reputation, but I never thought I'd say that about the town itself."

"It wasn't always like this. That evening we bumped into each other was an eye-opener. What does your boyfriend do again? Wasn't he writing a paper or something about feminism?"

"Oh, no, he's not a student. He's a reporter with the *Gazette*."

"The *Gazette*?" Beth nearly choked. "I must have drunk too much when we met and blanked that part of the conversation out!" She caught herself. "Sorry ... I didn't mean it to come out like that."

"That's OK. It drives him crazy too. He can't stand their editorial line, but he was also fed up with writing about hogs back home. He's finally been given an investigative story."

"What's the story? Are you allowed to say?"

"Sure. Have you heard of incels?"

"Those creepy guys who think it's their right to have sex with women?"

"You got it. Apparently, a whole bunch of them live at a weird college residence—called the Steel Mansion or something—out of town. Wyatt—that's my boyfriend—heard they're having an inaugural awards night on New Year's Eve and he's trying to get himself invited so he can go undercover."

"An *awards* night?! What, for all the horrible things they do?"

"I know, they're the worst. Oh, here's the professor—nice chatting. Let me know if you know any incels who could invite Wyatt to their party!"

After the lecture, Beth headed to Sisterhood House, where she was attending a committee meeting to plan a new budget push for the following year. She parked outside, thinking about her conversation with Emily. It upset her that despite everything she'd learnt about feminism's gains and the work done by organizations like Sisterhood House, she still let examples of such men get to her. *Why can't I be happy with what we've achieved? Just for a day.*

Get a grip, Beth told herself, and walked into the meeting room, to be greeted by Grace and Carly, who were waiting for the other committee members.

"Hi, Beth," said Grace "the others will be here soon."

Carly noticed Beth was pensive. "How are you doing?"

"I'm OK," came the half-hearted reply. "Sometimes I feel it's two steps forward, one step back with the women's movement."

"What's the step back?" asked Grace.

"Do you know incels? Those guys who say they're involuntary celibates because their right to have sex with women isn't being recognized?"

"I know them," said Grace. "They dress up hurting women as an ideology."

"A classmate told me today there's a bunch of them at some old mansion outside Mossberg. They're organizing an inaugural awards night for terrible things done to women. It's so depressing."

Carly pricked up her ears. "When's the awards night?"

"New Year's Eve."

"Will you excuse me for a minute? I'll just go to the restroom before the others arrive." Carly fumbled with her phone in the cubicle and sent a text: *Which of you has the roasting pan? Bring it to coffee after work tomorrow. Usual place.*

"BETH DEFINITELY SAID an awards night on 'New Year's Eve' and mentioned a 'steel mansion.' It's got to be the same place," said Carly, "and that's our date. It's the perfect time to attack. They'll all be there for the event."

"We should still try to confirm it." Seyram sipped her coffee.

"Imagine if all the residents have gone home for the holidays and we shoot up an empty building because we've got the wrong date," said Kate.

"Shhh, keep it down," whispered Carly, glancing around Whole Foods.

"It's an awards night, right? A big deal," mused Seyram. "They're going to have food and alcohol."

"The caterers!" said Kate. "A bunch of young guys isn't going to have a potluck supper. If we find out who's doing the catering, we might be able to confirm it with them."

"OK, but who?" asked Seyram. "Not Vegetarian. Not Indian. Not Thai. Not Chinese."

"Possibly Mexican. Possibly pizza. Possibly burgers," added Carly.

"They're not really awards night kinds of food. This is their fancy dinner for the year." Seyram looked thoughtful. "Barbecue!" she slapped the table. "It's the obvious choice. It's what Felix always wants to eat watching the Super Bowl."

"We just sold electrical wiring to Southern Ribs and Steak for an expanded kitchen. We could start by contacting them, but how do we confirm they're the caterers and what the date is?"

"I can do this," said Carly, who, despite lacking confidence in some areas of life, was supremely sure of her gift of the gab. She reached for her phone and pressed the number, waiting for it to ring. Kate and Seyram could faintly hear the conversation on the other end of the line.

"Southern Ribs and Steak," came a singsong female voice. "How can I help you today?"

"Oh, hi. I'm sorry to bother you, but my son is organizing a party for New Year's Eve, and I'm worried he hasn't ordered enough food. Could you possibly confirm the order? The address is the Opus Steel Mansion. It's his college residence."

"Just a sec … Let me see. December thirty-first … You must be Cody's mom. We've got an order for the ribs and steak banquet for fifty, plus desserts. Delivery at six p.m. Does that sound right?"

"Fifty people. Thank goodness. By the way, if Cody asks, would you mind not telling him I checked up? You know what kids are like—they don't want their moms interfering!"

"I hear you, ma'am," came the reply. "Have a nice evening."

"Done. Date, location, and number attending." Carly had a grenade-launcher glint in her eye.

48

IT WAS EIGHT THIRTY p.m., the Friday before Christmas, and Kate, Seyram, and Carly were sitting in Kate's living room.

"Thank God for cinemas," said Carly. "Summer's seeing *A Star is Born*. She's in love with Bradley Cooper and wants to be Lady Gaga."

"That's what Nana wanted to see, but she got outvoted by the boys. They're seeing *Black Panther* for the third time."

"Are you finished with the curries? Mom will be disappointed if there are leftovers."

"I cannot eat another mouthful," said Seyram. "Has she forgiven you for—what did the *Gazette* call it?—the *Outrage on Main Street*?"

"*Christmas Lights Shock Fells Crowd*," added Carly. Your mom's fainting scene almost upstaged the display."

"I'm sure that's what she intended," said Kate. "Anyway, Mom brought me the curries. That was her *I forgive you*. I told her she was the best cook ever, and that was my mea culpa. Not that I regret anything."

"Does D.T. know?" asked Seyram.

"Sales were up six percent on the same week from last year, and we're introducing a new line of *Dykes welcome* T-shirts, caps, and mugs, and starter toolkits for lesbians and housewives. He couldn't be happier. Meanwhile I've been interviewed by three gay magazines and the Northeastern Advertising Industry Journal."

Carly laughed, choking on her drink. "Kate Bajwa, I am so glad you are my friend." She got up and gave her a kiss on the cheek. "I'm going to get more wine. I'll bring you another Corona. Let's pull out the maps and figure out how we're going to do this."

Carly returned with the drinks and they stood around the dining room table with poster-size enlargements of Opus Steel House, downloaded from Google, as well as a large-scale map of the area, laid out under the light.

"Yesterday, I pulled every invoice for the mansion," said Kate. Over the past two years they've bought state-of-the-art surveillance cameras for entrances and driveways—even motion detectors. We know from Google images of the entrance that they've got a high chain-link fence stretching both sides, which probably means around the property. And we can assume no female has any chance of being admitted entry unless she's bound and gagged."

"What's more," continued Seyram, "although there's a firebreak trail from the rear, here, that leads to the boundary. The mansion may as well be against a cliff: they're snuggled into Fort Byrd property and only need to guard the front.

Carly took up the baton. "But we know they're going to have an awards ceremony, and everyone is surely going to be focused on that after it starts. We don't know the exact time, but my guess is by nine o'clock they'll be distracted."

Seyram was scrutinizing the large-scale map. "Look, here." She traced a finger on the map. "There's another firebreak to the west of the one leading from Fort Byrd to the mansion, only this one is on public land. The distance between the two trails, and then up to the mansion is about a mile."

"I can get wire cutters to get through the chain mesh between the first and second firebreaks," said Kate.

"And we can use my car," said Seyram. "It's got tinted windows so no one would recognize us, especially at night." She pointed at the map. "We can park on the first firebreak, then go through the woods to the second one. We'll have to get over this tributary that is in between, but the map shows it is narrow here at this point," Seyram tapped the map, "so we should be able to step or jump across it. Taking this route will add ten minutes to our walk, but it's safer than trying to park too close. Then we can approach the mansion on the firebreak leading from Fort Byrd. They won't be expecting anyone to come from the rear."

"This is sounding like a plan," said Kate. "If we approach while they're waiting for the awards to start, or just after, no one is going to be monitoring the surveillance cameras. And if they are, surely it's the driveway they're going to watch? We still need balaclavas and coveralls, though. They'll capture us on video at some stage when we approach the mansion, and the video will be stored somewhere. This means we'll be filmed, and we don't want to be identified."

"I'll burn the clothing in the kiln afterward." Carly turned to Kate. "Weapons?"

"The Berettas. The three from Giovanni's dad's armory."

"You remember, right, that I've fired a gun *once*, other than the grenade launcher?"

"And that I *didn't* shoot the lions," added Seyram.

"We don't even need to kill them. We want to break up their party and send a message. Destroy the whole residence if we have to—like the frat house. Which brings me to how we're going to do it. You need a firm stance and a strong grip, but if we rest our forearms on something, like a window ledge, we'll be fine. Seyram, tell us what you found out and I'll explain."

"I got a book out of the library on local historic homes, although funnily enough it was checked out and I had to get the library to recall it. It had photos of the mansion's exterior and interior, as well as a floor plan. The only place that could fit fifty people for an event like a dinner or ceremony is the ballroom. Here's a copy of the floor plan."

"I can't see them being anywhere else other than the ballroom at that moment," said Kate. "Creep up to the external walls of the ballroom and shoot out the windows. When they realize they're surrounded, I want them to *freak*; to shit their pants and scatter. Afterward, we throw in a few of your grandfather's Molotov cocktails and the place should go up in smoke."

"There's another problem," said Carly. "It's New Year's Eve. How do we get away from everyone?"

"I've thought about that," said Kate. "The council refused to fund any public events, but businesses downtown are paying for a kids' fireworks show along the river at nine o'clock and then another for adults at midnight. The council hasn't cottoned on yet that a whole different demographic is actually going out more than before. The fireworks will create the perfect cover. You two need to take the family along, lose the kids and Felix, then we absent ourselves for a couple of hours and return after ten."

"We'll be able to say honestly that we had an exciting time," said Carly. "What about an alibi in case we're caught on CCTV or we get interviewed by that FBI Agent? We know he's onto us."

Kate thought for a minute. "We just say we were fed up with the carnival crowd and drove out of town to have a quiet drink to celebrate. It's not much of an alibi, but it's vague enough to work."

49

WYATT PULLED UP to the gates of Opus Steel House at six thirty p.m., his allocated arrival time on New Year's Eve. He'd worked all afternoon with Henry Konig, going over the information and observations the *Gazette* needed for an article. Wyatt left the building to go home to shower and change with Konig's final words ringing in his ears: "Son, I want that story if it is the last thing you ever write!"

Damp, dark, leafless trees hung over the double gates and along the driveway, creating a tunnel effect, toward the mansion, which was out of view.

Having finally secured an invitation to the awards night from Cody, he was having mixed feelings about what he was about to do. From his internet searches, from viewing chat sessions on the dark web, and an initial WhatsApp conversation with Cody, who had cautiously agreed to meet him on condition of anonymity, Wyatt had learnt that he didn't like these guys. The chat with Cody had got him the invitation, but it had been an unsettling experience. Cody had asked him about his sexual activity and had been fishing for signs that Wyatt may, in fact, not hate women.

Wyatt also felt out of his depth, ethically: compromised by his undercover status—he wasn't used to hiding who he was— but also needing to say horrible things he didn't believe about women, in order to ingratiate himself with Cody. He wondered whether he was cut out to be an investigative journalist after all.

He pressed the buzzer and waited for a response. Two security cameras on poles, one on each side of the entrance, whirred to point directly at him, and Wyatt could see another camera directly above the buzzer itself.

"Yes?" came a voice.

"Hi, it's Samurai Twenty-Four." It was the alias Wyatt gave himself on incel chats. No one used their real name, and Samurais 1 to 23 had already been taken. "I'm here for the awards night."

"What's the code?"

Wyatt had nearly forgotten he needed to give a password. "V for Victory."

"Just a minute. I need to check the list."

Wyatt waited in trepidation, visualizing the gates as a mouth opening to devour him.

50

At eight fifteen p.m., Seyram, Carly and Kate rendezvoused as planned on a downtown backstreet. They could hear the noise of the happy crowd in the distance.

"Any trouble getting away?" asked Kate.

"Summer said bye the instant we arrived, then vanished."

"Nana did the same, then Kofi begged Felix to take him to the jumping castle. Easiest escape ever," said Seyram.

"Remember, phones off from now until we're back downtown," said Kate. If we get split up, we send a WhatsApp tomorrow about the roasting pan, with a time, and meet in Whole Foods."

They drove through the backstreets to get to the Mossberg River Road. There was no traffic: people were already safely at the fireworks viewing venue or another destination, or staying home in fear. Seyram turned into the side road, put the car into low gear, and drove quietly along the firebreak. After parking the car, they changed into their coveralls and caps in silence then entered the woods.

After about ten minutes, they came up against the fence. "Hand me the wire cutters," said Kate, squatting beside it. In the forest around them, light snow mixed with dead leaves on the forest floor. Everything was still.

Snip. Snip. Snip.

"It's so loud," whispered Seyram. "Can't you do it more quietly?"

"Shhh," whispered Carly. "Just hurry."

"Shut up, " replied Kate in a low voice. "I'm doing the best I can. Here, you two go through. I'll pass you the guns and the spare magazines—we've got four each—then I'll come."

The smell of damp earth met them as, in turn, they bent low to clamber through the hole in the fence.

"Look, I know it feels spooky, but no one is going to be in the woods," said Kate. "They'll all be at the dinner or watching it from a video control room. Let's make a beeline for the firebreak that leads up to the mansion and get to work. Keep the flashlights off so our eyes adjust."

An owl hooted, making them jump. Despite the cold, they were all sweating. Their vision improved with every step, allowing them to better navigate trees and logs, and to step on rocks to cross the creek. After five minutes, they stepped out onto the trail leading to the mansion, its lights emitting a glow in the distance.

Crack. A branch snapped nearby.

They froze. "Don't move," whispered Seyram. Ever so slowly she brought the Beretta off her shoulder and flicked the safety catch. *Click.* Seyram pointed the barrel toward to the noise.

Crack. Another branch snapped.

With no time to discuss what to do, Carly made an executive decision. She mustered the strongest, loudest, deepest, voice she could. "Who's there? We've got you surrounded!"

Silence.

"I said *who's there?!*"

"Ms. Schumer??" came a tremulous voice.

"*Beth?*"

"Yes. It's me. Don't shoot."

Carly thought quickly. "You, and whoever is with you, step out onto the trail. Put your hands in the air." Carly turned to Seyram and Kate. "Keep your guns on them until we're sure." It was the most authoritative Carly had ever been in her life.

Beth, Tanisha, and Bao stepped out onto the firebreak, their hands in the air. They saw three dim figures in coveralls on the opposite side, moonlight glinting on gunstocks.

Carly switched on her flashlight and shone it in their faces, giving each a hard look. "You can put the guns down," she said to Seyram and Kate. Then she asked the three young women, "What are you doing here?"

Faced with a Ms. Schumer who was completely different to the friendly artist, Beth's voice betrayed some doubt. "Remember I told you about the incels and their awards night?" Beth spoke haltingly. "We decided to do something about it. Um, what are you doing here?"

Carly looked at Kate and Seyram. "The game's up."

"Let's just tell them," said Kate.

"We're here to do the same thing," said Seyram.

"Do you have weapons?" asked Carly.

"Molotov cocktails," replied Beth. "We were going to throw them through the ballroom windows."

Carly's eyebrows rose in surprise. "How do you know about Molotov cocktails?"

"My family's Finnish," said Beth. "The old folks used to throw them at the Russians."

"This town needs more Ghanaian and Punjabi blood," muttered Seyram to Kate.

A low rumbling that at first sounded like distant thunder could be heard advancing up the trail.

"Everyone, shush," said Kate. "Someone's coming."

"Oh, she's with us," said Beth. "We figured we needed some backup."

"She's in a car?"

"Er, not exactly."

Beth pulled out a flashlight, pointed it down the firebreak toward the rumbling, and flicked it briefly several times. A large military vehicle with a small cannon on the front approached, stopping ten yards away. The hatch to a short turret popped up and a head emerged out of a Stryker combat vehicle."

"*Tank Girl?*" queried Kate.

Carly squinted in the dark. "No, it's Beatriz. Hi, Beatriz."

"*Carly?*" said Beatriz.

Kate was exasperated. "Folks, this isn't a coffee klatch!"

The owl gave another hoot.

"Jesus, even the owl's in on it! Beatriz, good to meet you—I'm Kate. This is Seyram. To cut a long story short, we're all here to take out the incels. We've got Beretta M12s and Molotov cocktails, but you're obviously army. What's your plan?"

"It's OK, Beatriz," said Beth. "They're on our side. We literally discovered each other a few minutes ago."

Beatriz sized up the situation, noting the Berettas. Unexpected support. "The ballroom is where we think the awards presentation is going to be held. It's the only room anywhere near big enough. French doors lead from there onto a terrace and the back garden. I'll drive the Stryker through the back garden, up onto the terrace and into the ballroom. Then I'll climb back to the gunner's seat and let rip with the machine gun."

"I'm sure this is a dumb question," said Carly, "but … the ballroom's French doors onto the terrace, aren't they too small for the Stryker to get through?"

Beatriz realized she hadn't been clear enough. "Oh, when I said *drive it into the ballroom*, what I actually meant was drive it through the wall of the building."

"You mean … like … smash through it?"

"Affirmative."

Kate was taken aback. "I missed my calling."

"It's what I'm trained to do."

"Um, another dumb question: won't the building fall down if you knock out the wall?" asked Carly.

Tanisha piped up. "I got a book from the library about local historic homes—although some asshole recalled it while I had it—including Opus Steel House. The floor plan showed structural columns everywhere in the front and center of the building. Knock one of those over and the whole thing would crash down. But the ballroom isn't structurally important for the rest of the building. As long as Beatriz doesn't knock out corner columns or the beams connecting them, the roof won't cave."

"When I'm done," added Beatriz, "I'll reverse out onto the terrace, set the interior of the Stryker on fire with one of the Molotov cocktails to destroy any DNA, and abandon the vehicle. Beth, Tanisha, and Bao will throw remaining Molotovs into the mansion to burn it down."

"What about you getting back to safety?" Carly could see Beatriz was capable but couldn't help worrying about her.

"I know Fort Byrd like the back of my hand. Every culvert and bush. Once I'm back on base, I'll be able to return to barracks without being seen—and the guards' attention will be on where the Stryker went through the fence."

"Carly, let *us* do this," said Beth. "Really. Give us the guns and we'll mop up after Beatriz has finished and we've thrown the Molotovs."

"You can use a machine gun?"

"We took up Mayor Konig's offer of automatic weapons training for young people during his so-called emergency. We had loads of practice time because guys stopped coming when they saw us at the shooting range."

"They were worried about our intentions—that we might go postal on them," said Bao. "We've been practicing for a couple of months now."

Kate, Carly, and Seyram exchanged glances.

"They've had more firearms training than us," said Seyram to Kate and Carly.

"We've also got a better weapon," said Tanisha, patting the nose of the Stryker, "and Beatriz is an army gal who knows what's she's doing."

"What about you three?" said Carly, looking at Bao, Beth, and Tanisha. "Do you have a getaway plan?"

"We'll cover Beatriz when she leaves the Stryker, then retreat together back along this trail. Beatriz goes through the fence, and we're parked across the stream behind us, two miles away, the opposite direction from where you came. We've got a car at a trailhead. We'll be fine."

"OK, you've convinced me," said Carly. "Make sure you burn your clothes and shoes afterward. Good luck."

Seyram, Carly, and Kate took their guns and tossed them the short distance to Tanisha, Bao, and Beth who, in perfect synchronicity, slung the guns over their shoulders, pulled balaclavas down over their faces, and turned to fall in behind Beatriz, who revved the engine. The Stryker growled past. Kate, Carly, and Seyram melted into the woods and headed back to where they'd parked the car.

51

GARY, THE MASTER of ceremonies, had come to Mossberg from Cleveland for the New Year's Eve event and was being hosted by Cody and the other incels at Opus Steel House. The event was being livestreamed on the dark web, but to protect identities they had decided to make it a masked gala for people in attendance in the ballroom and for those at home who decided to turn on their cameras. Gary had plans to turn it into an annual New Year's Eve celebration of who they were, as well as an annual reviling of what they hated.

It was also Gary who had decided on the awards and judged the entrants. He'd enjoyed making up the award categories: Best humiliation of a dumpster; Longest lasting (before deletion) sex pic on a teenager girl's social media; Best violent porn … the list went on. There were twenty categories and the competition had opened for nominations a month earlier. Gary would read out the finalists, then announce the winner. It was going to be fun.

The evening started with attendees sitting down at two long tables laden with a medieval feast: platters of pork ribs and steaks, stuffed roasted chickens, plates of fries, bowls of sauce, trays of slaw, mini kegs of beer, carafes of wine, and dozens of pies and tubs of ice cream on side tables for dessert. In turn, each incel stood up and made the same declaration:

that they deserved sex, hated women for denying them, and hated men who had been selected by women for sex. Dinner continued until nine, when eating and drinking was paused for the awards announcements.

Gary stood and walked to a podium adjacent to the table. He surveyed the group and gave a smile. His laptop showed the live feed, which captured the grand dining tables and himself at the podium, all of which was made possible through the internet wizardry of some of the members. This was an empire in the making. After a few minutes of introduction—mostly comprising angry laments about continued virginity—it was time for the awards ceremony to commence. "Without further ado, we move to the first category of the evening: Best humiliation of a dumpster."

Applause and whistling washed through the room, and the online chat pinged with thumbs-up and clap emojis from across North America.

Gary looked into the camera, "And now—drum roll—the moment we've been waiting for …"

On cue, to the left of Gary's image being livestreamed, a portion of the wall crumbled as the front of a military vehicle appeared through it then advanced into the room, its turret reaching high to the ballroom's gilded ceiling. The incels, their brains accustomed to computer games, didn't register that this was an actual clear and present danger, and continued cheering. One even fist pumped, calling out, "Cool!" The giant hole framed the Stryker for a few seconds before what was left of the wall crashed to the ground.

Inside the Stryker, Beatriz left the driver's seat and climbed into the gunner's chair, popping the hatch, singing softly "… doin' it for themselves …" She angled the Stryker's machine gun toward one end of the long dining table, paused for good aim, and gave a small exhalation … "*This* is what I forgot to say to you."

52

PAH-PAH-PAH-pah-pah-pah-pah-pah-pah-pah-pah-pah-pah-pah-pah-pah!

The noise was deafening, the effect spectacular. Ricocheting bullets zinged around the room. Online, viewers saw bullet tracers stream from the Stryker, raking the table from left to right, and back, and back again, then back again. The podium was shot to pieces in a hail of bullets, Gary falling from view. Incels dived under the table, ran for the door, or toppled backward on their chairs. The steaks, chickens, and ribs were shredded; wine, beer, ice cream, and pies splattered over the walls; windows at either end of the ballroom were shot out; and the twin chandeliers shattered into a thousand shards of glass and their raw electrical wiring sparked. From outside came bursts of automatic gunfire and the shouts and yells of escapees. The entire scene was shown live.

After setting the interior of her Stryker alight with a Molotov cocktail, Beatriz made her way through the woods to the perimeter fence with Fort Byrd. While the military police were busy establishing a crime scene, half a mile away she cut a hole in the fence, slipped through, and made it back to barracks undetected.

OVER THE NEXT twenty-four hours, a team of US Army criminal investigators and the FBI descended on Mossberg and set up a joint command. Their preliminary theory, based on location, victims, and the use of a Stryker, was that an army versus college fight over girls had spiraled out of control. When debriefed on this hypothesis, Mayor Konig and Chief Delaney, whose refusal to listen to Agent Fincher's warning had haunted them ever since the fraternity explosion, begged the investigators to consider the possibility it was the handiwork of a murderess.

"*Girls* couldn't have done this," scoffed the investigators.

"You don't understand," said the mayor. "In this town, women can be serial killers too."

ONE YEAR LATER

53

"HONEY, THE COFFEE'S READY," Fincher called to his wife, Sara, as he poured two mugs and walked to the armchairs in the living room. It was eight on Saturday morning, and he could hear their daughters watching TikTok, peals of laughter floating down the stairs from their bedroom. When he'd drunk his coffee, he would start to make pancakes. It was their ritual before the tasks of the day—housework, the supermarket, training at the skate rink, pestering their daughters to clean the rabbit hutch—took over.

Fincher was happy, mostly. One of the FBI's highest ever rewards had been posted the previous day for information leading to the arrest of the person or persons behind the Mossberg killings the year before; five million dollars. It had taken months of work to get the FBI to agree to this amount, almost as many months as the FBI team had spent trying to find clues about who had carried out the killings. But Fincher also became pensive when thinking about the investigation, especially the unresolved questions about what appeared to be the killers' final attack—on Opus Steel House. On this particular morning, he decided to embrace his mood by playing music. He reached for his phone to stream a track into the living room and selected Hiromi Uehara's "Old Castle, By the River, in the Middle of the Forest."

No longer on the ground in Mossberg looking for evidence, Fincher had been reassigned to intelligence analysis work behind the scenes in the Pittsburgh office. He relished having his weekends back and the return to a Monday-to-Friday schedule. It was a move sideways rather than up, but he had predictable hours, rarely needed to travel, and could pick up the girls from after-school activities when Sara, an attorney, had to work late.

"Here's the mail," said Sara, retrieving it from the hallstand where it had been left the day before. "You got your *Week in Review* magazine." She bent down and kissed him on the head, handed him the magazine, then walked to her own armchair with the weekend newspaper, which they still had delivered to the front door.

Fincher was an avid *Week in Review* reader. He pulled it out of its plastic sleeve, and turned it over to look at the cover. Puzzled, he opened the magazine to the explanatory editorial inside. Fincher suddenly choked, then snorted as hot coffee came out his nose. He grabbed for a tissue.

"Are you OK?" asked Sara.

Fincher sat totally still staring at the magazine.

"Ted!" Sara was alarmed. "Are you having a stroke?"

Fincher shook his head but didn't say a word, just stared at the magazine. Finally, he broke the silence. "It's *Week in Review*'s Person of the Year. Take a look." He turned the magazine toward Sara, his face pale.

Sara looked at the trademark framed cover and read the title:

PERSON of the YEAR
THE UNKNOWN ASSASSIN

The editorial inside explained that the "Unknown Assassin" who had murdered young men in Mossberg had been chosen as its Person of the Year due to their ... *legacy of disruption of established patterns of American life; acts that made an entire community alter its perceptions of safety and how men and women could—and should—interact; a social shock at the local level having repercussions across the nation.*

Because the number of assassins and their identity—including their gender—remained unconfirmed, the magazine had chosen a kind of *Charlie's Angels* montage of three individuals in silhouette: a woman in the center holding a machine gun, a man to the left holding a bundle of dynamite, and a person to the right, whose gender was undefined, with a baseball bat over their shoulder.

Fincher's anger was volcanic. "Are they making fun of us? They think this is a joke? I will never buy this magazine again!" He flung the magazine at the wall, although it fell short and landed on the cat.

His wife got up to soothe the cat and retrieve the magazine. "Ted," remonstrated Sara, "Person of the Year doesn't necessarily mean a good person. Vladimir Putin, Ayatollah

Khomeini, Henry Kissinger, and Hitler all got Person of the Year, and how many deaths are they responsible for? The honor, if you want to call it that, is about the impact someone had, for better or worse, on the world. They even gave it to 'The Protestor' a few years back. It's not an endorsement of murder or, need I say it, a judgment of your investigation." She bent and kissed him again on the top of his head. "Teddy, I know you're upset those women were never charged, but don't take it personally. I keep hearing stories about Mossberg and the impact those killings have had. The assassin *has* disrupted life in America."

"Sounds like you're on their side," huffed Fincher. "I *know* those women did it. If those local cops hadn't been so useless, we would have gotten the evidence we needed to put them away for life."

"It's the weekend. Remember what we agreed? No work talk. Let's just read for a bit and finish listening to the music, then I'll help you make the pancakes."

Fincher gazed at his wife, his temper subsiding. "I love you, honey. Honestly, what would I do without you?"

Sara had barely read a paragraph when she returned to the debate. "Doesn't part of you even grudgingly respect those women?"

"You're asking me to admire murderers. I'm a cop."

"They were smart."

"They were deadly," countered Fincher, refusing to look up.

"They were motivated."

Fincher couldn't resist the bait. "They took the law into their own hands. That's un-American."

"Ted, that's *totally* American! Communities taking care of themselves because the government doesn't."

"The community of women?"

"Now you're being sarcastic. No one ever questions it when men protect *their* community interests. They just say 'Oh, men's interests are the community's interests.' *Week in Review* was right: those women disrupted established patterns of American life, and it made men pissed."

"*Pissed?* I think you mean they put men six feet under! In the police force we call that dead. And you're a lawyer: defend your institution."

"I'm also a woman. We've waited a long time for men to stop sexual assault. They didn't."

"So you *are* on their side!" Fincher was incredulous.

"I'm not on their side. I wished you'd caught them and I were their defense attorney."

"That's their side."

"I would use the institution of the law to defend them, as is their right."

Fincher harrumphed. "You might still get that chance if the FBI's reward brings an informant out of the woodwork. They haven't outfoxed everyone yet."

"So let's hope you get your man—woman—and I get them their day in court."

They smiled at each other; it was a standoff.

"Let's make those pancakes before the kids start complaining."

They got up, and Ted went to Sara, put his arm around her, and scooped her in close to kiss her. "You drive me crazy, you know. But you also drive me wild."

WYATT BELL WAS in *Week in Review's* editorial room when the decision about Person of the Year was made. He hadn't been hurt in the attack on the incels because Cody at Opus Steel House had discovered through his own sleuthing that Wyatt was a reporter. Doing surveillance outside the *Gazette* one evening, Cody saw him leave work and greet Emily with an embrace. Their relaxed intimacy signaled that Wyatt was no incel, and he was never allowed through the front gate the night of the awards dinner.

Emily had applied to the PhD program in Public Health at New York University. She had been accepted and, after she graduated from Mossberg College, she and Wyatt moved to Brooklyn over the summer. On a whim and a prayer, Wyatt had emailed his CV to *Week in Review's* investigative journalism team. In a stroke of serendipity, the team head was from a Midwest farming community and his curiosity had been piqued by this farm boy who had graduated from writing about pork futures to writing about the Mossberg killings, and who also had the gumption to ask *Week in Review* for a job.

Thus, Wyatt found himself in a room, as part of a program to expose junior employees to editorial decision-making, surrounded by the magazine's most senior staff deliberating on who should be Person of the Year. The editors had narrowed down their candidates to "The Feminist" and "The Refugee," generic individuals who throughout the year had reminded the world of causes, rights, and values. Arguments raged back and forth about who it should be, when—true to character in being self-repressed until he could no longer take it—Wyatt blurted out, "How about making it "The Unknown Assassin"? You know, from those killings in Mossberg? It has the feminist angle, as well as the desperation and hope of refugees trying to change life."

The editors loved it.

THE PRESENT DAY

54

MOSSBERG HAS CHANGED. Mayor Konig failed to get reelected; Judge Nossel, an elected judge, also failed to have his term renewed; Chief Delaney left and got a job elsewhere; the *Gazette*'s board retired Henry Konig, convinced a new editorial approach with insight into the changes happening in the community was needed. The population had lost confidence in these men's ability to maintain law and order for everyone.

A female judge now presides over the local court and Mossberg has recruited three female police officers. Detective Schultz is still there, mostly deskbound, glaring at the female officers—one of whom is his superior—when they walk by. Trooper Chase is the liaison for the station's LGBTQIA2S+ outreach and led a small group of police officers in Mossberg's first Pride Parade.

The killings themselves stopped. Assaults and harassment still occur occasionally, but overall reports have dropped dramatically. Some families with sons moved out of town and registrations in male sports have declined, but female enrolments at the college and in sports have boomed. Downtown Mossberg has become a regionally popular destination for entertainment, restaurants, and weekend getaways. Moh's Kebabs is thriving.

No one has yet been arrested or charged over the deaths that occurred, and the FBI's five-million-dollar reward remains unclaimed. The FBI maintains an open file, but there is continued internal disagreement about whether the killings were ever connected in the first place.

Tulip Sorenson got a job with the Fox Network as its youngest ever news anchor.

Beatriz is still in the army; she retrained as an M1 Abrams tank engineer.

Tanisha, Beth, and Bao stepped back into college life and never spoke of what happened. They graduated and left Mossberg but have stayed in touch with each other.

Seyram sold the clinic. She enrolled in a PhD in comparative religion, and for her dissertation is analyzing different spiritual traditions' approaches to combatting gender-based violence. She is currently doing her fieldwork in Ghana and Nigeria. The family is with her.

Carly's dinner sets doubled in price. When Summer finished high school, Carly used her extra income to fund a two-year solo study tour to Oaxaca, Cuzco, Ouagadougou, Kampala, Bukhara, Kandy, and Rotorua.

Kate still runs Downtown Hardware. Its *DYKES WELCOME* sign is the most photographed landmark in Mossberg, and a café opened across the street to serve tourists. She broke up with Tulip after eight months. "I'm surprised it lasted that long," said Carly. "What did you even talk about?" asked Seyram. "We communicated in other ways," came the retort. Kate didn't mind them poking fun at her. She'd got her groove back.

Seyram, Kate, and Carly remain friends.

NOTES

"Triumph of democracy": In 2021 in Canberra, Australia, women marched in their thousands on Parliament to protest sexual violence and lack of progress with reform. Australian Prime Minister Scott Morrison described it as a "triumph of democracy" because in other countries they would have been "met with bullets."

"We're not like those moms who are driven to kill a man because their kids were abused": In 1981, a German woman smuggled a gun into the court where the man who raped and murdered her seven-year-old daughter was on trial and shot him dead. In 2014, a British woman went to the home of a neighbor, a convicted pedophile, whom her three sons had identified to the police as having sexually abused them and stabbed him to death.

"And women walk around in yoga pants!": In 2016, a man in Rhode Island, USA, wrote to his local paper, the *Barrington Times*, lamenting that yoga pants "do nothing to compliment a woman over 20 years old" and create a "spectre" of women "coping poorly with their weight or advancing age." He complained that yoga pants wearers cause him to struggle personally with women's "physicality." Women responded by organizing marches where they wore yoga pants, including a parade past the letter-writer's house.

"The case for the defense focused on Colette Fieldhouse's behavior at the party": This incident is loosely based on a real case in 2017, in which a seventeen-year old girl got invited to a birthday party in a small town in Australia. When she arrived at the party, she kissed her (female) friend on the lips. The girl was later raped. Lawyers for the defendant described the kiss as "making out" and "breaking boundaries," questioned her on whether she would have had that kiss if she hadn't been drinking alcohol, and focused on the clothing she wore and the fact she was silent while being raped. They argued these things suggested consent and reduced the culpability of the perpetrators, who were found not guilty.

"Last week in that library a man pulled his penis out and urinated on one of the couches!": I was once in a student lounge at New York University when a man did exactly this.

"Why couldn't you just keep your knees together?": In 2016 in Calgary, Canada, a judge asked a sexual assault victim this question during the trial of the alleged perpetrator. The judge later apologized for the comment.

"Pushed for comment by the media pack outside the court": This paragraph is loosely based on the trial and light sentence of a perpetrator of sexual assault on an unconscious woman on Stanford University campus in California in 2016. The perpetrator's father wrote a message to the judge in the case, stating that because of the stress of the trial his son would never again be his "happy go lucky self with that easygoing personality and welcoming smile" and that he should not have to go to jail for "twenty minutes of action". In response to criticism of his words, the father wrote a statement to *The Huffington Post*: "My words have been misinterpreted by people. What I meant with that comment is a 20 minute period of time. I was not referring to sexual activity by the word 'action.' It was an unfortunate choice of words and I did not mean to be disrespectful or offensive to anyone." See *Time Magazine*, June 6, 2016, online article 'Read the Letter the Stanford Rapist's Father Wrote to Ask for a More Lenient Sentence'.

"They joked they were a wolf pack: howling in unison when they spotted a woman up ahead …": I once knew a man in Canberra, Australia, who told me how he went running with a group of buddies and they would harass women. "We're like a pack of wolves!" he said with glee. In Pamplona, Spain, a group of men who worked together to sexually assault women, called themselves *La Manada* (the wolf pack). They were put on trial in 2016.

"Want me to grab you by the pussy?": You guessed it—Donald Trump's comment about women in 2016, that he could "Grab 'em by the pussy."

"Sydney Brown. She worked in a bar on Main Street": This incident is loosely based on a case from Melbourne, Australia, in the early 1990s, when a woman was raped late one evening. She fled her attacker, climbing a fence to escape him, falling down on the other side and breaking her leg. Another man found her lying there with a broken leg and also raped her. The second man was arrested, convicted, and jailed. I don't know what happened to the first.

"The judge even said that it should have been explained to the victim that pressing charges would ruin the boy's life": During the trial of a sixteen-year-old boy accused of sexually assaulting a sixteen-year-old girl in New Jersey in 2019, the judge presiding over the case said this.

"Or, last month in Canada, that man who pleaded *guilty* to sexual assault, but the judge decided there should be no conviction because it would have hurt the man's career": In Montreal in 2022, a judge gave no punishment to a man who pled guilty to sexual assault charges. The judge said that "a conviction would have particularly negative and disproportionate consequences for [the perpetrator], since he would have difficulty traveling outside the country, which could possibly hamper his career as an engineer."

"… feminists in Saudi Arabia are probably more interested in being allowed to drive than in ditching the headscarf": Women in Saudi Arabia were legally permitted to drive in June 2018.

"The fellas were real upset about damage to their vehicles": This comment is based on a lecture I attended where researchers from the UK presented results of a survey of fears held by young men and young women. Women's greatest fear was being raped; men's greatest fear was damage to their car.

"You fucking sluts! You drive off and don't even talk to us!" This is based on a conversation with a woman in Melbourne who told me how she and her friends had not wanted to engage with two guys who were insisting on talking to them. Initially, the guys called them something like "chicky-poo" or "babe," but after ninety seconds of no response, told her she was a "fucking slut."

"… teach [young men] how to be more streetwise": In 2021, the Police Commissioner for North Yorkshire, UK, was asked about the rape and murder of a young British woman by an off-duty police officer who tricked her into getting into his car by showing her his (genuine) police badge as she was walking home in the evening. The commissioner said women should be "streetwise" and know "when they can be arrested and when they can't be arrested," suggesting the victim could have prevented what happened to her. He resigned after a public outcry.

"Women's rights are human rights and human rights are women's rights": Hillary Clinton said this at the UN Conference on Women in Beijing in 1995.

"I will not be lectured about sexism and misogyny from this man.": Australian Prime Minister Julia Gillard said this in Parliament in 2012, in a rebuke to the Leader of the Opposition, Tony Abbott.

"We should all be feminists" is the title of a book-length essay by Nigerian writer Chimamanda Ngozi Adichie.

"… an argument broke out between women who said they should march as Jewish lesbians and others who said they should march as lesbian Jews.": This comment is based on a scene from the documentary *Treyf* by, and about, two Jewish lesbians who met at a Passover Seder.

Chi Omicron Kappa: The incident involving this fictional fraternity is loosely based on a real case in Sydney, Australia, from 2000. A gang of about a dozen boys, led by a teenager, raped teenage girls by tricking them into meeting the gang alone. On one occasion, the gang leader's younger brother tricked a sixteen-year-old female friend into meeting him in a park, so that his brother and the gang could rape her. The gang leader was sentenced to twenty-eight years in jail.

"In fact," continued Konig, "just last night my own wife Jenny and I spoke, and she said to me 'You have to think about this as a father. What would you want to happen if it were our girls who had been victims?': This is a real quote from Australian Prime Minister Scott Morrison, who was trying to explain how, although he'd previously paid little attention to sexual assault, his wife had reminded him that he had daughters, making him realize that sexual assault was bad after all.

"… surely you're not saying that people need to have children to have a conscience? … and surely having children doesn't guarantee a conscience, anyway?": This was the response from a famed and fierce campaigner against sexual assault, Grace Tame, to the previous comment from Scott Morrison—that his wife's reminder he had daughters, made him realize that sexual assault was bad after all.

"Wasn't it an incel guy behind that attack in Toronto earlier this year?": In 2018, an incel deliberately drove his car along the sidewalk in Toronto in order to murder women. He was convicted of eleven deaths and received a minimum sentence of twenty-five years in jail.

"… attack in California in 2014 that killed six": An incel carried out this attack in California in 2016, murdering six people before killing himself.

"The *New Yorker* had an article about incels recently," said Carly: See "The Rage of the Incels," by Jia Toletino, *The New Yorker*, May 15, 2018.

BOOK CLUB TIPS

Suggested questions for discussion:

- Could you identify with Carly, Kate, and Seyram's friendship, or with them individually? Why?
- Should they have been caught?
- Were there twists in the plot that surprised you? What were they?
- Do you have a favorite passage or sentence? Why do you like it?
- A central theme was sexual violence. Does the book make you think differently about how to respond to it?
- The book uses dark humor to make fun of some of the crazy things that have been said about feminists, women, gender, and sexual assault. Does the humor work here? Do humor and satire help you cope with upsetting things?
- Mossberg became a community where women were not scared to go out alone. What else could be different in such a community? What would your community look like if women were not afraid to go out alone?
- The book highlights some generational differences between women. Do you think younger women, who may be more comfortable with aggression and assertiveness, view the book differently to older women?

- Carly, Kate, and Seyram used violence to change Mossberg. Is violence ever justified to change society? Could similar ends be achieved without violence?

Meals prepared by Carly, Kate, and Seyram:

Seyram's meal where the main characters are all introduced:
- Pear, gorgonzola, walnut, and spinach salad (try a Dijon mustard and olive oil dressing, with salt and pepper to taste)
- Grilled whole tilapia fish (whole tilapia can be big; one is probably enough for two people)
- Grilled vegetables (your choice)
- Jollof rice
- Shito sauce for the fish. (The sauce is very spicy, so not to everyone's taste. If you don't want to make it, it can be bought from West African grocery stores or online)
- English Trifle for dessert

Carly's meal where she invited Seyram and Kate around to reflect on what they had done:
- Arugula, cranberry, almond, and parmesan salad (try a honey, lemon juice, olive oil dressing)
- Fettuccine with mushrooms, and a garlic and parsley sauce
- Herb bread
- Baked pears for dessert

Kate's meal where they discuss how the police are onto them and how they need a signal that they need to talk. (This is really Kate's mom's meal, because she brought around the food for Kate):

- Samosas
- Vegetable pakoras
- Lentil soup
- Lamb curry (try lamb vindaloo if you like spicy)
- Goat curry (try rogan josh with goat)
- Mango chicken curry
- Paneer tikka masala
- Vegetable malai kofta
- Dal
- Naan bread
- Rice
- Gulab jamun, coconut rasgulla, and jalebi sweets for dessert.

The following drinks were the characters' favorites:
- Sauvignon blanc white wine for Carly
- Corona beer with lime for Kate
- Any kind of mocktail for Seyram
- Kate's mom provided mango lassi for Kate's Indian meal
- Carly made margaritas when she suggested they attack the Chi Omicron Kappa frat house

The music list:

"Dreamer Girl" by Asa, from the album *Beautiful Imperfection* (2010). Played by Seyram when she is cooking for Kate and Carly and ignoring news about the court case.

"Blurred Lines" by Robin Thicke, featuring Pharrell Williams, from the album *Blurred Lines* (2013). Played by Branson Vanburg when he arrives at Coates Ravine for his morning run. (If you prefer a feminist parody watch "Defined Lines" by Auckland Law Review on YouTube).

"What's Up" by 4 Non Blondes, from the album *Bigger, Better, Faster, More!* (1992). Played by Carly when she argues they're on the right path and should continue their attacks.

"Shotgun" by George Ezra, from the album *Staying at Tamara's* (2018). On the radio in Cooper Hanson's car when he's cruising around with Sheldon Nossel, shortly before they are attacked.

"Havana" by Camila Cabello, featuring Young Thug, from the album *Camila* (2018). Played in the nightclub when Wyatt and Emily meet Beth, Tanisha and Bao.

"Sisters Are Doin' It For Themselves" by Eurythmics, featuring Aretha Franklin (1985). Hummed by Beatriz when crashing the incels' party in the Stryker combat vehicle.

"Old Castle, by the River, in the Middle of the Forest" by Hiromi Uehara, from the album *Spiral* (2006). Played by Fincher when reflecting on unresolved questions about the attacks.

ACKNOWLEDGEMENTS

THANK YOU TO the beta readers and sensitivity readers who generously gave their time to provide feedback: Alexandra Mills, Bill Kokkaris, Carrie Thomas, Claudia Halbac, Debbie Bell, Dornuki Jenkins, Evalynn Mazurski, Heather Marvell, Helen Moriarty, Jill Dobson, Leanne Jones, and Saba Din. Thanks as well to my wonderful copyeditor, James Bean AE, for his thoughtful and insightful advice; to proof-reader, Andrew Nest, whose eagle eye caught things I'd missed or not considered; to Margaret Curry for tips on golfing; to Gillian Flaherty for our instrumental conversation about young men and their navigation of gender and society; and to Merrily Weisbord, Sina Rahimpour, Kathy Main, and Ramin Rohanizadeh for advice and assistance on the cover design. Any errors are, of course, my own.

ABOUT THE AUTHOR

MICHAEL NEST GREW up in rural Australia. After spending his twenties studying, travelling, and doing development assistance (foreign aid) work, he moved to New York City to do a PhD that included research in D.R. Congo and Zimbabwe. He has previously published four books. *The Democratic Republic of Congo: Economic Dimensions of War and Peace* (2006) won a Best Academic Title, 2006 award from the American Library Association. *Coltan* (2011) focuses on the exploitation of natural resources in Central Africa. *Still a Pygmy: the unique memoir of one man's fight to save his identity from extinction* (2015) is a collaboration with Mbuti (Pygmy) activist and businessman, Isaac Bacirongo, and is the first memoir ever published by a Pygmy author. In 2017, Michael moved to Montreal, Canada, he collaborated on an investigation into one of Canada's most famous missing persons cases. This research was published as *Cold Case North: the search for James Brady and Absolom Halkett* (with Deanna Reder and Eric Bell; 2020) and won SaskBooks' Creative Publishing Award, 2022. His day job is preventing fraud and corruption. *Take Out the Jocks* is his first novel.